Praise for Megan Crane

"Crane's start to her Fortunes of Lost Lake series is a charming romance featuring a delightfully brainy heroine."

—*Booklist* (starred review)

"From its engaging setup to its endearing and quirky characters and the incredible Alaskan setting, I recommend *Bold Fortune* to romance readers who enjoy second chance romances, fish out of water tales, stories where opposites attract, or those set in the beautiful remoteness that is Alaska."

—Fresh Fiction

"A long adrenaline rush punctuated by sweet and sexy interludes . . . Crane takes her appealing characters on a breakneck adventure around the world. A well-balanced mix of romance and suspense makes this a sure bet for series fans."

—*Publishers Weekly* on *Special Ops Seduction*

"Megan Crane masterfully combines romance, suspense, and a dash of family drama in *Special Ops Seduction*. . . . A strong sense of place, whether it's the wilds of Alaska or the vineyards of California, draws the reader deeper into this irresistible and emotional story."

—*BookPage*

"Filled with mystery, suspense, and romance, *Special Ops Seduction* will have readers interested from the first page until the last."

—*Harlequin Junkie*

"*Special Ops Seduction* is a compelling, perfectly balanced read. There is just the right touch of romance, action, camaraderie, and suspense."

—Fresh Fiction

"Megan Crane's mix of tortured ex–special ops heroes, their dangerous missions, and the rugged Alaskan wilderness is a sexy, breathtaking ride!"

—*New York Times* bestselling author
Karen Rose, on *Seal's Honor*

Titles by M. M. Crane / Megan Crane

The Fortunes of Lost Lake Series

BOLD FORTUNE

RECKLESS FORTUNE

Alaska Force Novels

SEAL'S HONOR

SNIPER'S PRIDE

SERGEANT'S CHRISTMAS SIEGE

DELTA FORCE DEFENDER

SPECIAL OPS SEDUCTION

Reckless Fortune

A Fortunes of Lost Lake Novel

M. M. CRANE

BERKLEY ROMANCE
New York

Berkley Romance
Published by Berkley
An imprint of Penguin Random House LLC
penguinrandomhouse.com

ISBN: 9780593335406

First Edition: September 2022

Printed in the United States of America
1 3 5 7 9 10 8 6 4 2

Book design by George Towne

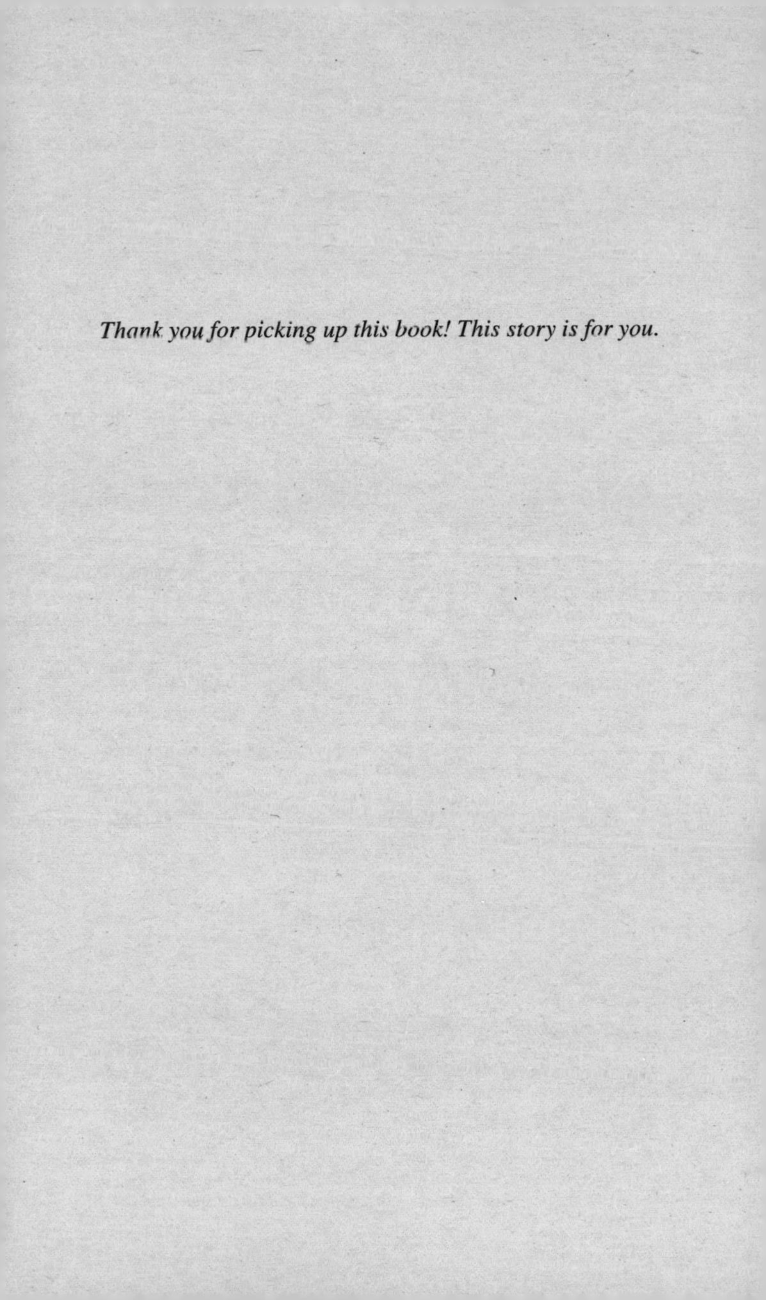

Thank you for picking up this book! This story is for you.

One

Bowie Fortune never backed down from a dare.

Especially not if the dare came from his mouthy kid sister, who might not be a kid any longer, sure, but the principle remained intact.

Bowie liked to think of his refusal to back down—no matter how ridiculous the dare in question—as evidence not only of the high standards he maintained, but of a life well lived. The only kind of life worth living, to his mind.

And he'd tried several lives on for size already, so he could tell the difference.

As he landed his favorite longer-range Cessna on what passed for a runway in the middle of spectacular Montana ranchland, he figured his life was looking just fine. No thanks to Piper and the challenge she'd issued him. But the Rocky Mountains down here in the Lower 48 were giving him a gorgeous early-June welcome, as if summer really was on its way. The sky was big and bright. The land was pretty.

You could do worse, the Bitterroot Valley had seemed to tell him as he came in.

He set the plane down sedately and bumped along the

countrified runway that was an upgrade from the gravel he was used to in Alaska. And laughed while he did it, because he laughed a lot more than some people considered appropriate—he laughed more the less appropriate they found it—and because *sedate* was not really his thing.

Mail-order brides weren't really his thing, either, but here he was.

Bowie normally flew charter flights around the Alaskan bush for folks with a taste for the more thrilling things in life. It was a guaranteed adventure—and also something he would have done as soon as he got his pilot's license, without anyone paying him. That he got to call it his job never failed to make him feel like he was getting away with something.

He never forgot for a minute that some poor slobs had to sit in airless offices and go to tedious meetings all day, a fate worse than death as far as he was concerned. But then, Bowie was from Lost Lake, out in Interior Alaska, where it was an adventure to survive on any given Tuesday. Not to mention all ten and a half months of winter. He figured growing up off the grid the way he had was what had given him an appetite for taking risks the way folks in big cities took their buses and subways.

Compared to some of the things he'd done—most recently, flying like a lunatic through spring storms with a pack of equally fearless outdoor photographers, for example—this mail-order bride deal sounded pretty tame. What was pretending to be married, pioneer-style, for one measly little Alaskan summer with a virtual stranger next to the thrill of landing on a glacier at 7,200 feet or playing hide-and-seek in fog and rain with some of the tallest mountains in the world?

Piper had dared him to take part in this publicity-stunt-slash-contest being put on by a questionable collection of regional locals, mostly because, she'd maintained, he was too unruly and uncivilized to find himself a *date*, much less a wife. Even if the wife in question was fake and temporary, for the dubious purpose of a little prize money. Assuming they won.

I date plenty, Bowie had told her with a grin, sitting at the comfortable family dinner table in his parents' house at the far end of the lake one blustery spring night. *How and when and who is a little too much information for your tender ears.*

There'd been a lot of snorting at that from the rest of the disreputable humans he claimed as his own, but Piper had only smiled at him in that particularly sisterly way she had. As if she pitied him.

It was meant to get his back up and it did.

You've gone full mountain man and you don't even know it, she'd said sadly, with a shake of her head. *You've become the character you play on your charter trips.*

I beg your pardon. I do not play any characters. I provide local color and commentary, as requested.

But he'd been grinning lazily while he said that because maybe he did play a role or two. If he felt like it. He wasn't an *actor*, though. He could still remember the various attempts at community theater at the Mine. The Mine was the center of the lake community. It was a whole village except, unlike most villages, it was all under one roof at the head of Lost Lake rather than spread out around the lake or along a road. There were no roads. The Mine was the bar, the restaurant, all the shops, and a place to shelter from the inevitable weather, too.

Watching folks he knew parade around in costume, *orating* in a great big room he couldn't escape even if he was actively trying to pretend it wasn't happening, was the stuff of nightmares.

Piper had rolled her eyes at him. *You're going to die alone, eaten by wild animals, Bowie. Even if you tried to entice some poor woman to take a chance on you at this point, how would you get her to stay?*

Little sister. I don't know how to tell you this. Bowie had held Piper's gaze and let his grin expand some. *I'm very persuasive in the right circumstances.*

What would happen if you had to actually get to know someone? his sister had asked, as if that was an idle question and she wasn't directly challenging him. Because maybe Piper was a little bit of an actor herself. *No song and dance on a flight past Denali. No flying off at dawn. What if you had to let someone get to know* you*?*

Bring it on, Bowie had replied immediately.

The way Piper had likely known he would, because she'd smiled with a little too much satisfaction. *I'm so glad you're game, Bowie*, she'd murmured. Smugly. *Because there happens to be the perfect opportunity for you to prove it.*

And then she'd told him about the so-called mail-order bride contest taking place this summer. The rules were simple, according to Piper. The ladies who entered chose their men, after a stringent vetting process that would include home visits. Together, the so-called couple would spend the summer exemplifying the Alaskan frontier spirit by performing and documenting as many survival tasks and adventures, as well as good, old-fashioned frontier living, as they could. They were to post a picture every day and at least one video per week to a dedicated social media account, the better to advertise the charms of the area here, that, while remote and unspoiled as the locals liked it, could benefit from some more tourism in the summer months. The contestants were expected to promote the area and the contest, and any disreputable behavior would lead to disqualification, as would anything illegal or even distasteful in the eyes of the judges. The judges were a selection of local officials from villages in this part of the vast Interior who would get together and name one "best old-school frontier couple" at the end of the summer.

The mail-order bride part was a gimmick and meant as a throwback to how a lot of folks' great-grandparents had met out here, as no weddings would actually be occurring—at least not as part of the contest. What contestants did afterward was up to them.

When Bowie had suggested that might be the dumbest idea he'd ever heard, he discovered that said dumb idea had come about thanks in no small part to his own brother, the unofficial mayor of the unincorporated Lost Lake community. Quinn had been more than happy to discuss the whole thing in detail, even though Bowie thought it was about as foolish as that time Mia Saskin, known as Grand Mia to one and all around here, had decided they should have an Adopt a Bear contest. All fun and games until the bears in question took exception to being tracked.

With both Piper and Quinn going on about the mail-order bride thing, a lot like they were in cahoots, Bowie had been backed neatly into it. He'd had no choice but to laugh like it was his very own idea and sign up on the spot.

Then act like he'd enjoyed every minute that had brought him out here to Montana to collect his fake bride for the summer, in the hope they might win some money if they made it all the way to Labor Day and proved themselves the most old-school Alaska while they did it. Whatever that was.

He laughed again now as he climbed down from the cockpit and took a deep breath of Montana.

"Idiots," he muttered into the stillness, though it was hard to say which idiot he meant. There were so many involved in this that it was hard to choose.

But it was done now. He'd chosen to fly down and pick up his bride for the summer because he could, and maybe because he'd wanted to both get his head straight with the nice, long flight as well as get to know the woman in question before they just . . . lived together. In his house.

Besides, there was no denying it was pretty here, and he'd always been a sucker for a pretty place with the wild still in it. Montana had that going for it. It was gorgeous by anyone's standards, if a little soft by his. For one thing, there were roads. He'd seen them as he'd flown south. A person could drive anywhere, right on out to the interstate if they had a mind to. All the way to the sea or anywhere else that appealed.

Not like up in Lost Lake. There were no roads, only preferred tracks, rugged vehicles, and a lot of willpower, depending on the tricky Alaskan weather, to make it down to the nearest small village from their hardy little community. The town of Hopeless sat on a bend in the epically twisty Upper Kuskokwim River and had been named, originally, to indicate the state of mind of the gold rush hopefuls who had not gotten what they'd trekked all the way out into the hinterland to find. These days the locals figured the name kept undesirables—meaning, the kind of looky-loos who cluttered up the Southwest Passage on their cruise ships every summer—far away.

In Interior Alaska, roads were a luxury. But then, so was summer. Some years it was just midnight sun most of the night and gray skies all day. You made of it what you could. That was some real old-school Alaska right there.

Bowie let his feet get acquainted with Montana dirt while he stretched a little. He'd flown in over his would-be fake bride's family ranch today to get a feel for the place. He knew that he had to walk a ways to get to the main house, and he took his time doing it.

He told himself he was getting the lay of the land. Could be he was also putting off the inevitable trouble coming his way. Because Bowie loved himself some danger. Thrived on it, even. But trouble he avoided like the plague.

And he'd never known a woman who wasn't some kind of trouble.

He had to figure that the kind of woman who would sign up for a bizarre contest in the boondocks was trouble with a capital *T*.

It was perfect walking weather today, with plenty of time to appreciate his last few moments of untroubled freedom. A pretty day in the kind of coy spring that marked most northern places he'd been—warm and bright with a punch of lingering cold beneath it. The Bitterroot Valley was putting on a show. There were carpets of wildflowers everywhere. The Rocky Mountains were flexing their rugged beauty on all sides, some peaks still whitecapped.

If a person had to live outside Alaska, Bowie thought as he walked, Montana wasn't a bad bet.

He walked for a good fifteen minutes along the little dirt track before he wound around to the house he'd seen from up above. Then he slowed, because as he approached, he could see folks were already gathered out in the yard.

Bowie wasn't the sort to turn down a parade in his honor, but somehow he guessed that floats and a marching band weren't where this was going.

He made sure his face was set in its usual amiable, easygoing expression, stuck his hands in his jeans pockets, and slowed his walk to a saunter. And he checked out the scene awaiting him from behind his standard-issue aviator shades while he approached.

The marines might not have been for him, in the long run. But that didn't mean he hadn't learned a few things along the way.

Like performing a little recon on all things whenever possible. He liked to *look* lazy and unbothered and infinitely unthreatening, but that was a lot easier when he already knew what he was walking into. In this case, he was going in blind.

Piper had laughed when he'd suggested that he should have the opportunity to personally vet the woman he'd be spending his summer with. A little theatrically, to his mind, there at her cottage where he had virtuously stopped by to help her out with a little springtime roof repair.

You're not the customer here, idiot, she'd told him scornfully, squatting back on her haunches on top of her cabin with the lake behind her like a bright blue frame, this side of the spring breakup that melted all the ice. She'd wiped at her forehead. *You're a contestant.*

He hadn't liked that much, but he'd run with it. *It's really not fair to the other contestants, though, is it?* he'd asked, treating her to his best charming grin.

Mostly because she was his sister, immune to his charm since birth, and his best grin usually made her roll her eyes. That time was no exception.

I don't know what makes you think you have a hope in hell of winning, she'd said, returning her attention to the roof. *I think what you should concentrate on this summer is a little information gathering. About yourself and how weird you've become.*

Bowie was under the impression that being weird was a favorite Alaskan pastime, and that his sister lived in a glass house of her own strangeness, but he'd only laughed.

While attempting to look wounded. *What? I'm a catch.*

Catch and release, maybe, Piper had replied, her eyes gleaming when she'd looked at him again. *I feel sorry for your poor mail-order bride, Bowie. Truly I do.*

If he was honest, Bowie felt the same. But probably not for the same reasons.

Personally, he would not have signed up to be a fake mail-order bride under any circumstances. Especially not to take part in this contest that a bunch of town leaders all along their stretch of the Upper Kuskokwim had come up with, mostly in an attempt to rustle up some measure of tourist interest in an area that was always going to be a little too off the beaten path—even for folks who liked that kind of thing. The contest had been trumpeted all over the radio waves for months now. *Reclaim Alaska's Gold Rush Grit!* the puff piece in the *Anchorage Daily News* had crowed, while also making it clear that everyone involved would be vetted thoroughly and made aware that it was all an elaborate game of pretend. That contestants would be judged on the difficulty of their attempted frontier projects—and also whether or not they worked—not on any actual marriages. *And maybe come away with the grand prize of $10,000!*

Bowie had been required to submit an embarrassing personal profile. He'd had to allow Bertha Tungwenuk, the mayor of Hopeless, to poke around his cabin and his private hangar, where he kept the only harem he'd ever need. His planes.

Quinn had been there, too, because while he was only unofficially the mayor of Lost Lake, he was actually the official representative of the community. A role he had always taken entirely too seriously. Though he sure had seemed to be enjoying himself on home inspection day.

You have to sign a waiver, you know, Quinn had said, his arms crossed and a smirk on his face that Bowie would have liked to take off with his own hands, but he was pretending to be civilized. Also he wasn't twelve. *You have to sign on the dotted line that you will, to the best of your ability, represent the Upper Kuskokwim well. You'll be subject to fines if you don't.*

Seems to me that representing something well leaves room for a lot of interpretation, Bowie had drawled.

Not so much, Bertha Tungwenuk had said, scowling at him. *No stunts, Bowie.*

I'm wounded, Bowie told them both. Neither of them had looked moved. *Maybe this is just the opportunity I need to settle on down and make something of myself.*

Also, Quinn had replied in the withering tone only a big brother could produce. *You might want to keep in mind that I'm one of the judges.*

Bowie shoved all that aside, because it was time to meet his so-called bride. No more pretending he wasn't hoisted up high on his own petard. No more hoping for a sufficiently painful, yet not actually debilitating, accident to allow him to bow out with his pride intact. It was go time.

There were three women standing outside in the yard, watching his approach in a manner he could only call unfriendly, and none of them was Autumn McCall.

Because he'd seen a picture of Autumn, his very own fake bride-to-be. And the little video to go with it, in which she'd talked too long and too close to the camera. None of the three women draping themselves bonelessly on the fence, the grille of a pickup truck, and the porch railing, respectively, bore any resemblance to that video. They all looked about six feet tall, for one thing, and he had gotten the impression that Autumn was more compact. And all three of them had the kind of glossy blonde hair, pouty lips, and slim hips that whispered of expensive places Bowie avoided like the plague.

Bowie was sure he would have remembered pouty lips and that much blonde in a video that he'd liked only because Autumn had mostly talked—very quickly and matter-of-factly—about all the pioneer-type tasks she planned to perform over the course of the summer. Without furnishing the to-do list for a potential fake husband that most of the others had.

"This is quite a welcoming committee," he said cheerfully as he drew close to the blondes.

"Less of a welcoming committee," said the blonde closest to him, arms crossed as she propped herself up against the truck. "More of a gauntlet."

"That's a little less friendly," Bowie agreed.

The closest blonde sniffed. The one by the fence stuck her hands on her hips, somehow managing to draw attention to her disturbingly long, oval-shaped, pale blue nails. He didn't know how a person got anything done with nails long enough to cause damage. Then again, that was probably the point. She didn't look like the sort of woman who concerned herself much with productivity.

"We don't like anything about this," she told him, the blue nails tapping out a beat at her hips. "We've been looking into you."

Bowie supposed there were some who might take offense to that sort of greeting, but he wasn't one of them. "That's smart," he said instead, and meant it. "Back in the day I guess a woman just answered an ad and hoped for the best. At least in this day and age you have the internet."

"Word is," said the third blonde from her place on the porch, studying him like he belonged under a painful sort of microscope, "you're something of an adrenaline junkie."

"Guilty as charged," Bowie replied happily. "Are you all angling for a ride in my plane?"

"There will be no adrenaline junkie-ing," said the first blonde severely. "Our sister is not a carnival ride."

"We're going to need her back in one piece at the end of the summer," said the second, just as sternly.

"You, on the other hand," chimed in the third. She let her words trail off. Then shrugged, with an admirable gleam of careless bloodthirstiness in her gaze.

"Message received," Bowie drawled. "I wouldn't want to call down the Furies on myself."

"See that you don't," came another voice. "They're a lot."

And then, from inside the house, slapping her way out through the screen door, marched Autumn McCall.

His bride.

Or anyway, the woman he'd be living with the rest of the summer.

Bowie felt a kind of chill run all the way down his back, and under different circumstances he would have called it a premonition. If he was flying, a near-shiver like that told him weather was coming no matter how blue the sky before him.

But today, under the Montana sun, he dismissed it, because this was all so ridiculous.

And maybe also because the word *bride* was settling in him in a way it never had before, especially when it wasn't accurate in this situation. She was not his bride. She was not *his*. He didn't allow that kind of thing, as a longstanding personal policy. Autumn McCall was like . . . a summer exchange student, maybe.

He told himself his odd reaction was heartburn from the significantly and gloriously fried food he'd tossed back at his last refueling stop, not that he usually suffered from that ailment.

Whatever it was, he forgot about it as Autumn marched off the porch and stopped when her feet hit the dirt, her hands finding her hips.

"Take it down a notch," she was saying, glaring at her sisters. Then she turned that glare on him. "And this is all wrong. You must know that. I'm hardly a mail-order bride if you're picking me up."

"I sometimes deliver packages," Bowie offered helpfully, going more genial in the face of all that glaring, as that was how he best needled the overly serious Quinn. "But I didn't think we were going for historical accuracy so much as the general metaphor of the whole mail-order thing."

"Metaphors are slippery," Autumn replied. Her mouth curved a little. "You'll want to watch them."

And that heartburn in Bowie's chest, because it had to be heartburn with all those dancing flames, seemed to get brighter.

Bowie had expected the hair, darker than her sisters and gleaming with bits of red here and there in the sunlight. He'd expected the hazel eyes and the generous mouth. He'd found her cute, if obviously overprepared for something he thought was idiotic, but he didn't care if she was cute or not. He'd picked her because she'd described herself as the kind of sensible pioneer woman his own great-grandmother had been. Ida Lathrop had taken one look at a grizzled miner in Juneau, married him while hardly knowing his name, and followed him out into the middle of nowhere, where by all accounts she'd proceeded to wrap him around her finger while also beating back the wilderness.

Practical, level-headed, and resourceful. That was his great-grandma to a T and that was what Autumn McCall had called herself. He'd thought that sounded useful. And out by Lost Lake, usefulness was always celebrated, because there was always work that needed doing.

Decorations like the blonde Furies were nice and all, but they belonged behind glass in places on the electrical grid where they could bloom like the hothouse flowers they were. Bowie liked to look at pretty things as much as the next man, but he didn't take them home.

He never took anyone home.

Maybe the truth was that he'd felt safe opening up his home to a woman who made him feel faintly protective, the way he felt about his sister when he didn't want to kill her. The whole way down here, he'd been congratulating himself on choosing the least objectionable candidate for a role he didn't actually want filled.

Sure, women were trouble, but he'd figured Autumn was the *least* likely to cause any. On purpose, anyway.

But he wasn't prepared for the reality of the woman he'd seen only in a video.

She was shorter than her sisters, though not *short*. He estimated she would fit right beneath his chin if he held her close—which he obviously wouldn't be doing. Ever. And she hadn't really touched on a lot of personal details in her video, but what was getting him the most was that she hadn't mentioned that hourglass figure.

That perfect, mouthwatering, *too good to be true except he was looking at her* figure that made him feel something like feverish.

She should have come with a warning label.

Because she made his mouth go dry, no matter if she was glaring at him. Hell, that only made her hotter. And Bowie might like a dare, but he had no interest whatsoever in torturing himself with killer curves he couldn't touch. Because this wasn't the gold rush and she wasn't really coming up to the Interior to marry him and even if she had been, he wasn't that guy.

He was a little concerned that he might be about to break out into a sweat, right there where her sisters could see. The blondes were all watching him closely, cataloging his reaction.

Waiting for him to indicate that he surely did notice that Autumn had a body of pure, delicious sin that he would have to somehow live with platonically for the next three months.

Waiting for a grown man to cry, more like it.

He'd thought their overprotectiveness was sweet. Now he got it.

Their sister was a time bomb.

In his profile, Bowie talked about his planes. He talked about the Fortunes' many generations out on the lake, carving their lives out of an uncaring, inhospitable stretch of Alaska that happened to also be about the most beautiful spot in the world as far as he was concerned. He'd said he wanted his "bride" to understand that the land and the planes came first, always. And that both required hard work and perseverance. His mother had told him he sounded borderline unhinged and off-putting. His sister had only sighed and mouthed *I told you so.* He'd been thrilled at their reactions, expecting that he'd weed out most of the contenders, but had been surprised when he'd still had almost too many to choose from.

That was how the coupling part of this thing worked. The lady contestants indicated which gentlemen they'd consider, then the gentlemen chose from among whoever had already chosen them.

Because, as everyone had been at pains to declare all over the ad campaigns, this wasn't actually the 1800s. The women weren't answering ads and delivering themselves into the clutches of whoever answered, come what may. There was absolutely no coercion or expectation of intimacy. There was only the summer and the upbeat pictures and videos they were expected to create to exult in the Upper Kuskokwim beauty all around them, along with regular wellness checks from the judges.

Bowie hadn't anticipated having any problems on that score. He hadn't been kidding when he'd told Piper he was good with his own dating—he just liked to make his own choices, and far away from home, where there could never be any blowback. He didn't do blowback, thank you. He'd been living hassle-free since he'd declined Uncle Sam's offer to re-up that last time.

He had also made a promise a long time ago to keep himself unattached, and he'd kept it.

And though he had spent his entire life, up until this moment, thinking that Alaskan summers lasted all of about thirty seconds, the three months stretching ahead of him now seemed like an eternity.

Because Bowie was a man who liked dangerous things. Killer curves topped that list.

You are boned, he told himself then.

It had the ring of finality.

His jaw was getting tight, so he forced himself to smile again. But he could see in the way Autumn was looking up at him that she'd caught the moment. She'd clocked him looking at her and freezing up. When those eyes of hers went wary, he felt a twist inside him, a lot like regret.

But he shoved it aside. Wariness was appropriate. The more wary she was of him, the less he would need to worry that he might succumb to temptation. He preferred enthusiastic invitations to lose his head a little—not that he could do that here even with an invite.

He'd signed that damn contract, promising he'd behave.

And even if he hadn't, he didn't do entanglements with complications.

Nothing about Autumn McCall's bombshell figure suggested good behavior was even a possibility.

"You don't actually have to do this, Autumn," Pickup Blonde was saying. "You can walk away right now."

"No harm, no foul," agreed Blue Nails Blonde.

"You should only do what you feel comfortable with," he managed to say, though he sounded like he was talking with glass in his mouth. He was more grateful than he wanted to admit that he had on sunglasses no one could see through, because he had the terrible suspicion that he was staring. *Gaping* at her like a teenage boy who'd never seen a woman before.

Next his voice would start cracking again and he'd have to take himself out.

"I'm not walking away, thank you." Autumn sounded unperturbed. Steady. It should have soothed him. But she was standing there in jeans and a T-shirt. A perfectly casual outfit, but the jeans hugged her butt and the shirt was enough to make a man weep, and he wanted to chew on his own hands. "And besides, you know as well as I do that it's high time Dad and Donna got some alone time."

That kicked off a chorus of blonde commentary and Bowie was pretty sure he heard the phrase *wicked stepmother* come up. More than once.

"I'm your stepmother, girls," came a voice from inside the house, and then an older woman stepped out, round and cheerful and unfazed. Followed by a man, clearly Autumn's father, who made no secret of the way he was sizing up Bowie. "But I'm not wicked."

"Fewer dramatics, please," their father said, casting a look around the assembled blondes. He moved forward, frowning at Autumn as he passed her, then stretching out his hand to Bowie. "Hunter McCall."

It was a relief to be *forced* to look away from the curve situation. He didn't know that he would have, otherwise. The older man's hand was firm and callused enough to suggest he put his own work into his land, which Bowie respected. He also didn't try to crush Bowie's fingers as they shook, though he continued to look suspicious.

He had every right to be, Bowie thought as he put in a valiant effort to stave off the great many images that wanted to flood his brain, all of them spelling out exactly the kind of trouble he didn't plan to allow himself.

Not with the unexpected bombshell he absolutely should not be taking home with him today.

It's fine, he assured himself. *Just don't look at her.*

"Bowie Fortune," Bowie replied to Autumn's father. He made himself smile. He tried to look like he meant it. "Not to worry. Your daughter is safe with me."

But to his surprise, Hunter McCall laughed.

"Glad to hear that, son," he belted out. "But it's not *her* safety I'm worried about."

Two

When a woman had three literal beauty queens as younger sisters and had spent a lifetime watching men walk into walls at the very sight of their blonde beauty, she grew used to *that look* she always got when the men in question finally looked her way.

Because there was always *that look.*

And not only from men.

People would meet her sisters and then Autumn would appear. And no matter how they tried to disguise it, there was always *that look.* It was made up of disappointment. Puzzled confusion. A very clear *What happened to this one?*

A question Autumn McCall had not asked herself since she was twelve. She had been plagued by puppy fat while her younger sisters were *already* stunning enough to make strangers stop to take their pictures. She'd waited in her parents' car while a photo shoot took place with her sisters outside of nearby Hamilton, her lovely sisters framed perfectly against the Bitterroot Mountains in the background, and had come to a decision.

She would not compare herself to them again. She would become good at something else instead.

And so she had. She had made herself her mother's helper. And after her mother died, she had thrown herself into the maternal role in the family even though she was only fourteen. She'd taken care of her sisters. She'd taken care of her father. She'd taken care of the house. She was fantastic at *taking care*. And she usually found *that look* funny when she encountered it. *No*, she would say with a laugh, *I'm not adopted. Supposedly.*

But not today.

It wasn't a *surprise* that she saw that same old look on Bowie Fortune's admittedly gorgeous face. Too gorgeous, actually, but she was still trying to process that curve ball. The look was par for the course. What was surprising was that she cared. Autumn had actually convinced herself that this would be the one arena where her sisters' beauty wasn't a factor.

She loved all three of them, but they were high maintenance at the best of times. Willa treated a chipped nail like a national emergency. Jade talked about her skincare routine the way some people spoke of religious services. And the baby, Sunny, had once cried when she found an inoffensive gnat in her orange juice. Like, last year.

They might have grown up in Montana, but if any one of the three of them attempted to go pioneer woman it up in Alaska, they would probably faint dead away at the sight of an actual deep-woods cabin, never to recover. They'd all left Big Sky Country for warmer weather as soon as they could and were unlikely to ever venture farther north. Not of their own volition.

Autumn had allowed herself to fantasize that this time might be different. That this time, she might shine for once.

That's on you, she told herself stoutly.

"You don't have to worry about my safety," Bowie was

telling her father. "I was in the marines for a spell. It taught me how to watch my own back, if nothing else."

"Thought about joining the marines," her father said, which was news to Autumn. And Donna, if her stepmother's expression was any guide. "Then I thought better of it."

Bowie let out a low sort of laugh that did disturbing things to the integrity of her knees. Autumn had to lock them to remain standing, and she was deeply disappointed in herself at the lapse. She was entirely too familiar with handsome men and their wiles, thanks to her sisters. Handsome men flocked around the three of them like mosquitoes and sometimes made the mistake of attempting to cozy up to Autumn as if she might give them access.

She never did, but that didn't keep them from their oily attempts.

The truth was that she had not expected Bowie Fortune to be *this* good-looking. She was . . . dismayed.

She told herself it was distracting, that was all.

Autumn blew out a breath and ordered herself to stop being distracted. She straightened her shoulders and got down to business. She marched over to the pickup where she'd stashed her bags earlier. There were two of them. One medium-size duffel and her little backpack.

Packing light isn't a virtue, you know, Jade had said last night, lounging across the better part of Autumn's bed in the room they'd shared when they were kids.

Neither is traveling with seventeen oversize bags for a quick trip home, Autumn had retorted.

Jade had grinned unrepentantly. *This is Montana. We could have six seasons before lunch. I like to be prepared.*

They both knew that it was Autumn who liked to be prepared and who, therefore, always was. What Jade liked was not being inconvenienced. It wasn't the same thing.

Autumn slid the strap of her backpack over her shoulder and pulled the handles of the duffel up over the same shoulder, too. Then she marched over to stand next to Bowie, her make-believe husband for the summer, who was significantly and unmistakably more attractive than he'd looked in his profile.

By about a thousand degrees.

It was the beard he'd had in the picture and video that he didn't have now. It was the baseball cap he'd worn shoved down on his head that had shaded his eyes. She'd expected a mountain man, like a great many of the men she knew around the Bitterroot Valley. She'd expected a known quantity, just a little bit farther off the grid.

He wasn't wearing a hat now. And he'd shaved sometime recently, though not today.

She was *dismayed*, Autumn assured herself, a little breathlessly. *Deeply* dismayed.

"Your dad makes it sound like you're something of a holy terror," Bowie drawled. She could see herself reflected in his sunglasses, and that was disconcerting. She looked smaller, as if he was taking her over, an idea she . . . did not hate the way she should have. He grinned wider, as if he knew exactly what sensations were careening around inside of her. "That certainly wasn't included in your profile."

"It's true," Jade offered. She was propped up against the front of the pickup like she expected a country song to kick up around her. "Make no mistake, she'll tear you up into little pieces."

"Noted." Bowie sounded unperturbed, his hidden gaze still on Autumn. She couldn't see it, but she could feel it. And something about that made her *dismay* even worse.

"She's ferocious," said Willa from her place at the fence. "No one around here dares to poke the bear. You should think twice."

Bowie Fortune only grinned. "Dangerous. Got it."

"'*The bear*,' Willa?" Autumn asked. "Really?" But her middle sister only shrugged.

"You better be nice to her," Sunny blurted out. In a rush of what sounded like temper, but was probably just her baby sister's usual oversize emotions. "Or I'll kill you myself."

"I'd let you," Bowie told her, a warmth in that low drawl that made Autumn feel almost light-headed.

She bent her knees a little more because she'd read that locking them could make a person pass out. That was probably what the light-headedness that felt like breathlessness was about. That or a bout of perfectly reasonable not-quite-panic about this huge thing she was setting off to do. More anticipation than panic, she decided as she stood there, bent-kneed.

Because it was high time she had a break from the McCall family homestead, love them all though she did. Her ulterior motives just made this entire mail-order bride thing make more sense, not that her sisters knew anything about that.

She'd been protecting her sisters for the better part of her life. It had been her job after they'd lost their mother, and in many ways, she'd loved it. She still did. But she was also looking forward to being herself for the summer. Just Autumn, instead of all the other roles she played here. But she couldn't tell that to her sisters. They wouldn't understand.

Autumn supposed she ought to have been embarrassed by their whole display, really. It was exactly the kind of drama that she hadn't missed when her sisters had all moved out, not that her father's tough-guy routine was much better. She wouldn't have blamed Bowie if he'd looked a little shell-shocked. Taken aback. Or even if he'd rolled his eyes at all of them the way she liked to do.

She wouldn't have blamed him, but she didn't think she would have liked him much.

Instead, his grin widened. "I'm glad to see that Autumn has so many defenders. I don't know that I would have showed up with this much fight in me if my little sister told me she was going off to do something like this."

But Autumn could tell, somehow, that he was lying.

"Right," she said briskly, before she lost control of her knees again. "I think everyone has said their piece." She smiled—tightly, maybe, but she smiled—at Bowie. "My sisters made a special trip up here to get those digs in. I hope you appreciate it."

"I surely do," he drawled, sounding more like a cowboy than a pilot.

And it wasn't until that moment, as she began to go around and hug everyone good-bye, that the true enormity of what she was doing hit her. The fact that she was getting on a plane with this strange and upsettingly attractive man to fly off to the middle of nowhere for the summer. Far away from the ranch, which she'd previously imagined was also the middle of nowhere. But Montana seemed like the bustling center of somewhere compared to Lost Lake, Alaska, which didn't even appear on most maps. And she'd tried really hard not to let the name of the supposedly nearby town that did appear on the maps get to her. *She* would not be hopeless no matter her circumstances, she liked to tell herself.

Typical Autumn, her sisters would have said with a sigh if she'd admitted she was suddenly questioning herself. Forever racing toward her objective without stopping to feel anything along the way.

That, of course, was why she very rarely told them what she felt about anything.

It made for a less dramatic life, but the flaw in her plan became clear now as all the things she hadn't permitted herself to feel began to swell up inside her as she walked around dispensing the necessary hugs. It wasn't so much her sisters themselves, who came and went with the seasons—and their whims. She had no doubt that she would see as much of them as ever. And there was no stopping their texts. But her father was a different kettle of fish. And so was her stepmother.

"I never meant to make it hard for you to settle in here," she said quietly to Donna as she gave her a hug. "I'm sorry if I did."

"It was never hard," Donna replied loyally, because that was the kind of lovely woman she was. No matter that it made her a liar. "I want you to have your shot at a life." Donna pulled back from the hug and eyed Bowie, who looked as if he could stand like that, minding his own business with his eyes on the Bitterroots, for hours. Days, even. "Though this does seem a bit extreme."

"That's the McCall way," her dad said gruffly. He hugged her in close, ruffling her hair as if she were still a toddler. "I like the look of him. But if he gets fresh, never forget your secret weapon."

Autumn couldn't help but smile, even as she blinked rapidly, trying to hold back the tears in her eyes. "I won't."

When she turned around, she saw that Bowie had hoisted up her bags and stood there. Waiting. "Ready to walk back to the plane?"

They'd all seen him land, out toward the northern edge of the property. It was an easy walk, but it was still a walk. "You don't want to take the truck?"

His grin never dimmed as he shook his head. "I figure you and I can take a nice long walk, while you're still safe here at home, and get better acquainted. Then you can decide if you still want to fly up to Lost Lake with me or not."

She didn't know if he said that because he meant it, or if he was playing to his audience. But either way, everyone made noises of approval.

Leaving Autumn to ask herself why it was that she wanted to take the truck. Not get acquainted at all, and simply charge forth into the summer before she could think too closely about it.

Well. She knew. *Welcome to your personality*, she thought drily. She'd been stuck with it for all these years, after all. She really shouldn't let it surprise her.

She waved one last time to her family, pretending not to notice the way her phone was already buzzing in her back pocket—thanks to Sunny, clearly, who was frowning as she texted—and then she marched herself over to Bowie's side, straightening her shoulders as she went. She glanced up at him to find him looking back down at her, so she nodded briskly. As if he was waiting for her to start things off.

That felt like a task, and Autumn was good at tasks.

It was much better than draping herself on things and *emoting*, like her sisters, and bonus: when she was done, tasks were completed.

This good-bye was now officially taking so long that she thought she might break out in hives or something equally unfortunate, so Autumn just . . . charged forward toward the path that wound back out to the makeshift runway in the distance. She didn't look back as Bowie fell in beside her without comment.

And that was how she walked away from the only life she'd ever known, into what could be described only as a reality show. However down-market and odd.

"I wouldn't call it down-market so much as peak Alaska," Bowie said when she advanced this theory. Mostly for something to talk about as they walked together, side by side, with only Montana's big sky as witness. "So, sure, odd. It's mostly just a publicity stunt. It might not shock you to learn that while there were a great many single men who liked the idea, there were far fewer women who wanted to go deal with some man's nonsense for a summer. No matter what they might win."

"How few?" Autumn suddenly panicked that she was the only one. Her sisters always said that, left to her own devices, she would run herself right off the side of a cliff before it occurred to her to look around for the stairs.

And she really hated it when her sisters were right.

"No more than a handful," Bowie said. "But that's a good thing, because there were only so many men who made the cut. Many disreputable characters had to be turned away."

"Fewer contestants means a better chance of winning," Autumn said prosaically. "I guess that's good."

She felt that searing sensation on the side of her face that meant Bowie was looking at her again, but she ignored it.

Just like she kept ignoring the buzzing phone in her pocket. Because if she didn't ignore these things, she was afraid they might consume her whole.

Or worse, she'd turn around and run straight back to the ranch house.

Where she would carry on living exactly the way she always had.

And as panicky as she felt—and it was almost certainly panic and not excitement, she could admit that—she didn't want to keep on living the same way she'd been living her whole life. She really, truly didn't, because Donna was right. She needed to *live*.

She also intended to do her family a particular service along the way, but the living part was key. There were other ways she could have tried to get the ten thousand dollars she needed.

The walking helped remind her that she meant to do this. Exactly this, exactly what she was doing. Her own little adventure. And it was starting off like this, with her feet on the earth. The big, bold sky above. It was hard to really give in to panic when she had those two things that had saved her more times than she could count.

So she kept walking. Bowie kept sauntering along beside her.

And for a little while they walked along the path quietly. Together. And it was almost nice if Autumn didn't think about too much besides the walk. It was a particularly beautiful day, sweet and whispering of summer. There was still a chill in the air, but the sunlight was warming it away. The Bitterroots rose before them to the west, imposing and beautiful. She couldn't imagine what it was going to be like to make sense of a horizon without them and the Sapphires to the east. She'd spent her whole life with these mountains as sentinels and silent guardians.

She told herself it was imagining life without them that was making her feel a little unsteady.

But Autumn didn't do *unsteady.* She was the rock of the family.

"If you don't mind my saying so," she said, because she was a *rock* and her knees were like *steel* and he was not the mountain man she had been expecting, "you don't exactly strike me as the sort of person who would normally sign up for something like this."

"I don't strike you as a man of adventure?" Bowie let out a laugh. "I'm crushed."

Autumn looked back over her shoulder to double-check what she already knew. That they'd walked around the bend, so they were no longer visible from the house. She stopped, and he did, too, not even bothering to set down her duffel as he looked at her.

"I didn't expect you to show up looking considerably different from your picture and video," she said, and she didn't try that hard to keep the accusatory note out of her voice. "A man named *Bowie* is supposed to look like an old hunting knife. Not like . . . you."

"I think they have a word for that," he said.

Though she noticed he sounded entertained. As if he had laughter layered into him, so that it was even a part of the way he stood there, sunglasses still hiding his eyes and his bomber jacket hanging open so she could see the T-shirt he wore with the name of an old rock band emblazoned across the chest. DEF LEPPARD.

But at least he didn't appear to be laughing *at* her.

"The word is catfishing," Autumn informed him. "I figured that since you were vetted, you couldn't be an ax murderer."

"Here's hoping."

"It was a very beard-centric photo but I assumed that if you looked different, it would be in the opposite direction. Like maybe the photo you sent was from a decade or so ago."

"Nope." That grin of his was a lazy sort of curl, and she could feel it *inside* her. "I'm just me."

"But that's the problem." Autumn found her hands on her hips and didn't do a whole lot about reining in her scowl. "You're too good-looking. Why on earth would someone who looks like you do something like this? There must be something wrong with you. What is it?"

For a moment he seemed stunned. But then the next moment, Bowie tipped his head back and laughed.

He laughed and laughed.

Until he had to take off the shades to run a hand over his face.

And it was like getting poleaxed.

It had been bad enough when she'd walked outside. Yes, he was attractive. Entirely too attractive. She had been completely unprepared for the sight of Bowie Fortune in the flesh.

He hadn't even been doing anything. He was standing there in the leather jacket and the shades. He'd had his hands in the pockets of his jeans. He wore weathered old boots and he smiled too much.

But her first glimpse of him had knocked the breath right out of her.

And now that he was laughing with the Montana sunshine cascading all over him, Autumn was forced to face the grim truth.

He wasn't attractive. He wasn't even good-looking. Those were pale words to describe him.

He was like the Bitterroots, her favorite mountains.

He was spectacular.

He was tall and rangy when she'd always thought of pilots as being short and stocky. He was all lean muscle with a certain carelessness in the way he held himself that made her whole body want to start shivering and maybe not stop. The rock band logo faded to insignificance when it was that flat-planed chest that really drew the eye.

And he had the face of a goddamned fallen angel.

His cheekbones were operatic. His jaw was sculpted and his mouth was distractingly mobile. He had dark hair, none of it receding or gray. And he had eyes as deep as a Montana night, a dark blue that made her feel something like hushed inside.

This was a *disaster.*

"Nothing's wrong with me," Bowie said, and she must have made a face at that patent untruth because he laughed again. "By my reckoning, anyway. Ask around and you might get a different answer. But the simple truth is that my sister dared me to do this, so here I am."

"Do you always do what your sister tells you to do?" For some reason she found that extremely hard to believe. It was his eyes, maybe. There was a wildness there that made her think of clear nights out here, where there were very few lights and the stars took over everything. "That's not how things went in my house, but all families are different."

"I never do what my sister tells me to do." Bowie looked incredulous. "She's my baby sister. It's a point of pride to act like she can't possibly know what she's talking about, no matter what it is. She *dared* me."

"Dared you," Autumn echoed. "Is that a thing? Really?"

"I don't back down from dares, Autumn."

Well, at least if he had to be beautiful, he was also a fool. That was some comfort. She could manage that. Probably. "At least your reasons for doing this are more foolish than mine. I guess that's something."

"I believe in the judicious application of foolishness whenever possible," Bowie drawled, all dark blue eyes and that lazy grin, and she wasn't sure she was prepared for this after all. The pioneering part, sure. But the man? She really hadn't thought enough about the man aspect. In the general sense of sustained proximity to one. She'd figured that handling her father had been good enough practice. Maybe she'd been kidding herself. "Why are you doing it?"

She noticed that he did not rush to tell her that she was entirely too good-looking for this enterprise. And she hated herself for noticing it, even as she told herself she had to admire him for his honesty.

Though *admiration* was not exactly how she would describe her reaction.

"Let me guess," Bowie continued in that cheerful way of his that she was beginning to think was not, in fact, all that genuinely cheerful. "You're in it for the fame."

She sighed. "I'm not sure that appearing a few times in a newspaper in Alaska qualifies as fame."

"I don't disagree, but it's more fame than not appearing in the *Anchorage Daily News*. Besides, everyone in Lost Lake will know your name. That's something."

"Lost Lake. Population . . . What? Twenty brave souls?"

"That's only if you count all the folks who claim they live in the Mine," he told her. Helpfully. "Twenty is a stretch, depending on the time of year."

"People live in a mine?"

Bowie's impossible eyes gleamed. "Not exactly. You'll see. But you still haven't answered me. Why are you doing this? And while we're on the topic, what exactly is the secret weapon your father mentioned and does it draw blood?"

Autumn would have sworn that Bowie hadn't been paying that much attention to her good-byes, or what was said. She was going to have to remember that he apparently noticed everything.

She opened her mouth to tell him exactly why she was doing this, but stopped. Her teeth clacked shut. He was doing this on a dare. A *dare*.

He didn't deserve to know why she was really doing this. Because it was earnest and she *felt things* and the thought of him *grinning* at her reasons made her toes curl up inside her shoes. She couldn't do it.

"I'm doing it for the prize, of course," she said, and when his eyes narrowed a bit, almost like he could read her, she shook her head at him. "What other reason is there to enter contests? I find it so disingenuous when people get on these reality shows and act as if they're absolutely *flabbergasted* by the notion that they might actually have to compete. I think it's lies. Pretending, anyway. I won't stoop to that level."

He was quiet for a moment, though nothing about the way he was looking at her *felt* quiet. Certainly not inside her body. "Do you watch a lot of reality shows?"

"I've been forced to watch a lot of reality shows," she corrected him, warming to the topic. And this new *reality show* persona she was taking on. It was a lot more fun than the sentimental truth. "My stepmother adores them. Which is why I can tell you, without the slightest hint of self-pity or bad feelings, that when she decided to marry my father and move into our house, she had very specific goals. Among them was getting me out. And she studied her shows well, because she achieved this goal in less than a year."

Donna would howl with laughter if she heard Autumn say something like that, because she was the least competitive woman on the face of the planet. She was undemanding, compassionate, and always, always thought the best of everyone she met. If sunshine were a person, it would still be dimmer than Donna.

But Bowie couldn't know that.

"Why do you live at home anyway?" he asked. "Aren't you too old for that?"

"What I'm good at is keeping house," Autumn said. "People look down on that skill, but it doesn't make it any less of a skill. Sadly, the kind of jobs on offer for my talents are usually for maids, not housekeepers. There's a difference."

"That does not sound like the kind of can-do attitude that made Alaska great," Bowie observed, but his eyes were dancing. "We make our own jobs out in the bush, Autumn."

"Besides," Autumn continued, ignoring his comment and the *dancing eyes*, "my father is a very particular kind of man. He likes a woman to take care of his house. And for a long time, I was the only applicant for that job, because he was a mess. So I did it, because I'm good at it."

Bowie didn't actually step away, but still, it felt as if he did. There was a distinct wall between them, suddenly. As if the temperature dropped around them.

"I am not that kind of man," Bowie told her, the dancing light in his eyes gone as if it had never been. Not that he looked any less beautiful without a smile on his face. On the contrary, he looked like someone should cast him in bronze. "It's summer. We don't have to be cooped up inside, on top of each other. You can do your thing and I'll do mine. I don't need caring for or keeping. That's the kind of thing that made me leave my mother's house when I was seventeen, with a waiver so I could join the marines before my eighteenth birthday. I've been taking care of myself ever since. Happily."

He said that very seriously. She could see he meant it.

"Then maybe you should have thought twice before entering a contest for a mail-order bride, fake or not," Autumn replied drily. "Especially when demonstrating pioneer spirit *together* is literally the entire contest."

"Pioneer can mean a lot of things," Bowie replied, still looking grave. No hint of that smile at all.

"I already have a number of projects planned." Depending on things like terrain and whether or not there were fish, but she didn't get into all that. The point was, she was prepared for the frontier-type tasks they'd need to film.

"If you really want to win the so-called grand prize," he began, not sounding all that interested in her projects.

But that was ridiculous. "It's ten thousand dollars. Not ten dollars, ten *thousand*."

Now he smiled, but she could see the difference. This smile was practiced. "I just want to make sure that there are no misunderstandings between us. As long as we're on the same page, I don't see why the whole thing can't be an adventure."

"The same page," she repeated.

"So no one gets the wrong idea."

She was about to ask him what a *wrong idea* might be, but then she got it.

Autumn stiffened in horror. "This is not *romantic*, Bowie. Not on my end."

And she wrestled with the twelve-year-old within, who wanted to point out that her sisters had never had a man *let them down easy* in their entire lives. But she shoved that away, because she was going to have her summer. She was going to have her adventure. Her *life*.

Even if she had to pretend she was a reality show character to do it.

"I wasn't suggesting otherwise," Bowie said, but he had been. She knew he had been. She'd been the duckling in a family of swans her whole life. It wasn't like this was the first time one of her sisters' suitors had rushed to make sure Autumn didn't *get carried away*.

Maybe later she would take the time to investigate why this time hurt a lot more, but this wasn't the moment.

Right now she had to pretend to be the win-at-all-costs reality show person she'd told him she was.

"My entire purpose in life is finding my way to a Caribbean beach," she told him. As if she was talking into a camera with dramatic music playing and her name emblazoned across the screen. "I intend to drink piña coladas, keep my feet sandy, and maybe, every other Tuesday, think about wrapping myself up in a sarong and testing out my flip-flops. *Maybe*."

"The Caribbean," he said, like he didn't believe her. "By way of Alaska."

So Autumn had no choice but to channel every amoral reality show contestant she had ever voted against. She drew herself up and tried to shake her head sadly, as if her machinations were far above his paygrade.

"Bowie." She said his name supervillain style, which was still less patronizing than the way he'd said, *So no one gets the wrong idea*. Then she tried to smile the way Jade did when she was getting ready to break men's hearts. "I'm willing to work hard to win this thing. But I want to be clear. I do intend to win."

Three

It was late—but still light, because welcome to Alaska—when Bowie finally landed just off the lake on the private runway he'd built himself to accommodate all the flying he liked to do. Or might one day like to do.

It had been a long flight, plus the usual refueling stops. But Bowie was used to being a charter pilot—not a *character* he played but a job he happened to be good at, thank you—so he kept up a running commentary on the various sites of interest they flew over, especially once they made it to the Denali region. His would-be pioneer bride, who was apparently in it to win it whether he liked it or not, looked out the windows from beside him in the cockpit and took the expected pictures of the tallest mountain in America as he flew them over the Alaska Range and into the Interior.

He would have been surprised if she hadn't.

But it wasn't until they made it to Lost Lake that Bowie really paid close attention to her responses. Because Denali spoke for itself. Pretty mountains had been astonishing humans for centuries. What Bowie really cared about was her reaction to his home, because she'd be sharing it with him for the next three months.

Not just her *reaction*, he corrected himself as he taxied to a stop on his gravel. *Any Outsider's reaction.*

Tonight the sun wouldn't set until just after midnight. That meant that visibility had been excellent as he'd flown in. He loved the approach from the east. He'd followed the Kuskokwim as it wound around past McGrath, before dropping elevation to meander along through the pristine wilderness. Eventually he flew in over Hopeless, the closest thing to a town around, hunkered there on the banks of the river. Though he supposed that in some places, calling the sparse collection of buildings and the population to match a *town* would make folks laugh. Down where *towns* could be thousands of people. Hopeless was small, there was no denying it. But it was still a booming metropolis in comparison to the community arranged around Lost Lake to the north.

The lake itself was big, stretching out from its source in the hills to the east, where Bowie's ancestors had followed rumors of gold and signed on to mine it. But when the vein they'd tapped had proved disappointing, the corporation had cut and run. Bowie's great-grandfather had banded together with a few others here to buy the land and, even more important, the mineral rights. The story went that the fat cats had laughed all through the deal, so sure that they'd been swindling the dumb miners who wanted this useless piece of land.

Joke was on them. All these years later, the descendants of those not-so-dumb miners had new and improved corporate types sniffing around constantly—though usually from a distance. Each one promised the moon and stars, if only they would sell off those mineral rights.

They hadn't. Yet.

But in the meantime, they'd gone ahead and created the Mine in what had been, historically, the big main building of the failed gold mine in the census-designated place known as Old Gold. Some of the successors of the original families still lived in the little buildings, once upon a time miners' cottages, stacked up along the hill. Together, over time, the original miners who'd settled here and their offspring had taken that old mining building and made it theirs.

A whole town in one room, people liked to call it. It was especially useful in winter, when folks could hunker down, get their shopping done, hit the bar, grab some food, buy an ATV if they had half a mind to, and even bunk down when the weather turned foul the way it often did. In summer, they opened up the big, wide doors and let the warmer air in.

Bowie had been to a lot of towns, but he found he liked the one they'd built themselves the best.

The Fortunes had found even the few people who frequented the Mine a little too much of a crowd for their blood. They'd moved out farther, all the way to the other end of the lake, where the original cabin his great-grandparents had first built still stood. And there were other houses now, other Fortunes. His older brother Quinn and Violet—Quinn's woman from California, of all places—who'd come up in January and stayed put. His parents, up in the rambling old house at the end of the lake that the family added to with each successive generation. His sister, Piper, who lived in her own cabin and shipped her version of pioneer goods all over the world.

Bowie didn't like to brag, at least not privately, but he considered the Fortune part of the lake the best. No contest. But when he glanced at the woman beside him, all he could see was the same poker face she'd been wearing since they'd left Montana.

Afraid of flying? he'd asked her when they'd settled into the cockpit.

Not in a normal-size plane, she'd replied, her voice clipped as she'd gazed out the window before them. *This appears to be the kid-size version.*

He'd laughed at that. *I think you mean fun-size.*

But he'd seen the way she was gripping her hands together, so hard her knuckles were white, so he'd kept himself in check as he'd taken off and started the flight home. No stunts, as Bertha Tungwenuk and his brother and a great many others liked to call his penchant for in-air dramatics. No tricks.

His reward had been seeing her slowly unclench as they flew, though the careful poker face remained.

"Home sweet home," he said now.

"I'll be honest," Autumn replied from beside him, still sounding measured, if marginally less remote. "I was expecting a shanty in the deep, dark woods. But that lake is beautiful. And if that's your house we just flew over, this is already a lot better than I was imagining."

"I'm almost offended." He wasn't, but he liked the way she looked over at him, as if to check.

"I watched a lot of those Alaska shows in preparation. Some of them are . . . Well. Pretty grim."

"I'm many things, Autumn. But never grim." He grinned to prove it. "Besides, most of those shows are set in the middle of winter for the maximum possible effect on Outsiders. I bet your Montana valley looks pretty grim around February, too."

She paused for a moment. Then, "I take your point."

He was still laughing about shanties, the deep, dark woods, and grim reality shows after he'd gone through his postflight checklist and brought the plane into the hangar so they could both climb down.

Autumn picked up both her bags and Bowie felt it would be undignified to wrestle her backpack off her shoulder, but he helped himself to the duffel again. He didn't mean for their fingers to touch, but he told himself that was nothing. Even though she let go of the duffel's handles like they were suddenly on fire. And then he led his blushing bride—for the summer, he reminded himself, and she wasn't really blushing—away from his beloved planes and toward his home.

Once again, he was a little more interested in her reaction than he wanted to admit to himself. But then, he didn't bring a lot of strangers home. Autumn was the first. A man didn't live this far off the grid if he wanted company.

Yet here he was, welcoming her in.

Something that was a lot like the kind of complications he usually avoided—but wasn't, he assured himself. Because this was a contest, not his personal choice.

It was important to make that distinction.

He led her down the long, covered path from the hangar to his house, but didn't go in the side door he usually used. Instead, he took her around the front so she could get a sense of the place. It was a tradition in his family to go off and build a cabin when the time was right, and Bowie had taken a lot of pleasure in his. He had picked out every log, shaped each room, and thought through exactly how he would use the space. Building this house had been an excellent project for a man who was finished with the service but not quite sure what to do with himself, back out here as a civilian.

He was more than a little proud of it. And he told himself it was perfectly natural to find himself interested in the opinion of a person who didn't know him. All she would see was the house itself, not all the whys and reasons his family and friends knew all too well, having helped him put this place together.

And having helped put him back together, too, now that he thought about it.

"I thought we were isolated in Montana," Autumn said as they cleared the side of the house. She stopped there to look out at the lake, still gleaming in the last of the day's light. It was eleven forty-five P.M. "But this is *really* isolated."

Bowie took that as an opportunity to stop fretting internally, not a good look for a former marine. "That's the Alaska promise." He stopped, one foot on the wide steps that led up to his front porch. "But to be clear, we have neighbors. My folks live up at the top of the lake. My sister lives between them and me. And if you look out across the lake, you can see the smoke from my brother's chimney. Just isolated enough, I'd say."

She stood there a moment, her gaze on the lake. Then she turned to him, eyes a grave hazel. "And if I decide to make a break for it, but not to the bosom of your family, what then?"

Bowie couldn't help but admire a woman who could have spent her life fulfilling pinup dreams far and wide, but who had instead, clearly, committed herself to practicality. She was direct. No-nonsense.

He felt an unruly sensation wash through him then. It was all heat and need and an intense awareness. Bowie tried to ratchet his reaction back under control. Where it belonged. Sure, she seemed to push his buttons. All of them. Hard.

But just because a man had buttons didn't mean he had to let them work. He decided if he responded. *You either control yourself or you don't*, he reminded himself, the way his father used to remind him when he was a kid, all testosterone and questionable impulses.

He realized that he was looking at her a little too intently when she frowned. "Am I not supposed to ask questions like that?" she asked tartly. "This feels like the right time to tell you that my sisters have me on a very strict schedule of check-ins. The first one is in fifteen minutes, so I'm going to need to access your internet by then."

"Or what?" he asked. Not in a challenging way. But because he truly wanted to know what their plan was. It wasn't as if they could send in the local police. Alaska State Troopers had outposts in remote areas, but the nearest one to Lost Lake was off in McGrath, a bit of a flight away.

"They're very creative," Autumn said. "And as you discovered today, not even remotely afraid of causing a scene."

"I'm heartbroken that they didn't trust me."

"They actively distrust you, in fact."

"Fair enough." He held her gaze then, because he liked to joke around whenever possible but this part was serious.

"I'm not that guy, Autumn. I'm not going to hurt you. And I'm never going to keep you trapped here."

If possible, her gaze grew even more grave—but not like she didn't believe him. More like she did.

"You have any number of vehicles to choose from when you want to escape," Bowie continued. "ATV. Motorboat. Rowboat. Canoe. Hell, you can try out the snow machine if you want, though I do require a pilot's license if you want to fly a plane. But any way you want to get away from here, you're welcome to use it. Most vehicles have a key right in them. Turn it and go, no questions asked." He jutted his chin in the vague direction of the head of the lake. "The closest outpost of civilization is all the way on the other end of the lake. Once upon a time it was a mining town. Now it's . . . a village, I guess. Everyone there knows me, but no worries, that only means they'll be more than happy to take your side. You can go right now if you want."

"That's okay," Autumn said after a minute. "I have my secret weapon."

"A machete? Brass knuckles? A concealed-carry handgun?"

Her lips curved. "If I told you, it wouldn't be a secret, would it?"

"Definitely something sharp, then."

She let her lips curve only a little.

That settled, he led her inside. He showed her around and then waited for her to comment on the layout of thc place, the way his family did every time they showed up. *This cabin is built like a call for help*, Piper would say. But Bowie liked it. There was his arctic entryway to handle mud and frigid temperatures alike. Once inside, everything was built around the central room, where he had his big fireplace, his couches, and his big, pitched roof with as many windows and skylights as possible to let the sky in.

Everything branched off from there. He hadn't built a proper square, and he built a new little wing anytime he felt like it, so the kitchen was in one direction, the bedrooms in another. There was the covered porch where he liked to sit and look out over the lake. There was another screened-in porch next to it, because a man could take only so many mosquitoes. He had an outdoor shower for summer with a door that led right into a big bathroom inside, with a tub that he could actually soak in and the kind of shower he'd daydreamed about while stuck in unpleasant foreign places. He had a little hall that led out to his office, where he could access the hangar from the side door without having to go out into too much weather. The shop was in the other direction.

His latest project had been to finally get around to building the master bedroom he'd always wanted, up on the second floor out back behind the pitched roof of his great room, where he'd just finished making himself an even better porch. And bonus, he felt like he was camping while he slept.

"Did you build this yourself?" Autumn asked, running her hands over one of the logs that formed a wall. "Impressive work."

"I guess it's not a normal house. It makes sense to me." And Bowie never felt stiff or awkward, so he rejected the notion that he felt such things now. "Why don't you freshen up? I'll find us something to eat. I warn you now, my mother insists that we come to dinner tomorrow night. If you haven't taken off before then."

"I make no promises." Autumn looked so serious that he blinked at that—until he saw the way her lips twitched. "But I don't need to freshen up. And I'd love to see the state of the kitchen."

"I was in the marines," he told her. Maybe a little chidingly. Maybe more than a *little*. "They took the slob right out of me."

He might not keep his house in the antiseptic state some veterans he knew did, but he was neat. That suddenly felt crucial to make clear to a woman who had expected a dire shanty, but had come with him anyway.

And he took a kind of pride in that as Autumn followed him into the kitchen, which he'd made big enough to fit his family, since there was no keeping them away. Her eyes lit up when she saw the comfortable couch against one wall near his second fireplace.

"I love a couch in a kitchen," she said with a sigh. "So cozy."

"No matter how many times you tell everyone to go sit in the room that was made for sitting, they always end up standing in the kitchen."

"Every time," Autumn agreed, and smiled at him.

The kind of smile that could rearrange the stars, so wasn't he lucky that it was currently still light outside. Okay, a dimming twilight, but still.

He gave her what she needed to access the internet and she connected, then spent a few moments typing furiously on her phone. Then it was her turn to watch as he moved around, making them a quick meal of pasta with his mother's widely beloved meat sauce. Caribou meat, this batch, if he wasn't mistaken.

"I didn't make the sauce," he confessed as he poured it into a saucepan. "That's all my mother."

"You appear to know how to make the pasta." She came over to stand near the stove, her hip against the nearest counter. And he did not need to pay any more attention to her hips, God help him. "So that's good."

He let his eyebrows rise, and definitely did not look at the perfect hourglass line of her body when he had cooking implements to manage. "I can actually cook, Autumn. Or I'd starve."

"I'm sorry if I seem amazed." She tucked her hands in her back pockets as she *leaned* there, disrupting the universe. Making it difficult to remember how hard Bowie had always worked to keep his life free of disruptions. "I guess that might seem condescending, but that's not how I mean it. I've been doing all the cooking at my house since I was about twelve. I don't think my dad knows how to fry an egg."

"My mother used to tell us that there was nothing on this earth she liked less than a helpless male. Therefore she set out to make sure that she didn't raise any. We all had different nights of the week we had to cook for the whole family, and let me tell you, the taste testers gave vicious feedback." He glanced over at her. "So I can tell you with perfect confidence that my spaghetti is masterful, but my mother still makes the best red sauce."

He hadn't thought about the pressure of cooking as a kid in a long time. Though everyone—okay, maybe just Bowie—still talked about the time Piper had crumbled under the weight of expectations and passed out bread and butter.

"You sound close to your family," Autumn said, bringing him back to the here and now, in this bizarre undertaking he should have flatly refused to do the moment his sister had suggested it.

Bowie had never had the slightest urge to be a martyr and now he knew why. It sucked. But she was talking about his family. "Not, you know, *let's make the fake summer bride run a gauntlet* kind of close, I guess. But yeah. We get along okay."

"My sisters and I are close." Autumn moved away from the stove while the pasta bubbled and he stirred the sauce, so that the warm scent of oregano and tomatoes filled the air. She emphasized the word *sisters* as she went over and sat on the couch. "I would say we're all fond of my dad, but he kind of dropped the ball there for a while. A long while. My sisters left the minute they each turned eighteen."

"But not you."

"Not me, no. But now that Dad is married, there's no reason for me to stay. I was going to have to move out anyway."

He looked over, sure that he heard something there in the way she said that. But then, maybe on this first, strange night when the enormity of the whole thing seemed to sit on them both a little heavy, there was no point in pushing.

And maybe, a voice in him suggested, *you could not push every button presented to you the way you normally do, just because it's there.*

It was possible, he thought then, that this bizarre situation he found himself in—entirely his own fault, he accepted that—was actually an opportunity. To stop being the Bowie Fortune that everyone knew, and to be . . . whoever he wanted to be. Not the guy he was when left to his own devices. He'd had years of that. But whoever he was with just the two of them here, no one else around for miles.

Because he'd lived with his family for years. And he'd lived with the other members of his unit. Lately he lived all by himself. But he'd never shared his space like this. With one other human. He'd never intended to change that.

Maybe he was completely different one-on-one. Not just for a night, but for three months. Bowie supposed he'd find out, like it or not.

What he did not intend to do was admit to his sister that she'd had a point.

He served up two big plates of pasta and sauce and carried them over to the rough-hewn farm table that took up a decent portion of the kitchen space. Instead of following him right over, Autumn got up and set about cleaning up the stove, carrying the pots to the sink, and then running some soapy water in them. In a matter-of-fact way that suggested that was just what a person did when someone else cooked the meal.

He grabbed a shaker of Parmesan and the good salt, then met her back at the table.

They sat there beneath another one of his skylights while the light outside blurred into that deep summer blue.

"You told me you want to win because you want a tropical vacation," Bowie said after they'd been eating awhile, and he was finding the silence a little too much. It encouraged him to think a bit too vividly about other things they could do while not talking, and that was no way to maintain his self-control. "I told you my sister dared me. What do you think? Do we have a shot at this thing?"

Autumn laughed and Bowie liked that. A lot. She sat back in her seat with that laughter all over her. It was like every single feature on her face was perfectly and particularly situated to catch the light. He found himself thinking that a face like that would be useful in an Alaskan winter, when there was so little light to go around.

Then he told himself, sharply, to stop thinking such things.

"I'm pretty determined," Autumn confided. "And I have to think that the kind of man who would build a house like this—in the middle of nowhere, without a single attempt at being conventional, and including your own private airfield—is the same. So I guess the question is not whether or not we have a shot, but whether you think you can turn getting back at your sister into actually winning this thing."

"I'm a man of many talents," Bowie told her.

"That's pretty clear."

"Well, Autumn, I might have started this as a dare, but I don't see why we can't accomplish all of our goals."

She smiled at him, her eyes dancing in a way that made him feel downright new. And for the first time since he'd set off to go pick himself up a wife, Bowie thought this madness might actually be fun.

Assuming he could keep that driving desire to touch her to himself.

Because fun was one thing. Bowie was great at *fun*. But there was nothing fun about complicating his life with a woman who was going to be here until Labor Day. Nothing at all fun about creating a mess and then having to sit in it.

"You don't look sure," she pointed out, that laughter still all over her face.

"I'm sure," he told her, with more conviction this time.

And he was.

He was Bowie Fortune. He could make a war zone fun and come out unscathed. He had, more than once. And this wasn't even a war zone. It was a summer. A quick little Alaskan summer that would be gone before he knew it.

Why should this be any different?

Four

Autumn woke up when the alarm on her phone beeped at her, telling her it was six the way it always did. And then she sat up in a rush, because she'd completely forgotten where she was.

It came back to her slowly. This small room made of logs and cozy details. The handmade quilt and the thick, colorful rug thrown across the weathered wood floor. The woodstove in the corner. *Alaska.* The publicity stunt she was participating in for her own purposes.

Above and beyond and around all that, Bowie Fortune.

She sighed a little. Bowie Fortune was not what she expected. She looked around the room, scouring it for evidence that would make him more . . . palatable, maybe, but it was the same as the rest of the house. Well made. Thoughtful. She even had her own door leading outside. As far as she'd been able to tell on her tour yesterday, just about every nook and cranny of this house had its own door, even though that had to be drafty in the winters. Maybe he blocked them off then.

But clearly, Bowie didn't like the idea of being trapped indoors. Or trapped anywhere, maybe.

She filed that away as she got up, the wood floor cool beneath her feet. She pulled on her utilitarian wool socks—a staple in Montana and likely here, too—and padded over to the door, just to see what outside looked like at six in the morning.

She was sighing in wonder the next moment, because she hadn't realized last night that he'd given her a room that looked right over the lake.

There had been a lot of to-die-for views on her flight out from Montana yesterday, but she thought she loved the sparkling lake that was *right here* the most. The lake gleamed at the end of the gently sloping yard, making the dock and boathouse near the water's edge seem gilded in the prettiest imaginable gold. She stepped out onto the little square that was close enough to a porch for her purposes, wrapped the sweater she'd grabbed tighter around her, and breathed it all in.

All the smells were different here. The wrong flowers. A different breeze. And then, at the same time, it all smelled comfortingly the same. Evergreens and dirt. The sunlight was already bright. The air was cool and sweet. She couldn't see the tall, imposing Rockies, but the lake only got more beautiful the longer she looked at it, and she'd seen the hills as they'd come in.

Autumn had visited all kinds of places, but she'd never stayed anywhere but home for longer than a weekend or the odd week's vacation.

She fished her phone from the pocket of her pajama pants and sent a quick text out to her sisters, who had been up for ages in their ahead-of-Alaska time zones and had cluttered up the group text with over one hundred comments. Mostly about what *kind* of serial killer Bowie was.

He hasn't murdered me just yet, she wrote. This is the view from my bedroom.

She snapped a quick picture, getting in the wildflowers, the trees, and the crystal blue waters of the lake that seemed even more beckoning and beautiful in the morning light than they had late last night.

And she didn't wait for their responses—though she could feel her phone buzzing away. Instead, she turned around and went back inside to dress quickly, pulling on jeans, a T-shirt, and a trusty wool midlayer before she headed out to see what the day held in store.

She strode out into the house with her usual purpose, then stopped dead, because Bowie was already in the kitchen. She could smell butter on a griddle, one of the very best scents in all the world, but she couldn't really marinate in that the way she wanted.

Because Bowie hadn't bothered with a shirt this morning.

Autumn stopped dead in the doorway to the kitchen, because she wasn't prepared. It was too early. How could anyone be prepared for *all that* at this hour?

Not that it would have mattered what time it was. The problem wasn't the hour. The problem was the man.

She realized in that moment that she'd never given adequate attention to the beauty of a male back. Especially a back like Bowie's. She hardly knew where to look. There were all those muscles, slabs of them, that spoke to an active sort of life. He looked like he could pick up one of those planes of his if he wanted, and maybe toss it around some. He looked like the sort of man who could take his place in one of those summer action movies her sisters loved so much.

If she was honest, Autumn had never understood the way her sisters carried on about men, in movies or in life. Autumn had dated a little bit in high school and had found the experience unremarkable. In her early twenties, when it had seemed obvious that her life was going to stay the way it always was, she'd reconnected with one of her high school boyfriends because she'd wanted to make sure that she wasn't missing anything.

But it had been clear that she was missing nothing, and so, once she'd had the full experience, she'd stopped worrying about men and their parts and their *backs* and had gotten back to taking care of her family.

Yet never in any high school dating scenario, or even her short-lived experience with what was supposed to be passion a few years ago, had she ever felt anything like this.

And all she was doing was standing across the room, looking at Bowie Fortune's back.

He turned then, and even though she knew that last night hadn't actually been dark until after midnight and the sun had been up before her, she felt as if the morning light were breaking through *whole nighttimes* all the same. It poured in through the skylights and windows and lit him up like he was gilded, too.

It washed over a chest so mouthwatering it really should have come with a warning label.

There was just no getting away from that shocking, stunning beauty of his.

She was never going to be prepared.

It was so *unfair.*

At least she could trot out a reality show persona to fall back on in moments like this. It didn't matter what she, the actual Autumn McCall, might have said or done in this situation. It didn't matter that really, if it had been just her, she might have succumbed to her helpless knees and crumpled right down to the kitchen floor. What other reaction was a living, breathing woman expected to have when faced with that much astonishingly mouthwatering male beauty, right there in front of her when she hadn't even had a chance to get a cup of coffee?

But when she remembered that she'd told him that she more or less thought she was on an episode of *Survivor,* the path forward became clear.

"We need to discuss sex," she announced.

Autumn had always been good at projecting authority. The more unearned, the better. How else could a grieving fourteen-year-old fulfill her promise to her dying mother and take care of the whole freaking family? She'd simply acted as if she'd been taking care of everyone all along and they'd fallen in line.

She didn't see how one overly attractive Alaskan pilot could be more difficult than a grumpy widower and three obnoxious little sisters, who were still texting their feelings at her. She could feel the phone buzz in her pocket. Again and again.

It was only as the silence drew out that she registered the details that all that morning sun and his general hotness had obscured. Bowie looked a little . . . rumpled. *Slept in*, a voice inside her whispered salaciously, the way one of her sisters would. His eyes, still the color of a Montana night, were sleepy. That dark hair of his looked as if he'd run his hands through it, then let it do what it liked.

But as he stared back at her, clearly startled by what she'd said, the look in his eyes changed. There was a gleam there now that made her pulse begin to catapult around the base of her neck.

And make a racket in other places farther south, too.

Maybe she shouldn't have thrown out the word *sex* so starkly. As ever, that sort of thing occurred to her too late.

"*Do* we have to talk about sex?" Bowie asked.

Mildly.

Too mildly.

Autumn realized her delivery could have been better. And maybe her timing. Maybe the real truth was that she wasn't cut out to be an amoral reality show contestant. But she brazened it out, because that was what she did.

It was the only thing she knew how to do.

"We do," she said in the tone a field hockey coach might use, not that she was an expert on field hockey or coaches. But she thought she was hitting the right note of *can-do* forcefulness. "I think yesterday we were euphemistically dancing around the subject, but I want to be clear."

"Clear is good," Bowie agreed. "Who doesn't like a little clarity?"

She could hear all that laughter in his voice again and

was halfway certain she could see it on his face, too. But he didn't actually laugh. He just seemed to fill the room with it without even trying.

Trust a beautiful person to *exude things* effortlessly while everyone else had to work to even make a splash.

"No romance, no sex, and no parading around naked," Autumn said, in far more repressive tones than she might have used had she not started thinking of all the things that were probably dead easy for a man like him. "This is a literal eyes-on-the-prize situation." She flapped a hand in the direction of his naked chest. The whole mesmerizing sweep of it. "That's all very distracting."

"I'm touched that a cutthroat contestant like you allows herself the occasional distraction at all," he drawled. "Much less little old me."

Little old him. There was something about the way he said it—or maybe that he said it at all—that made her want to explode. And that was not her style. She wasn't a *yeller.* She didn't flush all kinds of colors and blow her top. She had proven that she could weather any storm with equanimity, living on an isolated ranch with her entire family all those years. She would have said she had been tested and had proven herself, but apparently Bowie Fortune was a different kind of test.

She refused to fail.

"We've hit the ground running," Autumn told him, back to her demented field hockey coach impression. "We need to get out ahead of it. Start as we mean to go on."

"Yes," Bowie said, and now he wasn't exuding humor so much as laughing outright. "All of those phrases are empty, yet somehow mean the same thing."

Autumn was beginning to worry that it was entirely possible that she was always going to be this uncomfortable around him. Always overheated, pulse rocketing around inside her, and her breath tangled up in the back of her throat. She was going to have to get used to it.

"I don't think you'd like it if I was walking around without a shirt on," she said, hoping she sounded reasonable and calm when she felt neither. "So why are you?"

And if she hadn't been standing there, staring right at him, perfectly capable of seeing that there were no hands around his neck, she would've thought that Bowie was being strangled.

"You're right," he said, in that odd, half-choked voice. "It would be terrible if you were walking around without a shirt on."

He seemed to be frozen where he stood, an arrested sort of look on his face and still the clear sense that something had him by the neck.

"Are you sick?" she asked.

Bowie cleared his throat. Twice. "I think the jury is out on that one, darlin'."

"*Darlin'*. Nice," she said brightly, when that was not exactly how she would describe her body's response to hearing him drawl an endearment. She might know that a man like him said *darlin'* indiscriminately, but tell that to each and every overly warm part of her. They were all clamoring for attention now. "That will definitely help set the fake-marriage mood."

"To clarify," he said, and she watched, more intrigued than she should have been, surely, as he dragged a hand over his face. "The marriage part is a gimmick. You know that, right? We're not trying to convince anyone that we're actually married. We're seeing if you can tough it out here for three months, do some survival stuff, and not run screaming back down to the Lower Forty-eight before Labor Day."

"I will not be running off screaming to anywhere," Autumn replied loftily. "I told you, I have every intention of winning. But since you're the one doing this on a lark—"

"I beg your pardon. A dare, not a lark. I do have some pride."

She didn't see what pride had to do with either one, but she waved it all aside. "Since you're the one doing whatever you're doing while I try to actually win the thing, an endearment here and there can only help. It sets the scene."

"Autumn." And she could see the blue in his eyes then. Or maybe she was hallucinating things because of the way he said her name. "Are you telling me you like it when I call you *darlin'*?"

It was as if everything stopped.

Again.

The things she was aware of seemed to take over the world. Her breath. The way he looked at her. Her feet against the wood floor. The way she held herself so still, like everything inside her was pulled taut—

He didn't move, either.

It could have lasted hours. Days.

But then Bowie broke the strange tension between them. He turned and scooped up a henley that she hadn't noticed hanging like a dishcloth on one of his cabinets. Because she hadn't noticed much of anything when faced with acres and acres of lean muscles and smooth-looking skin.

It felt like an ache to be released from that strange little spell, but then there was a new ache as she watched him shrug his shirt back on and return his attention to what he was cooking.

"No need to keep clutching those pearls," he said gruffly, not looking at her. "I don't normally wander around half-dressed. I dumped coffee on myself."

She pulled in a breath, not surprised and yet also dismayed that it was so shaky. "Coffee?"

He jutted his chin toward a counter across the kitchen from him and Autumn couldn't tell if she was grateful for the coffee itself or that she now had a task to perform that didn't involve gaping at his body.

Or, worse in some ways, trying to act like she thought she was some strategic mastermind, planning to somehow use the middle-of-nowhere local publicity stunt as a stepping-stone to . . . what? Extreme regional greatness?

Her problem was, despite all the reality show episodes Donna had made them watch, Autumn had always disliked everybody on every show. When clearly she should have been psychoanalyzing them all and taking notes.

But there was coffee. That was something. Especially when she added a little of the creamer he'd put out, took a sip, and felt confident that her synapses were finally firing. And that all would be well.

Or at least she might stop shooting her mouth off before she thought better of it.

One or the other. Just so long as she never again decided it would be a good idea to talk to Bowie about sex, of all things. When it was already all she could think about when she looked at him.

Before laying eyes on this man, she would have said—and often had—that the general human preoccupation with sex baffled her. She'd tried it. It was fine.

There had been no near-catastrophic internal explosions. It had been pleasant. Civilized. She'd found it profoundly interesting to welcome another person into her body, but she had not felt the need to welcome said person back.

She wasn't sure she'd really ever thought twice about her experience in the back of sweet Grady Harold's pickup since. But now, thinking about stretching out in the back of a pickup truck with Bowie Fortune made her break out in goose bumps.

This is the first day, she lectured herself, glaring down at her coffee. *If you can't pull it together, what hope do you have of winning this?*

And she really did want to win it. She *needed* to win it.

It was a $10,000 prize. And split in half, that gave her $5,000, the precise amount it would take to get her mother's jewelry out of hock.

Her father didn't know that Autumn knew he'd sold off the jewelry a year ago, just like he didn't know she knew why. He'd wanted all his girls at his wedding to Donna, dressed pretty the way Donna wanted it, but he didn't want it to cost any one of them a dime.

Because he was remarrying and he didn't think they'd like it. Maybe paying for the whole thing was a bribe.

But Autumn knew that her mother would have loved that he'd done what he'd had to do to get all the girls home and dressed as part of the wedding—and the new family they were making. She would have applauded the idea that items he'd once given to her in love could be used to spread that love forward. Autumn knew that in her heart. And also because her mom had told her, repeatedly, how worried she was about Hunter and what he'd do with himself once she passed. How sure she was that he would make himself a hermit, then waste away in his own misery.

He had tried his best to do it.

Autumn knew that their mother would have pawned the jewelry herself if she could, but she also knew her sisters would find that hard to take on board. Maybe even impossible. But Autumn had no intention of standing idly by and giving her younger sisters, who'd been coddled their whole lives, another reason to speak ill of their father. It was already bad enough they called Donna their *wicked stepmother*. Or sometimes even *stepmonster*, when Donna had never said an unkind word to another soul in all her life. The truth about the jewelry would be like a bomb dropped into the middle of the family.

And Autumn hadn't spent nearly half her life trying to keep the family together for something like this to tear them apart.

She was going to win that money. To save her family, and also because she knew her dad had only the rest of the summer to raise the money to get the jewelry back. Sweet old Mr. Daniels at the pawnshop in Missoula had extended the loan as long as he could, he'd said sorrowfully in the last message he'd left. Right there on the old school answering machine where anyone could hear it.

Autumn doubted very much that her dad had an extra $5,000 sitting around. Neither did she. But she could win it—and she would.

Beautiful men with astonishing backs notwithstanding.

"Breakfast," Bowie said gruffly, snapping her back to the here and now.

She was still standing at the kitchen counter in his uniquely rambling house in Alaska, her coffee mug in her hands. Pretending not only to be some kind of hard-hearted reality show person, but also that she was in no way overwhelmed by the man she was supposed to spend these next three months with.

She'd known that Alaska was far away from everything and she'd assumed the man she ended up with would be a project, because men always were. What was important was that she could access the internet so she could research things at will *and* never had to feel too alone here. She already had the texts to prove she wasn't *too* isolated. This was going to be fine.

Fine.

She turned around, trying to smile in a manner both professional and calming, whatever that was, but he wasn't hanging around waiting to see what expression she had on her face. He was already shouldering his way out through the back door, so she followed him.

And found him settling down at a table on yet another porch, this one covered. And with a view of that beautiful lake once more. It was brighter now. The water seemed bluer. She'd been staring at mountains her whole life, and loved tracking weather and seasons across their peaks, but water was different. She thought she could spend a whole lifetime staring at the surface of the lake, always different from the moment before. Three months of this seemed like a treat.

"Any chance I get to be outside in summer, I take it," Bowie was saying. "That's the kind of thing you hold on to, round about January."

"I hear you," she said, crossing to the little table to sit down with him.

"Before we got off topic with dress codes and anti-sex pacts," Bowie said, his dark blue eyes gleaming again, "my intention was to have a celebratory breakfast. It's a tradition in my family. When everyone gets together, we make pancakes."

"I'm delighted to qualify as '*everyone*.' "

She meant that to come out as offhandedly sophisticated. Arch and amusing, the way Jade always managed to sound. But she was sitting on an isolated porch with a gorgeous man and one of the prettiest views she'd ever seen, and she was no good at *sophisticated* or *arch.*

It was a little demoralizing to comprehend that she would probably make a terrible reality show villain. That she didn't have what it took.

Bowie only smiled a little, hopefully unaware of her internal struggle for the sort of sophistication that would be out of place here anyway. "Today we'll take a tour of the land and make sure you know how to operate the vehicles around here. You need to know how to get around."

"Yes," she agreed. "So I can go about my business, which is winning, and you can go about yours, which is . . . not hindering me from winning, right?"

Last night it had sounded like he would help, but she didn't want to sound too presumptuous.

He stopped in the act of forking fluffy pancakes on to her plate. "I can help. And I don't want you to feel trapped here, Autumn. It might be the Alaskan bush but the entire point of being out here is that it's not a prison."

"Right. And that."

She took the plate he handed her, piled high with pancakes drenched in butter, and decided she had never been so ravenous in her life. There were two syrup jugs on the table, one birch and one maple. Autumn reached for the maple but then grabbed the birch syrup at the last moment, because that seemed deeply, authentically Alaskan and why not dive in? She dragged the jug close, tipping it over the mound of pancakes until they were flooded with a spicy sweetness she could smell on the morning breeze.

"You might want to brace yourself," Bowie told her when she set the jug back down.

"For the impending sugar rush? Don't you worry. I can't wait."

His face changed. It got . . . not softer, exactly. But it made her feel softer. "Tonight my entire family wants to meet you."

He had talked about his family. He'd pointed out that they lived close by—or close by according to rural Alaska standards, anyway. He might have mentioned that dinner with them was expected last night, though all she could really remember was shoveling pasta in her mouth.

But she hadn't really thought about *meeting* his family. In the way a woman who came home with a man might expect she would. It made Bowie seem, distressingly, like a real person, not just the key to her plans for this contest.

It made her wonder what it would be like if she really had come all this way to marry him, sight mostly unseen.

No, she told herself sternly. *You are not wondering about that.*

"I guess that goes under the heading of things it's reasonable to expect brides to do, even if they're fake," she said after a moment.

"Even if it wasn't, it's not like I'd be able to hold them off. They're wily and determined." Bowie nodded his head toward the plate in front of her, pancakes, butter, and enough birch syrup to drown them both. "You might as well fortify yourself, darlin'. You'll need it."

Five

By the time they made it over to his parents' house that evening, Bowie had been given a great many opportunities to second-guess himself. Not only himself, but the self-control he'd always prized so highly.

Sure, folks around the lake liked to call him a daredevil and other, less entertaining, things sometimes. Everyone and their mother could tell a thousand stories about the risks he'd taken and what a thrill hound he'd been since he was a kid, but even when chasing the biggest adrenaline highs, Bowie wasn't reckless.

He'd spent a little too long in the service for that. Carelessness killed people. Sometimes it had killed people he knew. He might like to appear like he was wholly unbothered by the kinds of things that shocked other people, but that came from practice.

It didn't make him reckless. Ever.

But Autumn McCall made him feel reckless, and that was a problem.

Especially because she seemed completely immune to his usual charm. He'd assumed he could, at the very least, endear himself to whatever woman showed up here for the summer. But Autumn did not find him even remotely endearing, apparently. A fact she did nothing to hide. Every time he aimed a smile her way, she frowned at him.

It was enough to give a man a complex.

And it might even have been dispiriting if he didn't keep reminding himself that it was a good thing.

A *great* thing.

Because he would be taking the sight of Autumn in the early morning—padding into his kitchen with her face bare and her hair tousled, looking soft and warm from sleep—to his grave with him. Along with the instantaneous little fantasy life he'd lived there for a minute, imagining other scenarios. Of her waking up *tousled*, but because he'd left her that way. Of her coming to find him for more—

Yeah. It was a *fantastic* thing that she wasn't that into him.

He needed to keep reminding himself of that fact.

And besides, no man became a saint without a little bit of temptation. Or a truckload of temptation. It was the not giving into said temptation that mattered.

Or so he kept telling himself.

Especially as he and Autumn walked up from the water's edge toward his parents' house, after paddling their way here along the shoreline in his canoe. He could have done without the view on the way over. Not the glorious lake on a summer evening, the water like glass. The family of moose grazing as they passed. The birds wheeling around overhead. A fish jumping for insects. A perfect Alaskan summer evening, in other words, and usually he would have paddled along feeling right with the world.

But tonight he'd spent the trip staring at Autumn McCall kneeling there in the front of the canoe, like she'd been sent here for the express purpose of driving him round the bend.

And it was working.

Though he would die before he'd let his family see that. Especially when Autumn didn't even seem to notice her effect on him. She was too busy *looking* at everything, sighing happily when she particularly liked what she saw—like the baby moose—and otherwise frowning at him.

Always frowning at him.

He had to remind himself how awesome that was.

"You survived your first day!" Piper called out from up on the wide, wraparound porch of the house as they approached.

"With a joyful song in my heart," Bowie replied.

His sister made a face as she came down the steps. "I wasn't talking to you." She bounded across the yard to meet them, sticking out her hand toward Autumn as she drew close. With a big smile on her face. "Autumn. I'm Piper. I am *so* glad to meet you. If you're already thinking you made a terrible mistake, well. You did. But the good news is, the rest of us can help ease the blow of being forced to spend three months in solitary confinement with Bowie."

"She actually hero-worships me," Bowie told Autumn. "She just has a funny way of showing it."

Neither one of them responded to that. It was like he wasn't there.

"I have three sisters," Autumn was saying, shaking Piper's hand like it was a lifeline. And this after he'd taught her how to operate every ground and water vehicle he had. "Not one of them responds to a dare the way your brother does. I must know your secrets."

Piper smiled smugly. "Training."

And even though he had what he considered a proper sense of foreboding about the unholy union of Piper and this woman who he'd been up half the night trying not to fantasize about, Bowie left the two of them talking. Because he needed to put some distance between himself and those fantasies. He jogged up the stairs to find his brother and Violet sitting side by side on the summer sofa that they hauled inside when the weather turned. Nestled up cozy and cute the way they liked it.

"I still don't understand what you see in my brother," Bowie said to Violet, but he was grinning.

"I think it was all the snow," Violet replied as if she was taking him seriously. She shoved her glasses up on her nose as she turned her smile on Quinn. "It blinded me."

Quinn did not seem concerned about his woman's eyesight. His arm stayed where it was, not so much along the back of the sofa as it was around Violet, in her usual bright colors. Tonight it was her favorite. Pink.

"I was certain you would've run that poor girl off by now," Quinn said to Bowie.

"Autumn's a hardy Montana girl, used to wrestling bears and climbing mountains," Bowie replied, grinning even wider while he said it, because that was the only response he should have been having to his fake new bride. Not all the rest of the feverish stuff inside him, thank you. He kept thinking that if it weren't all so new and unexpected, he'd be dealing with it better. He wouldn't get tied up in knots just because she even *canoed* pretty. "It's going to take a lot more than a day in my company to run her off."

Quinn nodded. "So . . . two days?"

The good news was, Quinn being Quinn felt familiar. And that was a relief after losing his head the way he had the moment he'd laid eyes on Autumn, so Bowie went and leaned against the porch railing. Like he didn't have a care in the world, because that usually got his brother's back up. He compounded it by treating Quinn to the most carefree grin he had in his arsenal.

"Now, Quinn," he drawled. "We can't all carry women off and make them live in rundown shacks, hoping to run them out of Alaska."

"I miss the shack," Violet said, her face going dreamy the way it did when she was having her typical big thoughts. Bowie had never met another person who got paid to think, but Violet made it look good. "There's something so atavistically compelling about living in concert with the elements. Not forever trying to fight them off, but accepting them as part of your own experience. Letting them enhance you instead of attempting to bend them to your will."

And even though he was used to it by now, watching his previously grim and humorless brother look at his woman the way he did then, with all that affection and heat, almost made Bowie wish—

But no. That kind of connection and commitment wasn't for him. He already took care of a hangar full of planes. That was all the connection and commitment he needed.

He'd promised.

"If you're that into it, professor, we can always go spend a few days out there," Quinn said. "It's different in the summer. For one thing, there are more bears."

Violet shivered. "I'm not afraid of bears," she lied.

"You thought I was a bear," Bowie reminded her.

"I was realistically and appropriately concerned that the large creature crashing toward the shack was a bear, yes," Violet said primly. It had been their very first meeting. "I wouldn't call that *afraid.*"

"Obsessed, then," Quinn suggested.

Bowie was just happy his brother's attention had been diverted from him. And happier still when the front door opened and Bowie's best friend in the world stepped out, holding two beers in each hand.

Noah Granger was a different kind of brother to Bowie. They'd met in the marines and after they'd each done their stint, Noah had decided there was nothing for him back in Texas. Grumpy SOB that he was, he'd decided there were a few too many people around here, too. He lived even farther out than Bowie's parents, though he came in too often to be considered a true hermit. More like a hermit-in-training.

Bowie took one of the beers and waited as Noah gave the other two extras to Piper and Autumn, who'd made their way up onto the porch. Still talking intently. But when they went over to Quinn and Violet, Noah joined Bowie at the railing.

And for a moment they stood there quietly, watching as

Piper introduced Autumn around, and then did it all over again when Lois and Levi came around the side of the house. Holding hands, because his parents were still cute like that.

"Well," Noah said after a time. "Damn."

Bowie knew exactly what he meant. Autumn was all curves and unearned swagger. There was no getting past it. "Yup."

"That's a Grade A catastrophe."

"It is," Bowie agreed. He shook his head sorrowfully. "I blame you, Noah. You sat there, listened to me shoot my mouth off about this contest, and never once slapped me upside the head to keep me from doing something so foolish."

His best friend was unfazed by this attack. "If a man wants to dig his own grave, I get out of the way. Or give him a shovel."

And what could Bowie say to that? So did he. He took a swig of his beer instead.

There was a certain fatalistic pleasure in the whole thing, Bowie thought as the party moved down the porch to another set of stairs that led out to a small patio. Levi started flipping burgers on the grill while the others helped carry out the rest of the food from the kitchen. When the big picnic table was loaded up with the usual casual feast, they all settled in around it and he found himself next to Autumn.

Who didn't seem to notice where she was sitting, because she kept looking out over the lake and sighing happily.

Bowie couldn't blame her. He was used to it and he still found it beautiful. But she'd been doing it all day.

"Do you not have lakes where you come from?" he asked, reaching over her for the potato salad.

She looked at him, then down at her loaded plate. "We have all kinds of lakes. My favorite, Lake Como, reminds me a bit of this. We used to hike all around it and sometimes camp there when I was growing up."

"That must be why you haven't turned tail at the sight of Bowie's ramshackle house," Piper said. "If you're used to roughing it."

Autumn frowned. Not at him, for once. "I would not call the house ramshackle."

He was pleased to hear her defending him. Possibly too pleased.

"Piper has unreasonable expectations," Bowie said. "And also doesn't have a hangar attached to her cute little cottage."

"Piper is also grown," Piper retorted, taking the bowl of potato salad from him before he could spoon any on his plate. "And doesn't like squalor."

"I'm sure Autumn didn't come this far north to listen to the two of you squabbling," Lois said. She eyed the new arrival with her usual frankness. "I know why folks used to do the mail-order bride thing way back when. What makes a modern woman try it on for size?"

If Autumn felt intimidated by being the center of attention—much less in Lois's sights, a fate a great many locals went to extraordinary pains to avoid—she gave no sign. She put down her fork, considered the question, and took her time doing it.

"I can see the appeal, can't you?" she asked eventually. Even holding Lois's intimidating gaze. "All you have to do is answer an ad and be willing to uproot yourself, and just like that, you get a whole new life."

"Is that what you're after?" Levi asked.

Autumn smiled, but it was that reality show smile that Bowie had seen a lot of today. He couldn't say he liked it.

"Not necessarily," she said. "But I understand the allure in a way I never did before."

"How did you even find out about this contest?" Violet asked.

"I heard it on the radio." Autumn relaxed beside him, her shoulders inching down just enough to make it clear she'd had them up near her ears. "My stepmother and I were cooking up big batches of stew to freeze, and she likes to listen to the radio in the kitchen. They started talking about the contest up here, I started daydreaming, and here we are."

Bowie doubted very much that his nosy family would accept that as the final word on the subject, but the conversation moved along. Piper was excited about the summer jams she was making or planned to make. Noah made a passing reference to the projects he was working on, way out at his place, that he claimed he never wanted help with. Quinn always had a lot to say on the state of the lakeside community, though these days, it was less about how burdened he felt by that responsibility and much more of a conversation. Sometimes he even laughed, like Violet had gotten all her pinks and purples on him.

"I can't imagine moving to a place like this from a big city," Autumn said to Violet at some point. "Coming up north from rural Montana isn't really that much of a stretch. But from San Francisco?"

"There was some culture shock," Violet said, then laughed when Quinn shot her a look. "But all in good ways. Unlike most of the people at this table, I don't have anything against cities in general or San Francisco in particular. And the winter here is definitely ferocious, but I loved it. To be honest, I expected it to be worse than it actually was."

"It was much colder when I was growing up," Autumn observed. "Is it the same up this way?"

That set off the usual cavalcade of commentary on the changing climate, which everyone at the table had witnessed with their own angry eyes and happily blamed on the big, bad cities. Everyone except Violet, who wanted to cite studies. And usually did.

When Bowie looked over at Autumn, she had a satisfied look on her face, as if she'd known exactly the sort of storm she would kick off.

She only looked more satisfied when she caught his glance. "Not my first rodeo."

He could only incline his head in acknowledgment. "I'll have to remember how sneaky you are."

"I'm not here to make friends," she told him, but ruined the line that even he knew was classic reality show villain by laughing. "Though that's too bad, because I like your sister."

Bowie decided that it was beneath him to complain about the fact she liked Piper more than she liked him. He should have celebrated it. Instead, her laughter seemed to add to the enduring problem that was her, making her that much more shiny and impossible.

Get a grip, marine, he ordered himself.

"We need to remember to take our first-day picture," she was saying, because *she* wasn't impaled on her own laughter. "It's on the list, but I left all of that back at your house."

"Yes," Bowie said. Still *impaled*, and looking over to see Noah's knowing expression didn't help any. "Your list."

He'd had a fuzzy sort of idea of what the day would hold. After breakfast, he'd cleaned up, and had expected that he would show Autumn around, make sure she knew how to operate everything from an ATV to a canoe paddle. The generator, the emergency radio, the regular radio. He thought he might take out a map so she could get a sense of where the few trails they had around here were. How best to make her way to his parents' house—a long walk—or, if necessary, all the way down to the other end of the lake to the Mine. A much longer walk.

He had not been prepared for the way Autumn came charging out into the kitchen after breakfast, her arms full of materials he hadn't recognized at first.

Possibly because he'd been a little too caught up in looking at Autumn.

Because sure, there were the mouthwatering curves. He couldn't say he'd gotten used to them, because who could? But he'd been braced for the sight of them, and maybe that was why he had only then gotten around to noticing that she was . . . pretty. Just ridiculously pretty.

And, as if she had a personal commitment to test his limits—as if that were her entire purpose here, not some stupid prize—she had dressed herself in something other than the jeans and T-shirt. It was not exactly warm on a summer's day in Alaska, so she'd gone for the kind of practical, layered outfit that any woman Bowie knew would wear.

But it was the way Autumn wore it. Hiking pants that whispered when she walked, calling even more attention to her hourglass shape. Three competent layers on top. The T-shirt that she was wearing now, the long-sleeve midlayer with a hood, and the thin vest she'd zipped up when they went outside.

None of it was sexy. It was hardly lingerie.

And yet, once again, Bowie had found himself struck dumb.

Because he liked the women he took to bed fluffy and far away, and he liked all the women he knew here at home because they were as functional and pragmatic as he was. It had never occurred to him that a woman could be both practical *and* pretty. Not in a way that got to him the way she did.

Maybe that was why it took him a little too long to notice that she'd gone ahead and transformed his kitchen into a kind of office space. Then proceeded to deliver a presentation on how she intended to pioneer it up around here, complete with a list of daily and weekly goals that she wrote on the whiteboard she'd brought with her.

It wasn't a large whiteboard. But Bowie had discovered that a whiteboard didn't need to be large to do its work. Not with Autumn around.

"My list, yes," Autumn said now, looking at him in that

armored-patience way she had, like she was prepared to act cool while waiting for him to catch up. Prepared, but pressed, even here with all his family around. "I wrote down all the things we need to do today, but the first-day picture was in its own, separate box. Surrounded by stars."

"I remember the stars," Bowie offered.

"This is part of the contest rules," she told him, with more of that exaggerated patience. Which did not exactly inspire him to act like he knew what she was talking about. "We have to do a picture a day and a video once a week. On our dedicated social media account, which, as I told you this morning, I've taken the liberty of starting for us."

"A social media account," Piper said in tones of awe. Completely over-the-top, faked tones of awe, that was. "Will the mysterious Bowie Fortune actually allow himself to appear on *social media*? Is the world coming to an end?" But she laughed and answered her own question. "Of course not, silly me. That would be if Noah showed up on social media one day."

"If a picture takes a soul," Noah said with his usual poker face, though maybe a little more pokery than usual when it involved Piper, for reasons Bowie chose not to examine, "imagine what your social media does?"

"No worries then." Piper showed him her teeth. "Since you don't have a soul to lose."

"You actually do have to follow the rules, Bowie," Quinn chimed in from down the table, looking entirely too pleased with this situation. "I hope you don't expect special treatment just because you're my brother."

"Special treatment is not how I would describe the joys of being your brother," Bowie replied, but he was already standing up. He offered Autumn a hand and wasn't particularly surprised when she scowled at him, ignored his hand completely, and climbed to her feet. She untied the midlayer around her waist and shrugged into it, still scowling at him when her head came through. She brushed her hair back, then aimed that scowl toward the water.

"Actually, I think it would make a very pretty picture here. With the whole lake in the background."

"I'll be your photographer." Piper sounded overly excited, to Bowie's mind. Probably because, under any other circumstances, if she'd offered to take a picture of Bowie he would've laughed. And possibly thrown her into the lake for her trouble.

But there was no point signing up for something and then acting like a tool about it. He'd agreed to do this, so he was doing it.

And it has absolutely nothing to do with the fact that the woman looks like she stepped directly out of your dreams, said a snide voice inside him that sounded a lot like the expression on Noah's face looked.

But it was the first day. And he had signed up for this because he was too much of a child to walk away from a dare. Maybe he needed to get over that, but it didn't mean he had to act like a child now.

That in mind, he went over and stood next to Autumn. He expected her to put her arm around him, but she didn't, so he crossed his arms and matched her glower. He even suffered what Piper called *art direction* for at least five minutes longer than he wanted to before he declared the picture was well and truly taken.

"This is great," Autumn said happily, peering at her phone as Piper swiped through the photos. Neither one of them bothered to show Bowie. "He looks perfectly curmudgeonly."

"And you look skeptical, but cute," Piper agreed.

"I regret this already," Bowie said, but they waved him away.

As was customary on summer nights, after cleaning up from dinner they all found their way down to the lakeshore, built a fire, and then sat around, breathing in the sweet almost-summer night.

This was the good life. Even in the middle of the worst mistake he'd made in recent memory, it was still good. Because try as he might, Bowie could think of absolutely no downside to midnight-sun evenings by the water, even with a fake wife in tow.

Quinn took off first, because he'd promised Violet he would teach her how to fish. Levi and Lois went off on a walk.

Piper and Autumn were still making conversation, so Bowie kicked back on an old log he'd been sitting on for as long as he could remember and had another beer with Noah.

The way God intended on a night like this.

"You're in trouble," Noah pointed out.

Bowie lifted his beer in a toast. "That's been established."

"On numerous fronts," his best friend clarified. "And I can tell you know that."

"What's a summer in the grand scheme of things?" Bowie asked expansively. "And besides. There are a lot of lists."

"Says the pilot," Noah said, a corner of his mouth kicking up. "Because you don't love a checklist."

Which was right about the time Bowie decided it was getting on, no matter how light it was out, and he and the wife had better be getting home themselves.

And when they were launched into the water again and on their way, Bowie couldn't help but appreciate that they fell into paddling rhythm easily. Not like Quinn, who had to teach his city girl just about everything when it came to surviving up this way. Autumn McCall didn't need any teaching. Which was a good thing, because Bowie was no teacher.

But it sure did make him wonder what other things she knew.

Back at his place, they walked up from the water side by side, the late night's summer light making things seem almost eerie in the yard. Autumn stopped at the bottom of the little path that led directly to her guest room, and offered him a tight smile.

He had the sudden notion that she didn't want to walk into the house with him any more than he wanted it, because it was almost certainly going to feel like the very situation it wasn't. But the trouble with a realization like that was that it got him thinking about why she would want to avoid the end of the evening in a quiet house with him.

And he really, really had to let that go.

"Your family is very nice," she said.

"That's probably the first time anyone's called them that. And I think my mother will be disappointed. She goes out of her way to be as spicy as possible."

"They weren't as bloodthirsty as mine, so there's that."

"I think they were on their best behavior. I wouldn't count on that going forward."

This wasn't a date. They weren't outside some bar. It was a strange, artificial situation that had no bearing on reality, yet both of them had decided to go ahead and do it for their own bizarre reasons. He knew all that.

Yet he still found himself shoving his hands in his pockets and rocking back on his heels, like some kid.

"It worked." Autumn nodded, maybe too hard. "I think they're great. Particularly your sister."

"She is pretty fantastic," Bowie agreed. "Though I'd deny it if you ever told her I said so."

Autumn's tight smile loosened and became something warmer. More natural.

More dangerous.

"I would never do such a thing. I know how sister politics work."

And then they stood there, that midnight sun cascading all around them in a kind of silver glow. It made the hints of red in her hair gleam. There was a breeze tonight, and the hint of rain on it. Bowie thought that was a good thing. Too much of this blue sky and bright-sun summer and her *hair* and he might start forgetting where he was. And once a man lost his bearings, he lost himself. That was Piloting 101.

It was also Life 101.

"I haven't been in a lot of fake marriages," Bowie said, his voice a little too low. "But so far, so good on this one."

Her smile widened. "I have to agree."

He was never not aware of those killer curves, but, just now, all he could really focus on was her face. The arch of her eyebrows, the faint hint of a flush on her cheeks, and lips that he now knew were that particular shade of pink. Just naturally. The longer he gazed down at her, the more her cheeks pinkened to match.

And suddenly, he didn't feel at all like a kid.

Bowie felt very much grown, and he had an excellent idea of exactly what sort of adult activities would best suit the moment. More to the point, so did she.

He could see that same awareness all over her.

For a breath or two it felt a lot like the sun was still up and shining just to make sure there was no missing this moment.

"Good night, Bowie," she whispered.

With a little hitch in the middle of his name.

And he didn't have time to think too much about how that about ended him before she turned around and headed up the path to her room.

But she ran the whole way, then threw herself inside, as if she didn't trust herself around him another second.

And that was trouble. Bowie was all too aware of how much trouble that was.

But at least it wasn't only *his* trouble.

And somehow, that made all the difference.

Six

Autumn woke up on her second morning in Alaska to yet another barrage of texts and messages from her sisters.

Both in the family text and privately.

So at least that much was exactly the same as it had always been. The only difference was that now they were talking about what Autumn was doing instead of the normal topics of conversation:

I don't like anything about this, Jade wrote. What if he's only pretending to be nice to lure you into a false sense of security?? Only when you relax will he strike!

I think the heat in Arizona is going to your head, Autumn replied, still lying in her cozy Alaskan bed, the air in her room cool against the tip of her nose. Also, stop staying up half the night watching true crime documentaries.

Willa's texts were typical Willa. Which was to say, high drama. And all in capital letters.

I WILL WALK TO ALASKA IF I HAVE TO JUST SAY THE WORD ANYTHING THAT PRETTY IS SUSPICIOUS

No punctuation, of course. Willa felt theatrics transcended punctuation.

If you're walking to Alaska, Autumn wrote back, you'd better get started. There's not a lot of summer left and it's going to take a while from San Diego.

She wanted, badly, to ask which prettiness was particularly suspicious to Willa. Was it the photograph she'd taken of the lake yesterday? Or the photo she'd uploaded to the internet last night of her with curmudgeonly Bowie? But she didn't. Because it would only encourage Willa. Not to mention that Autumn herself did not need to think about Bowie any more than she already did. He was a distraction.

Sunny's text was also on brand.

Remember who the sharpshooter in the family is, she wrote.

The only possible response to that was a roll of her eyes, so when Autumn was finished actually doing that in the privacy of her guest room, she also sent one of those along to Sunny in response.

As for the family text, where they'd apparently spent the better part of the morning egging each other on again, she ignored it completely.

But it wasn't until she put her cell phone aside and stood up that she faced the fact that all those texts were a really great way to avoid thinking about the night before.

She hadn't expected to like his family so much, and she'd more than liked them. She'd admired pretty much everything about their life there at the end of the lake. Autumn loved her own family, but there was always some *issue.* There was always the current ranch problem, because that was life on a ranch, even one as small as her father's. There had been the absence of her mother, then the presence of Donna. Her sisters were either there to cause problems, or were off having problems the rest of them had to talk about. Sitting around eating dinner with the Fortunes, and down by the fire afterward, had seemed as natural as breathing and a whole lot easier than life on the McCall ranch.

Piper had welcomed her so effusively, mostly to poke at

her brother, Autumn understood. She was familiar with sibling dynamics. But then the two of them had gotten to talking, and it turned out that Piper, at least, had a ton of ideas for things Autumn could do to boost her pioneer profile and make whatever projects she did to impress the judges *look* amazing. Because surely anyone out here taking part in this contest had, roughly, the same sets of skills. Presentation had to count for something, and might even tip the balance when it came time to declare a winner. She'd taken notes on her phone.

Though what she chiefly remembered from the night—and had possibly dreamed about all night long—were the two times she'd gone breathless. First, when Bowie sat down next to her on the crowded picnic table bench, much closer to each other than they'd been before. She hadn't been ready. She'd spent all day with him, but hadn't known until that moment how good he smelled. As if he were made of sun-roasted pine with something more mysterious beneath. She'd wanted to nestle her face into the crook of his neck—and had stopped that line of thought, horrified, because it felt like such a natural impulse that she'd been afraid she would just start doing it.

Right there where everyone could see her.

There will be no nuzzling of necks, she had told herself sternly.

And she'd almost convinced herself that it was an aberration, that she'd been carried away with the easy conversation and pleasant welcome and had lost herself a little. That was all. But then the canoe ride back had felt hushed. Something like magical. Bowie behind her, a brooding force propelling them across the water while all around them the lake was clear and fathomless, the silvery light dancing over them through the trees, so bright despite the hour.

It had been enchanted. That was the only excuse she could come up with for that moment there in front of the house. There should have been a warning label or an appropriate folktale—*Do not tarry with beautiful men as the midnight sun wanes*, or something. Because he'd looked even more compelling after the long day in his company, his moody eyes unreadably dark, and the way he'd studied her as they stood there made her warm.

Much too warm for so far north.

Autumn wasn't exactly proud of the way she'd literally turned and run, but if she knew anything in this life it was that she never regretted taking the opportunity to regroup and rethink—especially when she wanted to do the exact opposite.

And if she'd spent some time buzzing around her room, alive with sensation and incapable of settling down, that was her business. It was still better than embarrassing herself by throwing her entire body at this man on her first day.

She dressed, bracing herself to face Bowie. As she walked toward the kitchen she was sure that he would bring up that moment, and the fact she *ran away*, and she would have to defend it. But in the way a reality show contestant would defend it, not the way she normally would. Because she was acting like a reality show version of herself, and she needed to remember that. Even if she had no idea how she was actually going to *do* that.

Just like she had no idea how she was going to listen to him let her down easy once again without reacting in a way she was likely to regret.

But it turned out none of that was necessary, because he wasn't there. He'd left a note in the middle of his kitchen table with instructions on how to fix herself the coffee she'd enjoyed yesterday.

Had to go on a run, he'd written, and she spent a little too much time trying to glean meaning from the bold slash of his obviously male handwriting. **Try not to burn down the house.**

"I haven't burned down a house yet," she muttered, offended.

She set the note aside, made herself some coffee—very carefully, because she hadn't used a fancy French press before—and then took herself on a tour of her new home. Bowie had showed her around already, but it was different to find her own way. And it didn't take her long to end up out in his shop, where he'd told her yesterday she could help herself to anything she found that wasn't obviously mechanical and likely an engine part.

But she had no interest in such modern conveniences. She'd seen his gill nets hanging on the wall yesterday, and had been pleased, because she'd planned to make one herself. So she could film it. Today, she gathered up all the extra line she could find to complement the stash she'd brought with her and hauled it out into the middle of his yard, where she could set herself up between two trees and enjoy the view of the lake while she worked.

That was where he found her later that afternoon. When he returned, not from what she had begun to think was a decidedly extreme jogging expedition, but by plane.

This time he touched down on the water of the lake and she found herself stopping and staring at how easily he did it, making it look perfectly natural. As if the plane were nothing more than a large, graceful bird.

But staring would only lead to the kind of conversations she didn't want to have with him, so Autumn returned her attention to her work. And she was still scowling, virtuously and ferociously, at the line she was weaving together when he finally walked up from the water sometime later.

And then took his time looking at her. Or what she was doing. Or maybe both.

"That looks like some intense knitting," he drawled, eventually, when she was on the third or fourth round of lecturing herself to simply *remain calm*. Something that had never before been an issue for her. "Are you making a sweater for a giant?"

"It's not a sweater." She turned to frown at him as he spoke and saw that, of course, he didn't think it was a sweater. That curve in the corner of his mouth gave him away. "But you know that, obviously."

"I do know that, yes. Mostly because I also know there are no giants around here. I've lived here my whole life. I would have seen a *giant*."

She decided to ignore that. Bowie Fortune in that bomber jacket, jeans, another rock-and-roll T-shirt—Van Halen this time—and those same mirrored sunglasses needed a great deal of ignoring.

Even though he set her heart to clattering. Or *because* he did.

"I am making a gill net," she told him, like the librarian she wished she was sometimes—but only so she could read more. She doubted she would enjoy the *dealing with patrons and cataloging things* part of the gig. "You have a few, so you should know it's a kind of net used for fishing—"

"This is rural Alaska. I know what a gill net is. You could have used one of mine."

"I wanted to make one myself. They're very effective at catching fish."

He didn't say anything for a moment and her hands stilled. She wanted to keep pretending she didn't quite see him, but he was pulling his sunglasses away from his eyes, apparently so he could really commit to staring down at her.

"You know what another great way of catching fish is?" He seemed to take too long to ask that question. Or maybe it was that she could see all that Montana night sky that passed for his gaze. "We call it straight-up fishing."

"I've seen your fishing rods. They look like they could launch a space shuttle. I don't really think that's the pioneer spirit, do you?"

"Remind me, how many pioneers had a generator so they could take hot-water showers?"

Autumn found that unduly antagonistic but chose to *rise above it*. "I appreciate that I don't have to heat water on a campfire. Really. And I'm not trying to have a fully authentic experience. I just think it's going to be hard to have a pioneer summer if I don't do any pioneering. That's why I put it on the list."

"I read a lot of things on your list, Autumn."

Bowie was holding her gaze with an intensity she didn't like at all. Because she liked it too much. She really should have come out against *too much looking* when she'd tried to have the sex talk.

His expression was . . . leveling. "If you want to do subsistence living, this is the place to do it. If you want a taste of that authenticity, you can go live in the dry cabin my great-grandparents built. The only way to get closer to land is to build a shelter with your hands."

She did not think it was her imagination that he looked at her hands then. Or that he found them wanting.

"I'll consider that," she told him, trying to match his overtly placid tone. So placid it tipped over into confrontational. "It would be more realistic. But I'm not entirely sure that realism is the point here."

"It's *a* point."

"Anyway, my gill net is coming along nicely. As you can see."

"Have you ever fished with a gill net before?"

"Don't worry, I get the concept," she said loftily. When in fact she'd watched some stuff online and decided it looked doable, which wasn't really the same thing. "What with it being a net, and all."

He looked entertained by that answer, which made her doubt it was as easy as she'd decided it was. But Autumn had decided a long time ago that doubt was for suckers, so she shrugged it away.

"I thought when you wrote that you were *on a run* that you were exercising," she said instead of continuing to debate her gillnetting skills. "Not flying a plane."

"If in doubt," Bowie told her then, still looking entertained, "you can pretty much assume I'm flying."

"Where did you fly today?" she asked. She nodded toward the lake. "Somewhere with water, I'm guessing."

He nodded. "I picked up some climbers in McGrath and took them up into the Alaska Range. There's a lake I know about seven thousand feet up that makes a good base for some more moderate climbs. Sometimes I can pretend I'm a hero and take sick folks to hospitals from hard-to-reach villages along the Kuskokwim. But today it was tourists."

She studied his face. "But you're happy no matter what, because you're flying."

"It's flying," he agreed, as if that was an explanation. And the smile he gave her then was different from the grin she'd gotten used to. Wider. Less about charm and more . . . *him*, maybe. It felt like a gift. "There's not a whole lot I can think of that's better."

She had the impression he didn't talk about himself much. Oh, he talked *around* himself and could fill the air with chatter. That much had been clear on the flight up. But what did he ever really say about the real Bowie Fortune?

Autumn kept her gaze on her weaving, her fingers tugging on the rope as she tried to look as if she was only half paying attention. So he wouldn't get spooked.

"When did you learn how to fly?" she asked, almost offhandedly.

From the corner of her eye she could see him shift his weight, then fold his arms as if he planned to be there awhile. And she wasn't even looking at him directly, so she couldn't pretend the giddy sort of feeling that moved in her then was about how handsome he was. It was just him. The simple fact he was near.

"I used to get in some trouble when I was younger," he told her, and his eyes gleamed unrepentantly when she glanced up at him. "You know how it is in a place like this. You make your own fun. And sometimes it's maybe too much fun."

"I do not know," Autumn countered. "Right about when most people were making their own fun, I was making school lunches for my sisters."

"You're obviously a better person than I am," Bowie said, but not the way people had said things like that to her in the past, like she should climb down off her cross. Bowie sounded cheerful. "There was an old man down in Hopeless who'd been a bush pilot most of his life. When he caught me sniffing around his plane one time, he told me I could either expect to get the wrong end of his shotgun or he could teach me a much better way to waste my time. And I don't really like getting shot, so I chose the flight lessons."

Bowie was leaning against the tree now, looking completely at his ease. Autumn continued weaving in her pieces of rope, feeling . . . hushed, somehow. She told herself it was the scenery. The man as well as the lake before her, stretching out lazily as the afternoon rolled on by. The sun was testing itself against some clouds, but that only made the sky above them seem more complicated.

She had the stray thought that she could listen to him tell her stories forever.

"It turned out, flying was even cooler than I thought it would be," Bowie said. "It was what I thought about while I was in the service, when the US Marine Corps had other things for me to do."

"Like getting shot at?"

He didn't quite smile. "Like that. When I came back home, I liberated the rattly old plane I first learned on from the junk heap and I started tinkering with it."

"I'm guessing you're good with engines, too."

Because she'd seen the evidence. The planes in his hangar, some of them looking sleek and new. Others clearly halfway through a tinkering process. And she had the thought that the Bowie she'd spent all day with yesterday would make a flirty little remark here, something about *how* good he was with engines, or his hands, or something.

But this Bowie actually looked serious. "That's the thing about Alaska, Autumn. If you don't figure out how to be handy, you're probably not going to make it here. In Anchorage, sure. But out this way, you live or die by what you can make. And make work, even when it shouldn't."

His words seemed to have a little too much weight, so

she laughed. "I'm not a city girl, Bowie." She shook her head at him. "You do know that most people consider Montana sufficiently rugged, don't you?"

"You have too many roads," Bowie replied, but he was grinning again. "Roads make you soft."

"I've been called many things in my life, but not soft."

She reached the end of the row she was weaving and tied it off. Then stepped back from her net and was suddenly aware, once again, that they were alone.

Entirely alone.

Just the two of them and the wind.

It wasn't like that had changed any since he'd brought her here. But every time she became aware of it again, it was like a ribbon of heat wound around her. Through her.

She could feel it now, a glimmering deep inside.

"What do people call you?" Bowie asked, his voice low. And she was sure she could see that same glimmering in his eyes.

Last night, while she and Piper had been talking about canning and herbs and the kinds of edible plant life around here, she kept feeling his eyes on her. She'd told herself it was just because she was a stranger here and he was keeping tabs, as anyone would. She'd tried to tell herself the same thing last night after she'd charged away from him, running off to her room to hide—to her enduring shame.

But here it was again, and it was hard to convince herself that she was making it up.

At the same time, she'd watched her sisters' many love affairs and epic crushes, so she knew better. She was here in Alaska for a reason. And this was not the reason.

Though looking at his jaw—still not shaved and somehow even more attractive for all that ruggedness—she wished it was.

"My sisters have a theme," she said, grinning broadly. As if there was no glimmering. No heat. "The word *bossy* gets tossed around a lot, but they like to dress it up. The Bossiest Girl in Ravalli County, for example, thanks to

Willa. Autumn of Our Discontent, courtesy of Sunny. Jade prefers Captain Bligh."

"Captain Bligh?" He laughed, and she shouldn't have let herself feel a pang that the moment, the glimmering heat, was gone. She should have been grateful. It was what she'd wanted, wasn't it, or she wouldn't have told him these nicknames. "Does that mean they actually managed a mutiny? I'll admit they looked like the mutinous type."

"They attempted weekly mutinies while we were growing up," Autumn said. "But I'm betting you know all about that yourself."

Bowie let out another laugh. "It sounds like my sister has been making scurrilous accusations."

"Are they scurrilous? She says your older brother, Quinn, was tapped to be in charge of the community here from a young age. And that you took that as a personal challenge."

"It wasn't the *in charge* part I minded. It was more the Quinn part." Bowie shook his head. "My older brother could teach joylessness to members of the Inquisition."

"He seemed perfectly delightful last night."

"You're talking about New Quinn. New as in the past six months. Violet," he clarified when Autumn looked at him quizzically. "She brightened up the place. And achieved the impossible, which is making my brother act like a normal human being. I keep expecting it to wear off, but if anything, he's getting happier. I won't lie, it's disconcerting."

"I'm going to take all of that as an affirmative." Autumn crossed her arms and stared at him like she was some kind of judge. "You, Bowie Fortune, did in fact attempt to mutiny against your brother's authority."

Bowie took on a philosophical expression, still leaning against that tree. He reminded her of the sort of dangerous outlaw who all the stories suggested was likely to come high-nooning into any given western town when the urge took him. And here she was, a born-and-bred western girl. Maybe she was a little too susceptible to that kind of thing.

"This is why I declined Uncle Sam's offer to continue my service to this country," he told her. "I'm just not any good with authority figures."

"Is anyone good with authority figures? Or are they only selectively good with authorities of their choosing?"

His dark eyes gleamed. "Six of one, half a dozen of another, and none of them are my big brother."

But it felt a lot like he wasn't talking about his brother at all. It felt a lot like he was telling her something critically important, to her, and Autumn found her throat entirely too dry. "I guess it's lucky, then, that you work for yourself."

"That and the fact Quinn and I aren't kids anymore," he agreed, the intensity in his gaze lightening. Autumn couldn't decide if that was a good thing or not. No matter how dry her throat was. "We don't try to settle things with our fists anymore. I guess it's different when it's sisters."

"The reason Willa has nails like scimitars is because she and Jade used to pound on each other," Autumn said drily. "And probably still would if Willa wasn't constantly armed."

"I stand corrected."

And then, once again, the moment held. Once again, that glimmering ribbon pulled taut between them.

Autumn jerked her head away and jutted her chin toward her day's work with Lost Lake lying pretty and bright beyond it. "We should take today's picture in front of my gill net. I already made some videos but this is exactly the kind of hardy, survivalist content—with a view—that people are looking for."

Bowie seemed to take a very long time straightening from the tree. And then another eon or so to slide his sunglasses back over his eyes.

Like he was made of honey and molasses, especially when he smiled. And this time, it was the kind of smile that made every hair on her body feel like it was standing on end.

Except in a good way.

Only she couldn't allow it.

And Bowie's slow grin didn't help.

"You don't want to get ahead of yourself now, darlin'," he drawled, and the grin didn't take away the fact that he was chiding her. Letting her down easy, once again, and it turned out it really did make her feel violent. "You don't even know if your Montana net works up here in the Last Frontier. Might want to make sure it does before posting it all over the place."

And then he sauntered off toward the house while Autumn stayed behind with her gill net, plotting 101 ways not to catch fish with it, but to *do something* about Bowie Fortune.

Seven

The net did not work.

Autumn would have described her reaction to that as *enraged* if she allowed herself to feel her own temper. Instead of shoving it down and locking it away because there had never been any point in competing with all the other big emotions around her.

But she seethed a bit privately, because it annoyed her that Bowie had been right. That she was, in fact, *getting ahead of herself.*

Over the next two days, Autumn checked her net morning, noon, and night. And a whole lot of other times in between, but the fish—that she could see with her own eyes swimming blissfully around in the lake—avoided the net completely.

"I'm sorry to tell you this," she told Bowie on Saturday morning, out in the hangar where he was doing something incomprehensible to one of his planes. *Tinkering*, he called it. "But if we were depending on me to feed us in pioneer times, we would be very, very hungry."

Bowie let out a very male sort of grunt from the raised platform he was on. He shoved his wrench in his back pocket, then turned to look down at her. "Good thing I have a freezer filled with food and a thing called a refrigerator, if you don't feel like waiting for something to thaw."

She rolled her eyes. "That's not the point."

"Besides, I thought you'd moved on from fish and were all about plant-based food sources."

His grin was nothing short of dangerous then, especially because what he was doing was so [illegible] him, maybe. *Male*, something in her whispered. Not that women weren't perfectly capable of playing with plane engines. But Bowie, in his jeans and a Springsteen concert shirt with grease on his hands and a little bit on one cheekbone, too . . .

Well. Autumn could applaud Rosie the Riveter internally and be glad that *he* wasn't Rosie at the same time.

"I'm glad to know that you pay attention to me when I talk," she said, with studied placidity. "I was beginning to think I was just talking into the void."

"Plant-based food sources are very important to a subsistence lifestyle and are, of course, more plentiful at this time of year," he intoned. Repeating, verbatim, one of the lectures she'd given yesterday. "But I'll ask you this. You spent hours yesterday collecting greens. They tasted good when you cooked them up, I won't deny it. Yet when you think back to last night's dinner, is it the greens you remember most?"

She could have said that she remembered the greens chiefly because she'd gone full hunter-gatherer and had foraged for them. It had taken all day. It had rained the day before and continued on into yesterday morning, but had tapered off. Then it had been warm enough to be humid, so she'd felt as if she'd been tramping around looking for seaweed. She'd come back to the house, sweaty and cranky—though she would have died before admitting that her back hurt from being hunched over and her hands were scratched up from the foraging part—to find Bowie in his rambling living room area, reading a book.

Autumn hadn't known, until that moment, that she'd

been waiting her entire life to see a gorgeous man reading a thick, well-loved book of his own volition. She'd had no idea *how much* she'd wanted to see such a thing.

But she did not intend to tell him that.

"I like a steak as much as the next person," she said instead, wrapping her hands around her coffee mug and nestling a little more deeply into the cushions of the sofa that she'd been delighted to find out in the hangar when she'd come looking for Bowie this morning.

Sometimes I sleep out here, he'd said gruffly from up high.

You sleep with your planes?

Not in any euphemistic sense, he'd replied, in that edgy way he sometimes had that made everything in her dance a little bit. *Sometimes I don't feel like walking back into the house.*

And for some reason, that had simmered between them for much too long.

"I don't think that's true, Autumn," he was saying now, and leaned against the nose of the Cessna. "The next person in this scenario is me, and I'm a dedicated carnivore. If I recall correctly, your position was that you didn't want to dilute the glory of the greens you'd gathered with meat from my freezer. And then ate all of yours anyway."

She had scarfed it down, in fact, because she'd been ravenous after a day of foraging, which no one had adequately explained to her was really just hiking and weeding thrown together, except with none of the views that made hiking tolerable and none of the flowers that made weeding more than a thankless chore.

That, too, was not something she planned on sharing with her fake husband, mostly because he'd acted as if it was *funny* that she'd been out in the bush looking for edible plants. As if she was that same overachieving goody-goody she'd always been accused of being growing up.

"I don't think it would kill you to at least *pretend* to be interested in the thing we're supposed to be doing here."

And Autumn realized that that came out a little less than friendly only when she heard her own voice in the air between them.

Oops.

"I'm here, Autumn. We're doing it," Bowie said, very calmly. Matter-of-factly, even, and he didn't look away while he said it. "But I didn't sign up for a *Little House on the Prairie* reenactment."

"I don't think anyone will confuse you for Laura Ingalls Wilder," Autumn said gaily. As if she hadn't gotten a little snippy. Because one thing she knew was that no one ever bent an inch if they thought someone was mad at them. It was all about honey and persuasion, and she'd learned how to be good at that. She didn't know why being around this man made her forget herself. "And no one's asking you to take part in any reenactments. But you could also not get in the way of my attempts to win this contest we both signed up for, whatever our reasons."

She thought he would argue. But he didn't. He only looked at her for a moment or two, then nodded slightly, as if he'd come to a decision.

"Fair enough," was all he said.

Then he jumped down from his platform, landing on the concrete floor without hardly making a sound. Something else that made her feel a little giddy on the inside.

"Are you going somewhere?" she asked, because he had that sort of look about him then, as he wiped off his hands with a rag.

"We're both going somewhere," he told her. "It's market day." Autumn must not have looked sufficiently delighted by the news, because he jerked his chin toward the door that led out to the little breezeway that connected them to the house. "The boat's leaving in twenty minutes, darlin'."

And then he sauntered off into the house without a backward look.

Autumn trailed after him. At a distance. He disappeared up the spiral stairway into his bedroom upstairs and she drained her coffee in a few big gulps, washed her mug and set it to dry, then headed for her room to change into her usual Alaska uniform. It was a cool morning, drizzling again, but when she'd gone down to the lake to check her gill net earlier, she'd seen blue skies off in the distance.

By the time she made it down to the dock, Bowie was already waiting—but not with the canoe she'd been expecting.

She frowned at it. "We're not canoeing?"

"Do you want to canoe all the way down the length of the lake? Let me rephrase that before you answer. It's a long way to paddle. Ten miles. And then there's the paddling back in a fully loaded canoe. If you feel like six hours of paddling, minimum, by all means, let's do it."

His brows rose in a clear and obvious challenge.

And Autumn wanted nothing more than to call his bluff and *demand* that they start paddling *this instant*, but six hours, minimum, gave her pause. Because she loved a challenge, sure, but she also knew that six hours of anything—even something as pleasant as canoeing—was inevitably going to hurt.

"The motorboat will be just fine," she said. And then, after a moment's consideration, added, "Thank you."

Bowie rocked back on his heels and regarded her for a moment that made her feel almost as humid as yesterday's foraging expedition. "Are you sure?" His voice was all drawl. It seemed to catch on every edge she hadn't known she possessed inside. "Will I have to hear all about the desecration of your pioneer values?"

"If you're lucky."

She watched as he bit back a smile at that, and found she was smiling herself. Then she climbed into the boat in the place he indicated, and that was better than thinking about *drawls* and *edges*.

But then they were speeding along the water, chasing that blue sky. She almost thought the sound of the motor was a shame, that it somehow shattered the quiet serenity all around them. Not that she planned to mention that, in case it was too *Little House* for him. And anyway, it wasn't as if the Alaskan grandeur all around them disappeared just because there was a sound.

Especially when the sun came out.

A great deal of the land in the valley where she'd been raised was unspoiled, or near enough. But the Bitterroot was built up in comparison to this. Autumn was no stranger to wilderness, but Bowie had actually had a point back when he'd picked her up. There were roads where she came from.

Out here, there was only Alaska.

There was no pretending that humans belonged here.

And Autumn liked the way the knowledge of that felt inside. Humans might not belong here in all this untamed wildness, but that didn't mean they couldn't eke out a life here. If they wanted. It made her want to sing songs about human ingenuity and determination—but she refrained.

Though she did amuse herself with imagining what Bowie would do if she just . . . *broke into song.*

The whole length of the lake, once they left Bowie's house behind, she counted only two other dwellings. And it was only when they reached the other end that she saw more signs of life. There were a bunch of cabins in the trees as Bowie began to slow down. They spread out along the side of the lake, but Autumn quickly returned her attention to the old mining town that sprawled there, up the hill from the lake and almost all of it bright red.

She'd seen abandoned mines before, but this one wasn't abandoned. The smokestacks had been painted a variety of colors, like little rainbows rising up from the cluster of red structures—houses, she thought—that fanned out from the biggest building at the bottom.

"Old Gold," she said when Bowie cut the engine and let them glide the rest of the way to shore.

"The one and only." He sounded affectionate. "It hasn't been an active mine since early last century. And even when it was active, it wasn't much good. If it was, the usual corporate types would still own it."

"Nobody likes corporate types," Autumn said, with deep feeling. Though her corporate ire was usually focused on the loggers who wanted access to Montana's forests, supposedly to reduce wildfires. Or the enduring western skirmishes over water rights.

"Not up here," Bowie was saying in agreement. "You can be sure if you see a fat cat, he's coming for your land. Luckily, your average fat cat mining boss isn't what you'd call intrepid. They're unlikely to come this far out into the backcountry."

"Someone must have been a little bit intrepid." Autumn jumped out of the boat into about a foot of water, and helped guide the boat toward the pebbly beach. "Looking for gold all the way out here."

"It was a gold rush," Bowie said, jumping out on the other side of the boat. "They looked for gold everywhere. When the gold didn't pan out, most of them beat a hasty retreat back to wherever they came from."

"But not your family."

"The Fortunes like an exercise in futility." His eyes gleamed and she told herself, sternly, that she was not to take anything personal from that statement. "It's genetic."

Together they hauled the motorboat up a foot or so, though Autumn doubted he needed her help. She did not allow herself to focus on all of that lean strength, however. She knew better. Surely she ought to know better.

They left the boat behind and crunched their way along rocky shore. Autumn liked the feel of her wet feet in her sturdy water shoes, because that feeling could only mean summer.

She marched along, trying to keep up with Bowie's long, easy strides without appearing to *scurry* after him like some kind of mouse. And because she was certainly not *scurrying*, she took the time to look around. There were other boats along the shore, pulled up the same way theirs was. There was what looked like a swimming area mapped out in front of a big boathouse, and a dock stretching out into the water. There wasn't a particular path up the side of the hill so much as the beginnings of a summer meadow, and Autumn quit worrying about keeping up with Bowie. She kept stopping to turn back and look at the pristine expanse of the lake stretched out behind her, until it bent around out of view.

They'd caught up to the blue sky, and it was beautiful now, with the sun high above and a faint breeze moving over her face. The land itself seemed to be basking in the prettiness, after all the long months of cold.

They crested the hill and headed toward the biggest red building. As they walked, Autumn could see the doors were wide open, letting the good weather in. Inside, there was what looked like any farmers' market anywhere, just all indoors. Autumn had a sudden pang of homesickness for her favorite farmers' market in Hamilton, where she liked to go on summer Saturdays, eat an English-style pasty from her favorite shop, and go home with all kinds of things she didn't know she needed. The Mine reminded her of home and she picked up her pace a little as they drew close.

There was a group set up outside, playing a collection of fiddles, guitars, and the odd accordion. There were kids dancing around in the dirt in front of them, and more than a few adults, as well.

Autumn felt as if she was looking at the perfect distillation of all the things she loved about western small towns. The people here looked like the sort of rugged individuals she liked best. Capable of hunkering down to do what needed doing, but for today, just folks out on a summer Saturday exulting in the kind of connections she thought people took more seriously when the rest of their time was spent in isolation.

It felt familiar to her here. Almost like home, even though it was so different. It made her feel better about coming here in the first place.

She couldn't wait to tell her sisters.

Autumn glanced up at Bowie. "Do we have a shopping list?"

He cast her one of those looks she was beginning to think of as particularly Bowie. Dark eyes bright with laughter and maybe a little heat, too. That amused curve to his mouth. "That's disappointing, Autumn. Taking practicality too far, I'd say."

"I have no idea what you're talking about. Not an uncommon reaction to things you say, by the way."

"It's appropriate to get at least a little giddy over the Mine." His voice was chiding. He shook his head, sorrowfully. "You basically just told me that if you stumbled over a unicorn in the woods, the only question you'd ask is where the blacksmith is located."

"How disappointing for you that my concern would be whether or not the poor mythical creature could walk properly. How dare I."

Bowie nodded with great solemnity. "I'm glad you see the error of your ways."

"*I* like to know the parameters before jumping into something," she informed him. "What if I get my heart set on dancing only to find out that you think dancing is the devil, have no intention of doing it yourself or allowing anyone else to, and all my wanting it is only going to make not getting it worse?"

"That sounds like a whole lot of living in the future to me," Bowie drawled. "You know what happens when you do that?"

"I do. You're appropriately prepared for the matter at hand."

"You miss out on the present." His eyes were glimmering then, in a way that made that same old ribbon pull tight inside her, making her heart get good and giddy, despite her attempts to prevent it. "Me? I prefer to stay put. Right here in the thing that's actually happening."

Autumn nodded. "You would say that. You're a man."

Bowie came to a stop, there at the edge of the small crowd outside the big, red building. "Autumn McCall." He didn't clasp at his chest in mock astonishment, but he somehow seemed to *suggest* the clasping. And possibly even some staggering back. All while treating her to a lazy appraisal that made her think it was a lot hotter here in Alaska than she'd anticipated. "That's downright chauvinist."

"Is it chauvinist? Or just my observation of the way people behave?" She shrugged, hoping all the sudden heat didn't show on her face. "Men are celebrated for living in the moment. Boys will be boys, and all that. Women, not so much. We're expected to have our acts together. And while we're at it, everyone else's act, too."

"I think that's something women tell themselves," Bowie said, and now he even *sounded* lazy and too hot. It really shouldn't have been allowed. "Fun fact, Autumn. You could just . . . not. No is a complete sentence."

And she knew he was just being ornery, shooting off his mouth, entertaining himself. He couldn't possibly know that he'd more or less driven a knife into her side with that comment.

She'd never thought she could say no. Because most of the time, she couldn't. She'd been too busy trying to make things okay when they weren't. When they couldn't possibly be okay, because her mother was gone and no matter what Autumn did, she couldn't bring her back.

That same old grief rose inside her, a wave she'd grown all too wary of over these past years. It could strike without warning. It could lay her out flat, if she let it.

Autumn refused to let it.

"I'll ask again," she said, and it was more fight than it should have been to keep her voice even. "Is there any sort of parameter here that I should know about? Or can I wander around and enjoy myself, in or out of the moment, as it pleases me?"

"Knock yourself out," Bowie replied, and everything seemed a little more hard-edged and glittery, suddenly, layered in and around that wave she still fought to keep at bay.

But he didn't do anything about it. Did she wish he would? *What are you even wishing for?* she asked herself.

His gaze stayed on her longer than necessary. So long that she felt caught up in all that dark blue until he turned and melted off into the crowd.

Autumn told herself she was perfectly happy to be left on her own. And it was true. *If maybe not the only truth*, she admitted when her body took a little longer to adjust to the absence of the man who made her feel nothing short of stormy.

She stayed where she was, listening to the band play for a while. Then she wandered inside to check out the Mine, which really was a unicorn of a place. A village inside of one big building, which seemed far-fetched until she remembered where she was.

Maybe this is my happy place, she thought as she soaked in the Lost Lake market. Something seemingly fanciful that was actually practical? That pleased her more than it should have.

The lingering current of grief inside her reminded her that she needed a happy place. That she'd been a little too busy worrying about everyone else's happiness for a little too long now.

You could just . . . not, Bowie had said, as if that was easy.

Autumn blew out a breath and focused on the Mine instead.

Inside, there were booths filled with interesting crafts, goods, and services, too. One old man, visibly drunk, appeared to be dispensing his two cents. Folks actually gave him two pennies and he barked out a whole lot of terrible advice, all of which made the recipients roar with laughter. There were jewelry stands. Paper goods. Fly-fishing lures displayed like precious gems. Pottery booths filled with gorgeous pieces of ceramic art as well as practical mugs and plates. To her shock, this far out from anywhere, she saw a full-size, gleaming espresso machine being used to make fancy coffee drinks at the counter, making her wish she was like her sisters and could stand all of that frothy stuff.

It was hard to tell what was part of the Saturday market and what was always here. She figured the bar was a mainstay and the little diner area, too. There were seating areas all over, including one arranged around the big fireplace, that she could see being highly coveted in winter given the often subzero temperatures around here. There was a section that looked like an actual store selling all kinds of necessaries, though particularly Alaskan in style, with bear spray next to the single-ply toilet paper. And only one kind of toothpaste, in an unreasonably large tube. Like a convenience store for survivalists, she thought, and made herself laugh.

No one would confuse the crowd here for one of any size, like in Caras Park in Missoula on a summer night. But it was more than the twenty people she remembered Bowie said lived around here. She could hear a Native Alaskan dialect being spoken, and figured it was Dinak'i, the language she'd read the Athabascan tribes spoke in this region. She confirmed that guess at a booth that proclaimed it held all handmade Athabascan crafts. She made a note to look up the culture later, so that maybe she could attempt to incorporate some of the ancient local practices into her small attempts at survival-type projects this summer. Or, more likely, simply be awed at the people who'd managed to live here for centuries.

She bought herself hot popcorn from a young-looking girl with a toddler on her hip, who raised her blonde brows like she expected Autumn to comment on it. Autumn did not. And then, having developed a thirst, she helped herself to a beer, too, scrupulously writing down her name in the honor system log that lay open on the bar surface.

Autumn McCall, summer resident, she wrote. Then, after a moment, she added, *care of Bowie Fortune.*

It was the beer making her warm, she assured herself as she set off again to wind her way in and out of the booths. Not any unnecessary fantasies about what it would be like to truly be *in Bowie's care.* And she was having a raucous little internal debate with herself when she came face-to-face with Piper, who was selling the canned and jarred goods she'd told Autumn about at dinner the other night.

A good reason to stop thinking highly salacious thoughts about Bowie was exactly this, Autumn chided herself. The high possibility that at any point, she might have to face the man's *sister.* She was embarrassed for both of them.

"When you told me what you did, I was picturing a pantry of some kind," she said hurriedly, before Piper had a chance to read anything on her face. She leaned closer to some of the jars, all carefully, happily labeled and sweetly presented. "Not this. Everything looks so delightful I want to buy it all."

"The internet would tell you that's branding," Piper said, with a smile, like she was confiding a secret. "But the truth is, I just like pretty things."

Autumn picked up one of the sweet little mason jars, filled with preserves and labeled PIPER'S PICKS. "And when pretty meets practical? With preserves? You're going to take over the world."

Piper smiled. "That is, obviously, my intention. As long as I don't have to go out there and do worldly things while I'm taking it over. I'm a homebody. But an aspirational homebody, if that makes sense."

Autumn straightened. "I've learned that I'm really good at keeping house. It's a skill. But everyone treats it like drudgery. All the jobs I've ever seen that involve housekeeping seem to be aimed straight at the drudgery, and who wants to spend their life neck-deep in drudgery? I haven't been able to figure that out."

Piper shifted on her stool and kicked her heels against the rungs. "That's why I liked growing up out here. It's clarifying because there are no jobs. So you either have to go off to the city to find one, or you have to make your own. Or live subsistence, which isn't so much a job as simple survival."

"I'm all for survival," Autumn agreed, her gaze caught by the booth next to Piper's, which appeared to be a pageant of camouflage and was doing a steady trade, all by people already wearing items in camo print. "But is it too much to ask that there be the opportunity to survive without *looking like* the thing you have to kill to live?"

"I feel that deeply," Piper said with a sigh, shaking her head at the camo brigade. "In my soul."

"And here I thought your soul was mercenary straight through," came another voice.

Piper smiled and waved the new arrival closer. It was a woman Autumn had last seen handling the espresso machine expertly. "This is Rosemary. She lives down in Hopeless with the rest of her disreputable family."

"What makes the Lincolns any more disreputable than the Fortunes?" Rosemary protested, though she was laughing.

"Land," Piper said, with a shrug.

"I guess that's true," her friend agreed, looking philosophical. "All we have is the general store. Though it is the *only* store around, besides the Mine."

But there was no time to debate the merits of a general store versus land by the lake, or what *around* meant when vast distances in the bush were in play. Because Piper was holding her hand out toward Autumn.

"This," she said, her voice weighted with *significance*, "is Bowie's mail-order bride. Autumn."

"I play a mail-order bride, but I'm not really one," Autumn corrected her, reaching out to shake Rosemary's hand—until she registered the look on the other woman's face.

Jealousy, unless she was mistaken. Pure, bright *jealousy.* Though not really *personal*, she thought in the next moment. It wasn't focused and it didn't feel malicious.

"You *know*," Rosemary whispered then, her tone something like reverent. "You have to tell us. Everything. We've been *dying to know* for our *entire lives*."

"I have not been dying to know," Piper told Autumn. "For the record."

Rosemary waved a hand, the starkly jealous expression subsiding into the sort of glassy adoration Autumn associated with her sisters and their much-worshipped teen idols. "You're his sister. Your reports on him have always been suspect."

"Because you don't actually want to know what he's like," Piper said with a laugh.

"I don't want to know what he's like with his *family*, no." Rosemary leaned in closer, her eyes sparkling. "Autumn, you have a sacred duty before you."

"I do?"

"She really doesn't, weirdo."

Rosemary ignored Piper. "Bowie Fortune has steadfastly refused to give any local girl around here the time of day since he was in high school. And his high school girlfriend went off to school in Denver and never came back. You are our only hope."

Autumn brightened a bit at that. She was good at *only hope* business. You could even say she shined brighter under such circumstances. "What do you need me to do?"

"Whatever you need to do." Rosemary reached out and grabbed Autumn's hand with both of her own. "Every woman in Lost Lake is dying to know *what he's like*. Romantically. Domestically. *All the things*. You're the only woman he's not related to he's ever let into his house, Autumn. You alone can gather the great many details that we all require—"

"Not all," Piper said repressively.

Rosemary sighed. "That *most* of us require to make it through another long, dark winter. Will you accept this sacred duty?"

Autumn opened her mouth to say that no, of course she couldn't *spy* on Bowie and report back—but then she closed it. Because she could see the man himself, standing near the bar with that affable look about him.

Until, that was, he caught Autumn's eye and everything . . . glittered.

Might as well live in the moment, I guess, she thought, while everything inside her seemed to dance. *Since he's such a fan of that.*

"Why, yes," she told a delighted Rosemary, and she only smiled when Piper groaned. "I accept."

But it was Bowie's gaze that stayed with her, dark like midnight and deeper blue besides. It was that look on his face from across the crowded room that made her smile when no one was looking, long after market day was done.

Eight

Step one was accepting the apparently unavoidable truth that he was, in fact, attracted to Autumn in ways that could only be called problematic.

Since he had no intention of acting on it.

Bowie had resigned himself to that attraction pretty much the moment he'd laid eyes on her, in person. But there were different kinds of acceptance. And maybe it had taken him a day or four to really face up to what it meant that he was *that* attracted and *still* planned to ignore it until she went away again.

Maybe he'd had a harder time with that than he thought he should have. Maybe he'd stayed up a sleepless night or two trying to get around it. Maybe he hadn't really wanted to face that this, right here, was the exact situation he'd spent his entire adult life trying to avoid.

He'd been real good at it, before Autumn.

Step two was figuring out how to spend an entire summer season living with her anyway.

And in the past two weeks since market day, Bowie had handled it the way he handled pretty much everything he didn't care to marinate in—by avoiding it.

But today was the summer solstice and he had no choice but to face his demons. If anything as pretty as Autumn McCall could be considered a demon, that was. Not that it mattered either way, he assured himself. Because today was the longest day of the year and that meant celebrations all over Alaska, many of which he'd personally experienced over the years, from Juneau to Moose Pass to Nome. It also meant Midsummer at the Mine.

"You don't celebrate Solstice?" he asked Autumn over breakfast. And he tried not to notice the way she moved around his kitchen, like she belonged there. Because she didn't.

He'd vowed long ago that no one would.

The truth was, he tried not to notice a lot of things about Autumn. Like the way she piled her hair up on top of her head in the mornings, showing him the many different shades of blonde and strawberry there. Her colorful socks. *Her.* She didn't even glance his way, too busy bustling around doing her usual morning things. Coffee. Always coffee. And sometimes, like today, a piece of toast.

He kept telling himself he wasn't noticing her and then it turned out he did.

"You keep saying *Solstice* like it's Christmas," she pointed out, her attention on the French press.

"In a way it is. It's the longest day of the year. The longest night of the year is usually right around Christmas. Two halves of the same whole."

She did look at him then, a slow, faintly baleful look that indicated to him—in case he'd somehow missed it—that he was doing that talking thing of his again. The very same talking thing that his sister insisted was a character he played. And now that Autumn was likely to claim the same thing, though she never put it quite like that, he found he turned himself into a Wikipedia page whenever possible.

Which he guessed didn't really go under the heading of not noticing her.

"I'm familiar with the concept of solstices," she said drily. "We like a long summer's day in Montana, too. But I think you know, Bowie, that people do not celebrate both the summer and winter solstices the same."

"We do," he replied. But when she continued to look at him that way he found himself grinning. Then leaning back in his chair as if he planned to lounge away the rest of the day when he knew he couldn't. "What? This is Alaska. We like a festival."

She blew on her coffee. "I would have said that you don't have enough people around here to have a festival, but I've been there on market day. People seem to come out of the woodwork."

"Folks like a gathering place. And better still, a reason to get together."

"Sometimes in the summer we drive up to Missoula," she offered, and he found himself parsing her tone to see if it sounded *wistful*. He should have wanted that, as it might mean she was thinking of blowing off this contest and heading home. Something she should also want, by his reckoning. "There's nothing like those long summer evenings. There are always concerts, and it doesn't even matter who's playing. We like to sit out and enjoy it all, with whoever else happens to show up."

"This is the same basic idea," Bowie said. "Except amped up to fifteen, because Grand Mia never does anything by half."

"I don't know what that means," she said.

"You will."

He spent the bulk of the morning in his office doing his least favorite thing in the world. Paperwork. But even the best job in the world came with some paperwork, and put it off though he might, Bowie always had to sit down and handle things. Like the books. And the other inevitable, annoying little things that cropped up in the running of a charter business. Still, when afternoon rolled around, he sat back in the chair, rubbed his hands over his face, and took a moment to congratulate himself on the fact he had a business at all.

He didn't advertise. He didn't do a single thing to drum up business. He relied on word of mouth alone. Some of it from happy civilians, like the photojournalist types who were in a neck-and-neck competition with the climbers for who was the most likely to risk everything for that perfect moment. And the rest of it was a trickle-down effect from some buddies of his down in Southeast, where they were living out their A-Team aspirations and not quite ready to let go of that special forces lifestyle. Bowie admired their dedication, but he preferred to pick and choose his charters, and to avoid anything that even looked like a mission these days. Still, somehow, between the odd job from his ex-military buddies and all the hard-core Alaska tourists, he'd been deep in the black for years.

A good thing, given summer was his busy season and he had the contest and Autumn to think about this year. If he didn't have that extra set by, he never would have been able to take her on the camping trip he'd agreed to the other night. When he could have just as easily taken a job and told her he was too busy for field trips.

He didn't really want to get into why he'd done that. He didn't really want those answers.

In point of fact, he was feeling pretty good about his ability to contribute to the thing they were both doing, as requested, when he wandered out of his office and found Autumn out in the shop, cross-legged on the floor, doing something with wire.

"Are you making jewelry?" he asked.

"Only if you consider setting traps a kind of jewelry." Her attention was on her project.

"Are you setting traps in the shop?" he asked, aware that he sounded . . . indulgent. He really needed to stop that.

She frowned over at him, predictably. And maybe Bowie

needed to come to terms with the fact that he liked that frown. He went out of his way to do things that inspired her to haul it on out, didn't he?

"Only if I wanted to trap a cocky pilot," she retorted.

"If that's your game, I don't think that wire is going to cut it."

She gave him a long-suffering look and he told himself that was better than any flirty reply she could have trotted out. "I'm preparing a variety of traps for our camping trip. I want to trap a selection of animals, so that I can do some tanning." When he only stared down at her like she didn't make sense, because she didn't, her frown deepened. "There are only so many times I can post about a gill net, Bowie."

He didn't want to think about the gill net. Because the truth was, he'd cast aspersions on her net making and had felt vindicated when, at first, she hadn't caught anything. Maybe it was a sign that this entire summer was doomed to the same failure. He'd expected her to give up. Not that he was necessarily rooting for her to give up. He'd given her his support, after all. He was here, doing this with her. But he should have *wanted* her to give up, surely, because that was a neat and easy solution to everything.

She hadn't given up.

What he'd learned about Autumn over the past few weeks was that *giving up* wasn't in her vocabulary. She'd moved her net all around until finally, she'd started pulling in fish.

Her first fish, she'd been so excited that she'd screamed. He'd heard that scream from inside the hangar and had taken off for the water's edge, breaking records he'd set when he was a seventeen-year-old in basic training.

But when he found her, she was not being eaten by a bear. She was down on the rocks, doing a dance with a rainbow trout. A literal dance, on top of the rocks, as if she were some kind of earth goddess.

Next time you scream like that, a bear better be chomping on you, he'd growled at her.

She'd continued her dance, unconcerned with him. *You weren't impressed with my gill net, were you? Shows what you know.*

Then he'd watched, astonished, as she let the fish go.

He'd ordered himself to walk away, but he hadn't. *Why would you go to all the trouble to catch that fish only to let it go?*

Because we don't need to eat it. Once again, she regarded him in that solemn way she had, as if he was what didn't make sense out here. *When I catch my fifth fish, we can eat it. Because I have to film it.*

He'd been so churned up inside that all he'd done was stalk away. He didn't really want to think about the daily pictures he'd taken with her under duress. Or the online account where, his sister delighted in telling him, he already had a fan following.

Granted, I think it's probably just the entire Saskin family, Piper had told him airily, referencing Grand Mia's many grandkids, who Bowie had grown up with. *You know that at least three of them have a crush on you.*

I know no such thing, he'd replied.

Because he'd gone out of his way to not notice such things. Not here. He *lived* here.

And he was all about keeping the place he lived free and clear of any entanglements or complications. Too bad he'd been incapable of backing down when Piper had brought up this contest.

He didn't want anything to do with it and yet, when the entanglement he'd never wanted caught her fifth fish and set herself up down on the rocky beach, there he'd been anyway. He'd gutted the fish, then cooked it over a fire Autumn built. They'd sat there and eaten that fish for dinner as the midnight sun shined down, using their fingers and the odd stick for utensils.

And now, looking back, it was hard to remember that she'd filmed huge chunks of that night. Because what Bowie remembered was sitting cross-legged down by the water, singeing his fingers a little and maybe his tongue, too, and not caring at all. Because she'd been sitting there next to him, laughing. Always laughing. That's how she always was when he thought of her. Never frowning, though he was partial to that frown, too.

Autumn laughed with her whole body. Her head went back, she shook a little, and it was like she *became* joy. Every time he saw it he lost his place a little. Every time.

That probably qualifies as noticing her, dumbass, he growled at himself.

"I'm serious," she was saying now, no longer focusing on her wire traps. "The camping trip is a good start. We need more bushcraft kind of things. I saw that one of the other couples over in Takotna is literally living in a lean-to this summer. We have to stay competitive."

"Let's put the competition on hold for the moment, killer," he replied, and sure, he didn't have to sound so lazy. Maybe he just liked riling her up. He could *see* her bristle and it entertained him. *Mea culpa*, he thought. "We need to get ready to go."

"Go? Go where? I thought we weren't leaving to go camping until tomorrow. Or the next day, depending on your schedule. Isn't that what you said?"

"I finished all my paperwork," he said, sounding even lazier and more mild than before, because she was neither. "We can worry about camping trips later. Tonight is the big Midsummer at the Mine party. You're not going to want to head over there in your work clothes."

She sniffed and put a hand to the plaid flannel shirt she was wearing as if it were silk. "If you're expecting me to produce a ball gown, you're going to be disappointed."

"I don't actually care what you wear," he said, which was less true than he wished it was. Especially now that he had *ball gowns* on the brain. Not the gowns, per se. But Autumn with her lush body in one of them. *Lord have mercy*. "I know that my sister and my mother like to take the opportunity of a festival to spruce it up a bit. But you do you."

And then he walked away before he could say or do something else he regretted.

That, after all, was how he'd ended up agreeing to take her camping. Obviously, when he was trying to maintain some kind of distance between him and his summer wife, the last thing in the world he needed to do was bring a *tent* into the mix. But they'd gone back to dinner at his parents' house one night and they'd all been sitting around the fire the way they always did when Violet had mentioned she'd never been camping.

She'd glanced at Quinn, then smiled. *Not on purpose, anyway. I don't think hiding out from a blizzard counts as a recreational endeavor.*

Depends, Quinn had replied, and they'd both laughed in an obviously private joke that Bowie assumed meant intimate relations he preferred not to picture.

But, naturally, that had led to a spirited discussion among all the Fortunes and Noah about where the best camping spot was and why, and then devolved into the usual stories about family camping trips in the past.

You've never really been camping in Alaska, Bowie had found himself belting out, because he was obviously a masochist, *until you've gone somewhere you have to fly in. Because if you tried to walk in it would kill you.*

I accept, Autumn had said from beside him. *Fly me somewhere treacherous, please.*

And without meaning to, because how could he back down when his whole family had been *staring* at him, Bowie found himself agreeing to go on an excursion into the deep, dark bush with the very woman who drove him crazy enough when he was avoiding her at home.

At this point, it's entertaining, Noah had said later that same night. Bowie had been staring into the fire, wondering where it all went wrong, while Autumn laughed with his sister, and Violet and his brother debated mineral rights issues with his parents.

I'm glad someone's entertained, he'd muttered.

Alternatively, his best friend had said, sounding downright chipper when most days he was nothing but grumpy, *you could just set yourself on fire. That might be more . . .* He'd laughed when he saw Bowie's face. *Expeditious.*

Bowie had hoped that Autumn would forget the whole thing. But she hadn't. Of course she hadn't. She'd talked about their camping trip the whole canoe ride home, her excitement bouncing off the water and back at them from the trees. She was still talking about it the next day. And the next.

Before he knew it, Bowie was dragging out the maps and talking to her about the perils of backcountry camping, especially in hard-to-reach places. Instead of alarming her, his warnings had seemed to make her more excited.

But that was tomorrow Bowie's problem, he told himself today after a quick shower to wash away the taint of office work. He went out to the front porch to wait for her and took a moment to remind himself that he had always loved Solstice. Here on the lake or anywhere else in Alaska, because only folks who knew the contours of a long, long winter with very little light knew how to celebrate the midnight sun at its height.

For that matter, he liked all the various parties his friends and family put on over at the Mine, because they usually became part of the lore out here. Though Midsummer at the Mine was his favorite of all the community events they put on here. It was a funny, funky little celebration that perfectly fit this place and these people. Bowie might find discussions about legal rights tedious outside of community meetings, but he loved this place. And these people. He'd lived other places but this was his only home. And this time of year, folks from down in Hopeless and sometimes even as far away as Nikolai, Takotna, or even down the Kuskokwim a ways in Stony River came to the party. Bowie liked all the same old familiar faces well enough, but it was always fun to have visitors. He was just settling in for a good trip down memory lane into midsummers past when Autumn walked around the corner of his house.

He took one look at her and was doomed.

Because maybe she hadn't thrown a ball gown into that duffel of hers that had somehow managed to transport a whiteboard, of all things. But she'd found a dress all the same.

"I forgot I packed this," she said happily as she strode toward him, as if she wasn't tearing apart the fabric of his universe with every step. "And you're right, we should always take the opportunity to dress up while we can. I can never be bothered in winter. Too cold, too many layers. But this is summer and that deserves celebration."

"Hear, hear," Bowie said.

Weakly.

Because Autumn's dress was red and slinky and as far as he could tell, was actually some kind of weapon. Maybe even the secret weapon she still hadn't disclosed. It clung. Everywhere. Bowie could only think that she apparently had no idea what that figure could do.

For a minute there, he thought he was actually seeing stars.

But no. It was only Autumn, in fire-engine red, like she was going out of her way to wreck him.

She kept talking to him as they walked down to the dock, but he couldn't have said what it was they were talking about. He made the odd assenting noise whenever it seemed necessary, and otherwise hurried her into the motorboat, because he needed the slap of the wind in his face and the roar of the engine to set him right.

It was a relief to pull the boat up on the beach below the Minc, because the minute he and Autumn set foot on land again, they were swept up in the swirl of activity and music and merriment.

And that was better than the two of them being alone with that *dress* in the mix.

Because the more alone they were, the less reason Bowie could seem to come up with to continue to maintain his distance. The more alone they were, the less he seemed to recall his own history.

"This is *fantastic*," Autumn breathed, her eyes shining, and then she drifted off into the crowd, where he knew she would wander around, soaking in everything. Because that was what she always did, every market day. And Midsummer at the Mine was more than a market.

He told himself it was a relief when she took off, though that wasn't how it felt. Not as he watched her walk away from him. He found himself rubbing at his chest like it hurt.

When it didn't. It *couldn't*.

"It's all that adrenaline-junkie-ing," came a voice from beside him as he walked up the hill. He didn't have to look around to identify the gravel-voiced speaker. There was only one Nyx Saskin. Short for Onyx, which no one had dared call him since approximately the fourth grade. "Giving you that heart attack after all."

Bowie dropped his hand from his chest, irritated that Nyx had caught him at it. Though it was better than one of his siblings.

"I expected you to be busy today." He didn't respond to the heart attack comment. "I thought it was a Saskin family requirement to work all of Grand Mia's festivals or risk excommunication."

"I've been working, never fear," Nyx said. "This year might actually be my masterpiece."

Bowie laughed, but as they made it up to the crest of the hill where the Mine sat, he had to change his tune.

"I know," Nyx said when Bowie let out an appreciative sound. "I've outdone myself."

Nyx was considered the artistic one in the Saskin family, so that meant his grandmother leaned heavily on him when it came to throwing these festivals of hers. Nobody said no to Mia Saskin.

Still, it must have taken them forever. There were posts stuck deep into the earth, all of them connected with strands of brightly colored lights. And even though it was daylight, and would stay daylight until almost one in the morning tonight, the lights gave everything an extra pop of color. All of the chairs and couches from inside had been pulled out and set into groups here and there, so folks could take advantage of the outside seating.

Every door and window in the Mine was pulled wide open, and inside, the big central space had been cleared for dancing. There was already a band playing, but this was midsummer. Anyone who felt like it could jump in, whether with an instrument or just with their own voice, and take part in the festivities.

The youngest member of the Barrow family, the defiant Victoria, was holding her own toddler's hand fiercely as she ordered children around through what looked to be the detritus of a potato-sack race. Bowie could remember all those midsummer games from his childhood. Relay races. Capture the flag. Shoving saltines in his mouth, then trying to whistle. Potato sacks, egg tosses, and three-legged races. And then, when everyone was sticky and on the verge of a sugar crash, down they'd go to the lake, where they'd swim, play Marco Polo like it was a grudge match, and basically exhaust themselves.

It seemed to him the next generation had it all well in hand.

But Nyx hadn't stopped at rearranging things. He'd created a long, covered terrace down the length of the area in front of the Mine, where folks usually parked their vehicles. It wasn't a tent so much as a kind of trellis. Branches and flowers wound together to stretch out over a very long table, where folks were setting up camp chairs.

"Grand Mia wanted a banquet," Nyx said, looking the

way everyone did when they'd been bulldozed into following the old tyrant's wishes, despite their own inclinations. "She's got the food covered. But I provided the banquet hall."

Bowie slapped his friend on the back. "It looks terrific."

He left Nyx and wandered inside to get himself a beer. Then he stood at the bar and drank, telling himself he was looking around, that was all. In a neighborly fashion, just seeing who was where. But the third time his eyes snagged on a flash of red that wasn't Autumn, he accepted the truth. He wanted to see what she was doing. He already knew what everyone else was doing, or would do, given the opportunity. Even Bertha Tungwenuk's troublesome cousins from Nikolai.

Bowie made himself walk around, greeting old friends. Especially those who had come in from far off, like his old high school buddy who lived down in Sleetmute. He sat a spell with each of them, to hear the stories that needed telling after so much time and distance. And he could remember trying to explain summers in Alaska to Karina a lifetime ago, all those daylight hours making each day into two days, at least. He'd met her on a beach north of Camp Pendleton and to a California girl, he might as well have been talking about Narnia.

You must be so sad when it gets cold again, she would say. Because she couldn't imagine that kind of cold.

But the truth was, fall came in almost like a relief. Because everyone exhausted themselves in the summertime, trying to make the most of every moment of light. You had to make up for all the dark months. And usually, Bowie did.

I can't imagine dark like that, Karina would say.

And he hadn't tried to explain it to her.

He was walking back across the Mine floor, weaving his way in and out of the groups of dancers, when it occurred to him what had just happened. He stopped dead, then caught himself before he let two octogenarians careen into him. He splashed a grin over his face and lifted his beer at Mary Joseph and Mary Louise Fox, gray-haired sisters who were dancing solemnly with each other, a nice respite from their usual squabbling.

"No, young man," Mary Louise said grandly. "There will be no cutting in tonight."

"We're good girls," Mary Joseph confided.

And the two women laughed so uproariously that Bowie did, too.

"I wouldn't dream of it, ladies," he assured them.

It wasn't until he walked back outside again, taking himself away from the merriment so he could get a breath, that he processed the fact that he'd thought about Karina that way. So offhandedly. As if she was a happy memory, nothing more.

He'd never believed that would be possible. It felt bittersweet.

Once upon a time, he would have considered it a betrayal. But he couldn't quite get there today. *Maybe*, came a sweet voice inside him that sounded like Karina's, though he wasn't sure he would recognize her voice any longer, *you're moving on*.

And he was still standing there, like someone had stuck a spike through his heart while he stared out at the lake, when Noah appeared beside him.

"It's not like you to be avoiding the party," his friend observed. "You're usually right in the middle of it."

"I'll get back to it in a minute."

He could feel his best friend's attention on the side of his face. Noah knew part of the Karina story. He was the only one who did. But even he didn't know everything.

Bowie had guarded the truth jealously. All these years, he'd kept it inside, because it was his. Theirs. But in all that time, he'd never thought of Karina so casually before. He felt off-balance.

He didn't like it.

Noah made a low noise. Likely of judgment. "Keep staring out at the lake like this, all brooding-like, and folks might start to mistake you for your brother."

Bowie grinned, because that was what he did. Then he made an anatomically impossible suggestion to his friend, and turned to head back into the party. The food was coming out now, tray after tray of Grand Mia's specialties that on non-festival nights, she doled out only as she saw fit. Tonight she had all her greatest hits on the table. And maybe it felt like another betrayal that he was hungry.

Maybe you stopped grieving a long time ago, came that voice inside him. *And all the rest of this has been stubbornness.*

He dismissed that, possibly a little stubbornly. Then he looked up, and there was Autumn.

And he couldn't think of another thing. There was only her.

That red dress. Her hair, swirling down around her shoulders. That pretty face, dominated by those eyes of hers, bright hazel, and interested in everything.

Autumn, who smiled when she saw him, then checked it with a frown.

Autumn, who turned right around and marched back into the big red Mine building, leaving him no choice at all but to follow her.

Autumn, who was alive, and more tempting than anything or anyone he'd ever seen, who whirled around as he followed her down the abandoned little hallway toward the bunkhouse section of the Mine and faced him as if she intended to fight him off with a scowl.

But he had no intention of fighting.

Because when he looked at her, he couldn't remember his own past, his own tightly held secrets. His bullheadedness and his vows. He looked at her and saw only her.

Only joy, even when she wasn't laughing, like joy was a gold thread and she was shot through with it.

And that was why, with the Solstice festival so loud outside that it made the wall seem to shake beside them—or maybe that was just him—Bowie walked straight to her.

"Bowie . . ." she whispered when he got there, but he didn't want to talk.

Maybe he couldn't.

He slid his arms around her, all those mouthwatering curves and the heat of her like a punch, and lifted her up those last, crucial inches toward him.

Joy, he thought.

And then he kissed her like his life depended on it.

Nine

He was kissing her.

Bowie Fortune was *kissing* her, but she had dreamed this too many times. So many times it probably should have embarrassed her.

Autumn told herself it couldn't be real. She must have fallen on her way inside, hit her head, and was possibly lying there on the ground, even now, in a coma.

Except this had to be the hottest coma of all time.

He claimed her mouth, but he did it softly, like he was setting the scene. Kissing her once, then again, until she was the one who was pushing forward, surging up against him, fisting his concert T-shirt—the Ramones this time—in her hands.

And every time she kissed him back, he deepened it, taking them to another level.

One of his hands palmed the back of her head. The other took a lazy journey down her side. Neither one of those things should have been remarkable, and yet together they were everything.

She felt like kindling, and he was coaxing her to burn. One kiss at a time.

And she'd dreamed this, but not quite like *this*. Her dreams of kissing him had been a delight, but they'd been paper-thin in comparison. Because the wickedness she'd sensed in him at first sight was exactly the way he kissed her now. Every stroke of his tongue set off new fireworks inside her until she felt him in her breasts, low in her belly, and deep between her legs.

The hand at the back of her head held her face where he wanted it, and he played with her mouth, tasting her, tempting her. Taking his time, but with an intensity that made her shake. The kiss went on and on, as if he were thirsty, starving, and only she could ease the hunger.

As if only Autumn could possibly kiss him back the right way.

He kissed her as if he'd been wanting to kiss her forever, though she knew that wasn't true. She remembered the way he'd frozen solid the moment she'd stepped out the front door in Montana. She knew what it meant.

But she didn't care—she couldn't care—because she was tasting him at last. The scrape of his jaw that felt as good beneath her palms as she'd always imagined it would. She found herself holding his face between her hands as the kiss got slower. Deeper.

Hotter.

So much hotter.

So hot she didn't understand why they weren't both incinerated on the spot. Particularly when it seemed they were teasing those flames, licking them higher, making them dance.

Autumn shuddered against him, sensation rising inside her like a tide.

Bowie pulled away but he didn't go far. His dark blue gaze was darker than she'd ever seen it before, like midnight in winter, and it made her pull in a breath to steady herself. But she didn't look away.

And she had no idea how long they stood like that. Holding each other the way they were, as if they always stood together this way. Her hands on his face. His hands at the back of her head and on her hip, holding her close to him. *This close* to smashing her against that long, rangy body of his, which was the only place she wanted to be.

It felt like a very long time they stood there, neither one of them breathing normally. It felt like forever.

She thought he would say something. Then she thought maybe she should.

But neither of them moved.

Bowie stepped back suddenly, dropping his hands from her like it hurt him. Then he looked at her as if letting go was tearing him apart.

Or maybe that was how she was looking at him, in this hushed, heated moment in a back hall where they were somehow all alone in the middle of a community-wide party. Even though she could hear so many people outside. The music. The laughter.

Her perilous knees signaled their uselessness, so she backed away until she could feel the wall behind her. And strangely enough, she felt absolutely no shame when she found herself clinging to it.

Once again, she thought that Bowie, who never ran out of things to say, would say something here. A joke, she figured. Something to ease the tension. To whisk it all away.

But he only looked at her for another too-long moment, as if even he was lost for words. *Tortured*, she thought. *He looks tortured*. Then he turned and walked away.

Leaving her standing there, inside out, and not at all sure how she was meant to put herself back together again.

And maybe at some point she would have to address the part of her that really, truly didn't mind that. Because she was the dependable, reliable McCall sister. She was not the sister who inspired men to *seize her bodily* and press kisses upon her, then leave her in a *torturous froth*.

Autumn couldn't say she disliked the fact that today, on the summer solstice, she got to be confused for that sister. She blamed the dress.

It was possible she clung to that wall for a lifetime or two. But eventually, her heart calmed down a little. Her pulse stopped threatening to burst straight out of her temples, her wrists, and that needy place between her legs. Even her knees seemed to rise to the occasion. She tested them by standing up straight and taking a couple of steps within reach of the wall. And when that worked, she walked the rest of the way down the hall to the bunkhouse. She wound her way through the dormitory-style setup there and into the toilets.

She was washing her hands when the door swung open behind her and a set of women came in that she knew by now were assorted Saskins.

"You better get out there and fill up a plate before it's gone," the most intimidating one said, peering at Autumn as if she was doing something wrong. The way she had since they'd first met at her first market day.

"I'm on my way," Autumn assured her, slightly worried there were rules she was unwittingly breaking. Like kissing Bowie Fortune in the hall, for example. There had to be rules against that.

"You have to forgive Silver," said the woman beside her. Her sister, Autumn knew. The whole family had the same striking features. "She thinks she's the boss of everyone."

"Oh, for God's sake, Amie," Silver said, but as if the description not-so-secretly pleased her.

The third woman, their cousin, was nodding. "I'm Team Amie on this one. We never run out of food. Grand Mia would die first."

"Thank you, Ruby." Silver did not sound the least bit thankful. "You have a lot of opinions for someone who spends most of her time in Fairbanks."

The three of them made her miss her sisters. And they were still bickering happily among themselves as Autumn slipped out the door and made her way back to the wide-open doors of the Mine.

She paused there, taking in the scene. Because she, too,

came from a place where summers were revered after long, cold, dark winters. No one wanted to miss even a moment of outdoor time, and they didn't. It wasn't unheard of to put in a long day at the ranch and then, even knowing they'd have to be up early the next morning, pile in the car to go into Hamilton. Where maybe they'd jump off the bridge and swim around in the river for hours, just because it was light out and they could. Sometimes they'd head all the way up to Missoula, the way she'd told Bowie. They'd sit down on the banks of the Clark Fork River and soak in every last drop of light, eating and drinking and listening to music and enjoying the last, best place they all called home.

Autumn had sweet memories of summers back home. But Midsummer at the Mine, which was written all across the huge banner that hung over the doorway she was standing in, took it to a different level.

She recognized quite a few people she'd seen on market day Saturdays, but there were more people here tonight. Family like Ruby Saskin in from Fairbanks, she assumed. And she loved that families coming together seemed to be another theme here as the longest day wore on. Folks didn't break up into their own little groups and sit apart. Whole families were settling down around the big, long table made up of what looked like every table from inside. Like they were all one big family here, beneath the bower's summer bounty with the glorious lake behind them, blue and inviting.

People were pulling up camp chairs to the table or dragging out seats from inside. They were passing platters around between them. Autumn could hear the sound of parents corralling their children and calling them to eat, sparking another set of memories. Her mother, calling out across the fields to bring them all running home, barefoot and red-faced and filled with that wild summer glee.

She concentrated on the view here, now. Past the boathouse down at the water's edge, around the shoreline to the right, there were little cabins here and there. And there were enough of them with vehicles parked in front to let her know that they were occupied. Seasonally, she would bet, as none of them looked sturdy enough to be winterized. Or not for an Alaska winter, anyway.

And everywhere there was a bit of flat land, there were tents. Some clumped together, suggesting a family unit, or friends. Others off on their own. There were tents set up on top of vehicles and others that looked as if they wouldn't be out of place halfway up a mountain. But there were enough of them to indicate making it up to this particular celebration of daylight was a priority. A destination.

A delight, Autumn thought, but maybe that was the kiss talking.

Most of the musicians who'd been playing along together inside had laid down their instruments and wandered over to find places at the table, but a couple of the men had come outside and sat themselves on the back of someone's ATV, like it was a stage.

And somehow, two old men in fedoras, playing dueling blues, were the perfect complement to the moment.

Autumn reached down to check the security of the belt of her wrap dress. Then she walked down toward the table, something hitching inside her when she saw Violet and Piper already there, and waving. To her.

Like she belonged here.

"We saved you a seat," Piper told her when she sat down. "And it wasn't easy. Maryam Fox tried to steal it no less than seven times."

"I find it fascinating that, given open seating, all the factions of the Lost Lake community still divide into their familial groups, even at a table that is clearly meant to stir them all up," Violet said, but she was talking more to the notebook she was scribbling in than to Piper or Autumn.

"Just wait until December," Piper said with a grin. "It's smaller, but in a lot of ways even better. And there's definitely more fraternizing between factions."

Autumn could have asked more about December, but

she was betting she knew. Another festival, but this one in the dark.

Of course, she wouldn't be here for that one.

And acknowledging that truth seemed to take something out of her. A big chunk she hadn't known she was at risk of losing.

"Are you all right?" Violet asked, her gaze sharpening on Autumn as she looked up from her notes. "You look . . ."

"Overwhelmed?" Autumn asked, and made herself smile, even though her mouth didn't feel like hers anymore. Her entire body was in a small riot, in fact, but she couldn't do anything about it. Even though she knew, with distressing accuracy, exactly where Bowie was sitting. As if he'd kissed her and now she had a particular, internal GPS, tuned to him alone. She could feel him, like a searchlight, sitting farther down the table with his parents and some of the men around his age who Autumn recognized, but hadn't met yet.

He didn't look at her once but Autumn knew he was aware of every breath she'd taken since she'd appeared in the doorway. Like he had the same GPS in him, too.

She had never found *GPS*, of all things, hot before.

"You're overwhelmed?" Piper asked from beside her as if, depending on Autumn's reply, she was prepared to flip the table to make her feel better.

"Only because I've never been to Midsummer at the Mine before," Autumn assured her.

Violet looked up and smiled. "Me, neither. It's extravagant."

It was, for more reasons than she planned to share with Violet, but knowing that she wasn't the only brand-new person here helped, somehow. Autumn grabbed the next platter that passed her by, taking the opportunity to pile her plate high with food. All the food.

She wasn't hungry. Or anyway, not for food. But she couldn't have what she wanted, so this felt like the next best thing.

Just to make sure, she had seconds.

And a tiny portion of thirds.

Followed by a generous helping from the cake tray that Maryam and Sylvie Fox passed around.

By the time she'd forked in her last, deliciously gluttonous bite, Autumn was so stuffed she couldn't take a full breath. That was fine with her, because what had breathing done for her so far? If there had to be breathlessness, to her mind, better it should be from all the glorious food rather than one too-beautiful-to-live man.

Who happened to kiss even better than the numerous dreams she'd had on the subject.

Much, much better.

She waddled over to one of the couches, sat down, and let the night wash over her. It was still light, of course, and would be for hours yet. There was dancing. Anyone around with a musical bent appeared to shake off their feasting by picking up their instruments to join in what should have been a cacophony, but what came across instead as a chorus.

Joyful, almost accidental, and maybe somehow more perfect because of it.

It was the longest day of the year, so Autumn waited until she felt like she could pull a full breath in, and then she danced in the summer light that persisted so long into the evening. She danced and danced, with people she knew and people she didn't. There were no steps, no formalities. People did what they liked, sometimes in couples, sometimes alone, sometimes in raucous groups.

She danced so she wouldn't have to think about that life-altering kiss. Or maybe so it could burn inside her while she moved, because it was all she thought about. She danced so that her body could quit its sensual assault, but the music and the movement seemed only to heighten the sensitivity of her skin. Of her . . . everything.

Autumn danced to pretend she didn't have that bright light inside her, letting her know exactly where Bowie was at every turn, but she knew.

She knew.

Not long before midnight, Autumn took a break to drink a lot of water, then prop herself up against one of the couches outside again. There was a breeze playing with the ropes of light that hung everywhere, making them dance and cast their rainbow shadows. And the trellis that covered the table was wrapped in lights, too, making it all feel otherworldly. As if this weren't the Mine at all, but some fantasy world she'd stumbled into.

Piper had told her that the party went on until the sun went down at last, and it showed no signs of stopping before that. There were only a few people outside with her. A couple cozied up in a big chair. A table of kids playing a boisterous game of cards. Otherwise it was just her and the body she'd fed and then moved as joyfully as she knew how.

And still, all she could feel was that kiss.

She could have texted her sisters and told them what had happened. They would have loved it—or hated it—with all their usual noise. That normally made her laugh. But somehow, it felt like a betrayal of the moment she'd had with Bowie to consider sharing it that way. She didn't even know what she would say. Thinking of what she could write in her head seemed to diminish what had actually happened. *Bowie kissed me. We kissed.*

It had been a kiss, sure. That sounded woefully quantifiable. Small and comprehendible.

When what happened was nothing short of a revelation. A song she'd never sung before with a melody she now thought she would never get out of her head.

And much as she'd tried to tamp it down with sugar, then sweat it out on the dance floor, the fact remained.

That kiss had changed everything.

Inside, she felt . . . seismic.

Still.

She blew out a breath, drained the rest of her water, and decided it was high time she sorted herself out. She had already decided that it was foolish to have designs on a man she had to live with for two more months, especially when she was trying to win a contest. More than foolish, it was directly asking for trouble. Courting disaster, even. Everyone knew better than to do such a thing.

And Autumn was nothing if not devoted to conventional wisdom.

But somehow, out here beneath strands of colored lights that made her own hands look like technicolor rainbows, she couldn't seem to sink back into any kind of conventional wisdom that would normally bolster her. Maybe because none of this was conventional at all.

Conventional wisdom would not have allowed her to join a mail-order bride contest in the first place. And if she had any wisdom in her at all, she would have taken one look at Bowie and called the whole thing off, because he was nothing if not a heartbreak waiting to happen.

Probably to her. Maybe right now.

Her breath got tangled up again at that, because it had been one thing to moon around over how beautiful he was, and how, really, he probably would have preferred to spend three months isolated somewhere with one of her sisters. Like every other man alive. She'd been sure of that since the day they'd met.

Except now she wasn't sure at all.

Because she might not have had a lot of experience. Some might even say that she didn't know a thing about men. And maybe that was true.

But she knew this man. Maybe not well. Maybe not the way his friends and family did, but she'd lived with him, night and day, for almost a month. And she knew that the way he'd kissed her, he hadn't been thinking of anyone else. He hadn't been wishing she was any other woman but her.

Her sisters were forever going on about who was a player and who was not, and Autumn had always counted herself lucky that she was never involved in the sorts of games that involved players in the first place. If she pulled out her phone and told her sisters what was going on, that's exactly what they would call Bowie.

But she knew that they were wrong. And that she would never be able to explain to them how she knew it.

It was the way he'd kissed her. It was the way he'd looked at her, as if he was tortured by the fact that the only thing on this earth that he could focus on was her. She knew that was what he'd been feeling, because she felt it, too.

Everything was different now.

So the only question she really had to ask herself was, What did she plan to do next?

Her own query seemed to kick around inside her like a lightning strike.

What do you plan to do next?

The wise move would be to pretend nothing had happened. To sink back into the routine that had cropped up between them as they awkwardly cohabitated. There was no question that if she was smart, that's what she would do.

No harm, no foul.

But she knew even as she thought it that she wasn't going to.

Because Autumn had been taking care of other people for as long as she could remember. Even her sweet mother before she'd died. She'd first gone into the hospital when Autumn was ten. Autumn had spent four years trying to fill in the gaps for her, and then, at fourteen, had done her best to take charge once Roberta McCall was gone.

What if? came a voice in her head.

A voice that sounded a whole lot like the way she remembered her mother's.

What if, just this once, Autumn thought about nothing and no one but herself? What if she focused on what she wanted *right now*? Not what was smart. Not what was practical.

But what she wanted the most.

What would happen?

Piper appeared in the doorway then and threw her hands up in the air when she saw Autumn sitting down. "What are you doing? This is the final push! We have to dance out the daylight!"

That sounded like exactly what Autumn wanted to do in this moment. So that was what she did.

She danced. She danced until she felt like the music was a part of her bones, and she smiled so wide and sang so loud that she was sure that if she looked in any kind of reflective surface, she wouldn't recognize herself.

When really, she felt more *her* than she could remember ever feeling before.

She danced and she danced, and when the sun finally went down as much as it ever did this far north, she took part in the long, wild cheer that seemed to raise the roof off the Mine and echo down the length of the lake.

And as night finally fell, a dark blue suggestion of the dark, folks began to clean up a bit and head off for their tents and bunks and cabins.

She stood there, out in the gathering almost-dark, waiting.

And sure enough, as if she'd conjured him up in her own mind, Bowie appeared before her. He looked as delicious as he had earlier, in his usual uniform of T-shirt and jeans, only now she knew how he tasted.

Now she knew too much.

"Ready?" His voice sounded rough, like all of those things inside of her.

"Ready."

And she felt as if she'd suddenly become a figure from a myth as she followed him down to the water's edge while above them, the moon rose over the lake.

She'd seen the lights he had strapped to the bow of his boat, but there was no need for them as the moon climbed higher in a sky that never quite got dark. Bowie guided the motorboat across the water with his usual skill, and it felt like flying. Her hair whipped around, the boat skimmed across the surface, and she was certain that if she looked down, she might find that she'd grown wings.

Back at the house, they walked up from the water together, and she felt that lightning inside of her.

What if? came that same voice inside. *What if tonight you do exactly what you want to do?*

"Listen," Bowie said gruffly, as if he could hear her mother inside her. "Autumn. I think we need to—"

"Bowie." She cut him off. "I don't want to talk."

He looked taken back. The moonlight drenched him in its soft light, emphasizing his truly marvelous cheekbones and making his eyes seem haunted. "That's all right. It'll keep."

"I want to go to bed."

He nodded, curtly, and she saw his neck move as he needed to swallow. Hard. "Fine."

"But I want you to come with me."

And if she thought about it, she would perish from embarrassment at the very idea of saying something like that. Particularly to him. A man who must have women fling themselves at him constantly. But she wasn't thinking about it, she was doing it.

She felt as if the moon above, and the long hours of daylight, were all wrapped around inside of her. She felt powerful. Wild and free in a way she never had been before.

As if she was claiming what was hers.

Herself, first and foremost.

And him.

She held his gaze in the moonlight, and she knew she wasn't haunted by a thing. "And Bowie, I want you to stay all night."

Ten

He should say no. Right now.

Bowie ordered himself to step back, to turn away from her, but he couldn't seem to move. He stood there, stock-still in the middle of his own damn yard, as if she'd turned him into stone.

He knew he was going to remember this moment forever.

Autumn McCall, the woman who wasn't his wife but was living here like she was, with her lips curved into something feminine. Mysterious. Looking at him like she wanted to gulp him down whole.

And he understood, in a way he never really had before, why it was that people had been performing sacred rites on nights like this for as long as they'd walked the earth. Because it meant something to acknowledge the change of the season. It meant something to bear witness to the turning of the year.

Just like it meant something to watch the woman he shouldn't want dance like she was made of pure fire and untamed joy, like she was something ancient and profound, wrapped up in a red dress that made his heart beat faster every time he looked at her.

And it meant something, too, that he was the one who'd kissed her back at the Mine. But now she was the one standing before him, offering him a night.

Bowie hadn't forgotten the secret he carried. He hadn't forgotten about Karina.

This was more complicated than that.

It was as if his ghosts were part of the moonlight. That smile on Autumn's face, the wild magic in her gaze.

He had never denied himself a good time. But he'd always balked at anything deeper. He'd always made certain to hold most of himself in reserve.

But they were all alone in an Alaskan summer night, and he'd indulged himself with a taste of her after all this time abstaining.

There was no going back from that.

Maybe he didn't want to go back.

They had sat at the same table, participating in the same ritual. And for all the fun of it, the community and the food, the music and the games, that's exactly what it was. A sacred ritual, bidding farewell to the light and welcoming in the dark again.

It suddenly seemed to Bowie that Midsummer at the Mine had been the opening act.

But this was the show.

And he didn't know if he was man enough to take on a woman who was looking him over like she wanted to eat him alive, but he surely intended to try.

Especially when that sensual, mysterious smile deepened. And she reached down to untie that dress she wore, then shrug it off.

So that she was wearing nothing but a little bit of lace and a whole lot of moonlight.

Deep inside of him, Bowie was dimly aware of all the objections he should have been having at this moment, but he would care about that later. He was sure he would care a whole lot.

The only thing he cared about right now was Autumn.

The only thing he could think, or feel, or see was Autumn.

"All night works for me," he told her.

Then he moved closer and wasted no time hauling her up into his arms.

The way he'd wanted to do, if he was honest about it, for some time now.

She let out a sound that might have been a laugh, but he was already walking toward the house. Carrying her, not to her little guest room, but through the front door.

A lot like this was a wedding night, after all.

He kicked the door shut behind them and pretended he hadn't thought something like that, because it was all kinds of wrong.

But it wouldn't have stopped him anyway. He didn't think anything could.

She was close enough to naked, and in his arms, and he understood two things with perfect clarity. One, this had always been inevitable. From the moment he'd locked eyes with her outside her father's house. And two, he might regret it in the morning—that was just as inevitable—but he intended to make sure he drank his fill of her anyway, all night long, as ordered.

Because he figured he was going to live on that memory for a long, long time.

He carried her through his house, regretting for the first time since he'd built it that it wasn't a simple square and easier to navigate. He held her tight against his chest as he took her up the spiral staircase that rose as if it were heading straight for the stars, then curved around to deliver them to the second floor he'd given over to one big bedroom.

Then, finally, he carried her over to the bed he'd lain in all these nights, thinking things he shouldn't and imagining scenes exactly like this one. He set her down on the mattress, then stood back.

"Don't move," he said, when she looked as if she was about to sit up. And he felt his mouth crook when she frowned at him, though he hadn't found much of anything funny since she'd turned up in that red dress. Because of course Autumn frowned at him even now, laid out on his bed like the pinup he'd always wanted, her hair tousled around her, her curves a lush symphony that begged for his hands, his mouth. Naturally Autumn, who had already seduced him, wanted nothing more than to scowl at him. "I want to look at you."

"I would have thought there'd been more than enough looking already," she retorted, in that huffy way that should not have gotten him hot, but here they were.

There was no getting out of the way of this thing between them. Lord knew he'd tried.

"There's been a lot of looking, I grant you." Bowie took his time toeing off his boots and getting rid of his shirt. He took his time, tracing the lines of her with his gaze, because she was a dream come true. Literally. Those big, glorious breasts. Her narrow waist. Then the flare of her hips that made him wonder if he was going to be able to hold on to his self-control. At all. "But you were always wearing clothes. Layers," he reminded her, as if betrayed by her devotion to merino wool. "This is better."

She flushed a little, then she scowled even harder, and there was no pretending that she was simply the physical embodiment of his most fervent fantasies, though she was. What made her impossible to resist wasn't her body, lush and gorgeous as it was. It was that she was Autumn.

Relentless, determined, unstoppable Autumn.

Even in his bed, wearing nothing but a bra and panties in a matching shade of deep lavender, she was 1,000 percent herself.

Bowie had never seen anything hotter.

"I really don't think—" she began, sounding cross and irritated, which only made him want her more.

"Autumn." He used his military voice and her eyes widened. Then she swallowed, hard. And was quiet. "I've wanted to get you naked since the moment I met you. It's been nothing short of a living hell and I do not intend to waste this time arguing with you."

"You've wanted to get me naked?" She sounded . . . shocked. Delighted. Both. "The whole time?"

"Baby, come on." He shook his head. "I've thought of very little else."

And this time, that rose and pink flush went everywhere. Bowie was shorting out. He was so hard it hurt and his hands kept twitching, as if they wanted to touch all that warm softness before him on their own. As if they thought he might not get the job done.

"I need you to help me out," he told her, almost solemnly. "The minute I get my hands on you . . ." He shook his head as if it was too terrible a prospect to speak out loud. "There's no telling what might happen."

"I have a pretty good idea what I'd like to have happen."

"We'll get there. Don't you worry. The question is, how fast."

"Oh." And there was such a wealth of disappointment and resignation in that one syllable that he almost laughed. "Well. I guess it's nice of you to warn me in advance. I guess that will make it less disappointing."

"You're not understanding me here." He was pretty sure he was smiling. Possibly ear to ear.

"No, I understand you. It's okay." He watched her make herself smile encouragingly, like she really wanted to be here for him on this. How a woman as stunning as she was could also be this cute escaped him, but she managed it. Easily. "How long have you had your . . . problem?"

He had no choice but to laugh at that. "I don't have a performance problem, Autumn. I have a *you* problem, but you can trust and believe that no matter how long it lasts, it will be spectacular."

She was still smiling like she was trying to be brave and *kind*. Very, very *kind*. "Like, a minute of spectacular? Is that what qualifies as spectacular this far north? Because I have to tell you, that does not sound remotely spectacular to me."

"I like to think that I don't have a weakness," he said, not sure if he was laughing or in agony. Probably both. "But the perfection of the female form . . . Well. I don't have any defenses."

"I'm still hung up on a spectacular sixty seconds," she said, sounding cross and Autumn-y again. His own little hit of pumpkin spice, sweet with a kick. "I don't think that's possible. I think, Bowie, that a lot of women have lied to you because you're pretty."

He was standing beside his own bed with a gorgeous woman splayed out before him, and he honestly didn't know if he was going to need to take a time out to howl with laughter for a spell. Nice though it was to know she thought he was *pretty*.

"I'm going to need you to shut up," he informed her, with that military edge again. "I'm talking about a perfect hourglass shape. Breasts that look like they're going to *just* overflow my hands. Hips I can't wait to hold on to while I sink into you." He smiled again, because she went silent and her eyes widened. "But first, what I need you to do is get naked for me."

"Why didn't you just say so?" she asked, a bit impatiently. "That sounds like a lot more fun than continuing discussions of your minuteman issue."

"To clarify, if all I have to give is sixty seconds in heaven, you're here for it."

She sighed as she sat up. "I don't think disappointment can actually kill a person, can it?"

Bowie was still laughing as she unclipped her bra and tossed it aside. But the laughter had turned to some kind of ache by the time she wiggled out of her panties and dispensed with them, too. And then she lay back, propped up on her elbows, naked and beautiful.

And here in his bed. At last.

He wasn't sure if he should fall down on his knees and praise whatever celestial being had allowed this to happen. Or whether he should simply throw himself down beside her and stop worrying about finesse.

That voice inside him that tried reminding him that he shouldn't be doing this at all was quiet, which was maybe more damning. It really should have given him pause.

But in the end, Bowie did what he'd been hungering to do for what seemed like a lifetime now, because this was the only night he got to have her, it was the shortest night of the year, and time was a-wasting.

He knelt on the side of the bed and grinned at her, because she'd gone quiet, too. She'd lost that scowl, too, and now she was all big eyes, that soft mouth, and the flush all over her that gave her away. He did the only thing he could.

Bowie scooped up her hips and lifted her toward him like an offering. Then he rolled himself between her legs and got his mouth right there, where she was scalding hot and slippery sweet.

And went straight to his head like moonshine.

Soon enough, she was crying out his name, and that was even more intoxicating.

But he liked the sound of it so much, he did it again.

And when he finally wrung out that last cry from her, he began to make his way up that marvel of a body of hers that he should have known was built to make him silly.

Hell, he had known. From day one.

But he couldn't find it in him to regret that now. The only thing inside of him was a need to please her.

More. Again. Over and over, until they were both worn out.

And then he wanted to start all over again.

But here and now, he focused. He tested the width of her

hips again, then tried to touch his fingers together around her waist and thought he almost made it. But by that point, he'd brought his face up level to her breasts, so he spent some quality time acquainting himself there.

Right where he'd wanted to be for near to a month.

And as he introduced himself to all the parts of her he'd been admiring all this time, slowly and carefully and with intent, she returned the favor. She kissed her way across his chest. She found his scars and learned them with her lips. She sank her hands in his hair and she buried her face in his neck, and she didn't look the least bit disappointed.

But he had the better deal. Because he got to listen to all the songs she could sing when his mouth found her nipple and he let his fingers draw patterns in her slippery heat.

And only then did he pull himself up over her, so he could kiss her neck, and feel the way she panted there below him. When she opened her eyes again, their gazes seemed to tangle. It was almost like they were back in that hallway, alone, with everyone he knew just there on the other side of the wall. But between them, all of this.

Because it had always been between them.

Because he'd been kidding himself, pretending that it would ever end anywhere but here.

She was breathing heavy, her eyes were wide and gleaming with that same heat he could feel in him like thunder.

That ache inside of him intensified, and it wasn't as simple as sex. Or need. Or any of the things he'd already done to her. Or even the things he had yet to do.

Because he wasn't ready. He wasn't ready for this. He wasn't ready for her. He had never intended to be ready. He had never intended for this to happen, and on some level, he knew that this, here, was the real betrayal.

But Bowie also knew that he wasn't going to stop. That he didn't want to.

Maybe later, he would beat himself up for that, too.

And it would be worth it, because that was how much he

wanted her. Like she was already a part of him and he was just playing catch-up here.

Bowie had no idea how he could possibly open his mouth and explain any of that. The tangle of it. The pain in it, but wrapped all around that, far brighter and better, the joy.

Even if it was only for tonight.

"Autumn," he began.

"I have to insist that you use birth control," she said then, so matter-of-factly and prosaically it took him a moment to process what she was saying. "I got my latest shot right before I came here, but that's only one kind of preventative. And I know it's all the rage to be swept away by passion, but I've always suspected that there is less sweeping and more not wanting to be bothered. And now I know that's true. Because this was very passionate, but I'm still in possession of all my faculties and I think you'll agree, we really have to *make sure*—"

Bowie shook his head as he looked at her. "You should know better, baby. That sounds like a dare."

He set about kissing her with everything he had, then. He revisited all the places he'd already discovered, and this time, made sure that she had no time to mount lectures on the topic of protection or anything else, because she was too busy falling apart. Shuddering and shattering, again and again.

And when she was soft and mindless beneath him, he reached into the drawer beside the bed. He pulled out protection and handled himself.

"But—" she began when he notched himself into her heat, though her head was thrown back and her hips rose to meet him. "We have to—"

"Autumn," he said, as if he was chiding her, even as he sank down on his elbows and buried his fingers into her hair. "I'm always going to have you covered."

Then he thrust inside of her at last.

And died, there and then, but what a way to go.

Autumn was lush and wild beneath him. The deeper he went, the harder he sank into her, the more she came alive. She wrapped her legs around him, tight, as if holding him close and telling him to hurry up in one.

So he slowed down.

Every particle of his being wanted to let go, to pound himself home, but instead, he went slow. Not because he was afraid of finding out that he was a minuteman after all. But because it was better to build a fire, one bit of kindling at a time, than it was to pour gasoline over everything and use a lighter.

Not when they were already burning this bright.

Bowie settled in. He bent his face to hers and took her mouth, deep and claiming, even as he moved inside her.

And he kept going until she began to break apart. Only then did he speed up. Only then did he let himself go, making her buck and shatter all over again as he joined her in that sweet free fall.

For a long while, there was only that shattering, as if they were tumbling end over end in space, wrapped up tight around each other.

Bowie didn't know if he fell asleep, or maybe passed out from the glory of it all, but either way she was tucked up beside him when he could think again. He rolled out of the bed, fully aware that there was not one part of him that wanted to leave her, and went into the bathroom. He handled the condom, threw some water on his face, and opted not to study himself in the mirror.

That was tomorrow's problem.

When he came back out, Autumn was sitting up, her arms wrapped around her knees. He took some time examining her face as he walked back to bed. He braced himself because he expected vulnerability. Distance. Maybe some kind of joke.

Instead, her eyes lit up when she focused on him and her smile got mysterious again.

"That was not a minute," she said. "That was a great many minutes."

Chastising him, he was pretty sure.

"I'm sorry to disappoint you, darlin'," he drawled. "I know how much you hate disappointment."

Her eyes gleamed. "I'm just fascinated by the psychology that would compel you to act like you expected to be really, really bad at that. When clearly, you're not."

"It's not like there's a grading system, Autumn. You either have chemistry or you don't."

"I don't think I've ever believed in chemistry," she said, but she was still smiling. "I was sure it didn't really exist. That it was just what people called all the beer they drank in retrospect. I'm so happy to be wrong."

And probably, he should start thinking with his big head. Probably it was time to lay down a little distance of his own. Because sooner or later, he would have to think about this, and he didn't think that was going to be pretty. He was a little bit surprised it hadn't already walloped him.

Then again, Autumn was still naked in his bed, he had the taste of her in his mouth and everywhere else, and he was already ready again.

He couldn't seem to think about anything but that.

So instead, he matched her smile with one of his own.

"You don't have to believe in chemistry. We still have it." He crawled up the length of the bed, watching her smile grow wider the closer he got. "But don't take my word for it. Let me show you."

And that was what he did. Over and over. Until the new light found them again, tangled up in his bed, to tell them it was morning.

He thought maybe they'd slept a bit, though there was no telling. She was spread out over his chest and he could see smudges from the night's exertion beneath her eyes, but that didn't take away from the brilliance of her hazel gaze when she finally looked at him.

Now was definitely time, he told himself sternly. He

needed to say . . . something that would sweep away the moonlight and any thoughts of rites and rituals and lay down the law. Something he'd never found hard before.

"There's only one thing that could make this better," Autumn told him, her eyes sparkling, brighter than any summer moon.

He shouldn't take the bait. He should do what he knew he had to, and end this here. Now. No matter how little he wanted to do that.

But instead he found his hand on her face and his thumb moving up, then down, stroking her cheek. "What's that?"

She beamed at him in that way of hers, as if all the light he'd ever need in the course of a dark year was right here, and he lost his place again. That easily.

"We get to do this *camping*, Bowie," she said, like it was Christmas morning and she already had the best presents, and how was he supposed to defend against that? Especially when she let out a little sound of delight. "How cool is that?"

Eleven

"Well," Autumn said a moment later, when there'd been nothing but silence. And what looked like all kinds of complications on Bowie's face to match it, not that she was *parsing*. Her sisters always made it clear that no one liked *parsing*. "This is awkward." But she smiled at him because the truth was, she didn't feel awkward. She felt amazing. "I had no idea that you were so opposed to camping. I hate to break it to you, but that seriously dents your Alaskan off-grid street cred."

For a moment she thought he wouldn't laugh, or that maybe he was planning to fight it off, but then he gave in and let one out. Maybe it was a rueful sort of laugh, but she'd take it. It was better than the way he'd stared at her. As if he was about to do a little bit of that heartbreaking she knew was coming.

Knowing it was coming didn't mean she wanted it to come *now*.

But instead he laughed and then he turned her over, still laughing, as he moved with her so he could prop himself above her. Beautifully, gloriously Bowie. And better still, he slid himself between her legs.

Where she was ready for him. Again. Always.

She'd had no idea that it was possible to be so . . . *voracious*. Even if she'd known that people out there could be, she would have found the notion that she was one of them hilarious. Before last night.

Autumn was fairly certain her whole life would now be divided into before a midsummer night in Alaska and after. She had already accepted that. But this was the first moment of *after* and she didn't have the slightest idea how to handle it. When she'd always known how, exactly, to handle *everything*. All her life.

"I love camping," Bowie told her, as if he was outraged at such an attack. But not too outraged. Because his eyes were gleaming again, in that way she knew now was pure entertainment. "I don't know what it's like down there in your soft, manageable Montana valley of peaches and honey and whatever else—"

"Yes. So manageable. We're known for that. That's why we have snow ten months of the year, temperatures that make people in warmer climates cry, and a whole lot of ornery grizzlies. Only some of them bears."

If Bowie got her little Montana State reference he chose to ignore it.

"Up here, everyday life is a lot like camping. You don't need to make such a big deal out of it."

"I bet you've always been this kind of guy, haven't you?" she asked, though she had to stop and suck in a delighted little breath as he moved, rubbing his length through her slickness. Using her own softness against her. "No matter the situation, you're sure a big deal is being made of it and you, by God, need everyone to know that *you* won't stand for it. *You* will remain detached at all costs."

She was a little breathless when she finished, and only partly because of the way he was moving against her. Teasing her. There was also that dangerous glint in his dark blue gaze, like all the Montana nights he was slandering.

"No matter what, I fly the plane," he drawled, and even

his voice seemed to snag in all the most interesting places inside her. "I don't conduct research on how other people want to fly the plane. I don't need to have emotions about it. I just do it. I'm glad you're catching on."

But he was leaning down as he said it, smiling as he set his mouth to the line of her throat.

"I understand if you're afraid to go camping with me," she told him, though it was hard to talk, what with all the heat careening around inside of her and the fact that she couldn't seem to stop herself from laughing. In pure joy. "Many people wilt before my indomitable spirit and determined nature."

"Darlin'." His voice was more properly a growl then. Inside her, it was like flame. "I don't wilt."

And then he set about proving it.

Turning her inside out with that same lazy skill he'd been using all night.

And Autumn finally understood exactly why people would choose to do something over and over again even when they knew it wasn't wise. He was that narcotic.

He also bore absolutely no resemblance to her poor post high school boyfriend, who she'd thought had showed her how all this worked. *In any respect.* And at some point, she'd promised herself repeatedly throughout the night, she was going to have to step back, take a breath, and possibly make a few bullet points about how woefully unprepared she'd been for the Bowie Fortune experience.

And how little it turned out she knew after all.

Who could have guessed that sex could be so different depending on who you were having it with?

It was even lighter outside when they woke again, tangled up in each other as if they'd slept that way forever. And maybe there was too much forever in her gaze, because one moment they were looking at each other, and the next he smoothed his hand over her cheek. Then kissed her. On the forehead.

Before she could frown properly at that, because it felt

dismissive, he was rolling away and then stalking off across his bedroom floor. She wanted to complain, but couldn't, because the view was magnificent.

"We'd better get going," he said over his shoulder. "Soon."

"I thought you said we had to pick out a place on the map." Autumn yawned as she pushed herself up onto her elbows. "And if I'm remembering it right, you also cast aspersions on my ability to pick a decent place at all."

"You're from the Lower Forty-eight, baby. I'm not casting aspersions. You just don't know any better." He stopped in his bathroom doorway to deliver that, complete with a grin.

"I'll have you know that I'm actually renowned throughout the Bitterroot Valley for my perception and discernment."

Bowie only laughed, then disappeared through the door. And before she knew it, she was up and on her feet, trailing after him into his bathroom. Where she could only admire the things she'd been too giddy and wowed all night to notice, like the fact that even his shower had a window with a view. Why not? It wasn't like neighbors were an issue here.

Something she reminded herself of repeatedly when she joined him in the hot water and he lifted her up, tilting her away from him so she had to brace her hands on that window as he made them both groan. All that heat and wonder, and none of the worry about ending up on the neighborhood social media page.

"It's going to be a little bit of a flight," he told her later, when she was wrapped in a towel, sleepy-eyed, and had never felt more alive in her life. "And maybe a little bit of a hike, depending. But don't worry, Autumn. I won't make fun of you when you get left behind."

"Liar," she replied cheerfully.

Even as she vowed to herself there and then that she would literally die before she lagged behind him in any fashion.

After she dried herself off, she left him up there in that sprawling, magical room. She made her way back down the spiral stairway to get ready. Assuming that was even possible after the wildest night of her life.

It was hard to sort through her own memories and accept that yes, that had been her. All over that man. Under him, beside him, before him. He was so *athletic* and she . . . had simply given herself over to the heat and the joy of it all.

"Focus," she muttered to herself as she charged down the stairs. "You can daydream over the campfire."

Right. Camping. That felt like a gift, because unlike the other off-grid-ish tasks she'd completed so far—or had tried to complete, anyway—Autumn felt pretty good about camping. She might not have been foraging for food her entire life, or fishing for her dinner, but she'd spent a lot of time camping. When they were little, they used to camp out on the ranch on summer evenings, toasting marshmallows and then falling asleep with sticky fingers. She remembered lying there in the tent she shared with her sisters, giggling while the Milky Way pressed in above them, heavy with stars.

She still liked to camp, especially when her sisters were home. Sometimes they'd hike up into the mountains and go too far to turn around in one day, just so they could set up a tent and marinate in being that far away from everyone.

But she'd never gone so far into the backcountry that she needed a plane.

She sighed a little to herself as she marched into her guest room and surveyed her things. Mountains were always tricky, whether in the Lower 48 or not, and always required careful layers. She preferred performance wool to fleece, because all it took was getting a fleece wet on a cold hike once—and then the miserable night that had followed—to turn her against it for life. She had her sturdy hiking boots and her favorite hiking pants, not too stiff and not too stretchy, that she'd been putting to the test for years. She dressed quickly, stashing what she thought she'd need for a week or so in her backpack. Long underwear and cozy socks. A knit hat because her head always got cold. All the bug repellant, because mosquitoes were considered the state birds around here for a reason, and she'd had a layer of DEET on her at all times since she'd arrived. Her trusty headlamp, because no one wanted to stand around holding a flashlight in the dark, and everything else she could think of that she might need for this adventure.

Then she stopped, standing there in the middle of the room, where she'd been attaching her sleeping bag to her pack, because *she'd had sex* with *Bowie Fortune.*

A lot of sex, in fact. More sex in the last twelve hours than she'd had in her entire previous life.

Surely she must be *profoundly* changed. Inside and out.

"You have to be," she muttered to herself. She hadn't even known her body could *do* the things he'd done to her last night . . . Though clearly, he'd known.

She told herself it was a good thing she appreciated knowledge as much as she did. *Yes*, came a voice inside, dry and amused, *you* appreciate *the knowledge he demonstrated so amply last night.* Otherwise she might be tempted to collapse into a giggly little ball right there on her thick rug. Or text her sisters in ALL CAPS and emojis.

Autumn wanted to pretend that she didn't do either of those things because she was so dignified and mature. But she was all too aware that the only reason she didn't was because it would defeat the purpose. Which was getting back to Bowie as quickly as she could.

Because she'd lived a very long life not kissing him, and not getting to roll around with him naked. And she couldn't think of a single reason why, having now done both—and a lot of both—she would ever wish to return to that previous state.

No thank you.

Her hair was damp, so she combed it out with her fingers, then braided it loosely on one side. Then she swung up her pack and headed out to find him.

Bowie wasn't in the kitchen, though she could see there was a fresh French press waiting for her. She smiled at that, absurdly touched, as if it were a bouquet of flowers. Although, in truth, she'd never understood the whole bouquet-of-flowers thing. She'd always liked her flowers best when they were connected to plants and in the ground where they belonged, so they could bloom again and again.

She carried her coffee with her as she wandered through the rabbit warren of the house, eventually making her way outside onto the breezeway. It was a cool morning. She fancied she could feel the hint of fall there in the breeze, even though it was, properly, the first day of summer.

Autumn didn't want to think about summer beginning, because she *really* didn't want to think about it ending. Not today. Not now.

Out on the lake she saw a pair of birds wheeling overhead. And she thought that right now, what she wanted was to go camping. Somewhere indisputably Alaskan, and hopefully inhospitable, because that could only make what she and Bowie were doing here seem that much more impressive. Because yes, she was looking forward to time in a tent and around a campfire, away in the wilderness with Bowie.

But she also still wanted to win.

She walked into the hangar, expecting to find him with one of his beloved Cessnas, but he was nowhere to be seen. Curious, she turned back around and retraced her steps. Once inside the house again, she headed for the one section she'd never really ventured near, set off to the side where it could be accessed from another door along the breezeway, though he'd told her he never used it. And that was where she found him, sitting in a room that was clearly his office. He was surrounded by mountains of papers, a computer screen, and all the other trappings of what was clearly an actual business. Not just a plane fetish.

Autumn could admit that she'd wondered.

He'd swiveled his chair away from the door so he could stare out the window. Another view of the lake, blue and beautiful and he was making low sounds of gravelly assent into his cell phone in reply to whoever he had on the call.

So she really couldn't do anything but stand there, quietly, and wait for him to be finished. It wasn't her fault that gazing at him made her feel . . . funny. In a whole lot of good ways, sure. Very good ways.

But in a lot of complicated other ways, too.

Because she hadn't missed that arrested look on his face when they'd woken up the first time this morning. And maybe if she was as forthright as she'd always believed she was, she would've gone ahead and asked him about it. But she hadn't.

She hadn't wanted it to end.

She still didn't want this to end. She might not have buckets of experience, or really any of note, but she didn't need much to understand when someone wanted to cut things short. She had been dizzy with desire and longing and wonder. He had been thinking about ways to let her down easy.

Autumn recognized that expression on his face. She'd seen it before.

And the truth was, she'd learned things about herself today. All of last night and all of this morning. She had always prided herself on facing facts. On marching, head unbowed, into any fray that presented itself. But today she'd wanted just a little more time.

Just a little more, before he took himself away again, out of reach.

Something inside her shifted, uncomfortably. She wasn't good at losing people. She figured that was par for the course after losing her mother at a tender age. But then she'd lost her sisters, too. One by one. And it didn't matter that she'd been so delighted to see them go. That she'd celebrated their reasons and their dreams, and the fact that they'd been so determined to get out of Montana. It had been hard to lose them like that anyway, one after the next.

And she loved Donna. If she'd been asked to choose the

perfect stepmother, she would have picked Donna every time. They'd all known her for years. She'd been a teacher in high school when Sunny had been a senior. No one in town had a bad word to say about her. She was kind and happy and smart. And somehow, she had still taken a look at grumpy Hunter McCall, and thought, *Yes. I can work with that.*

First she'd worn him down enough to take her on a date. That had taken a year. Then she'd let him take his time working his way up to thinking about marriage again. That had taken two years.

Autumn often wondered if this was how parents felt as they gave their children away to spouses, or graduations, or cross-country moves. Because she was happy for them. She was. But there was a part of her that mourned losing her place in her father's life, too.

Though now that she stood here in the doorway to Bowie's office, it all felt to her like a lot of whining. The kind of self-pity she certainly did not enjoy in others. She tried to tell herself that there was no connection between all of those things and the way she felt about Bowie Fortune. Even after she'd seen, with her own two eyes, that he wanted to be done with her, too.

She decided there and then, in his office doorway, that she would wrap that feeling up inside her until it was compact. She would put it away. Because she'd seen Bowie's look of disappointment the day he'd come to pick her up. He'd run the sister gauntlet and he'd ended up with the dud. That wasn't hurtful, that was just the truth. Besides, he was so absurdly beautiful—with that jaw that made her feel swoony—that she was sure he had sex like that all the time.

And that was okay. It was really, truly okay. She told herself that it was, a few times, until it took.

Because she didn't need him to treat her like she was one of her sisters. To fall head over heels in love with her. To send arrangements of absurd cut flowers to the house, to buy her expensive items she would never use, to write her bad poetry. She didn't need all those bells and whistles and gift baskets. She wasn't a beauty queen. She'd tried on one of Jade's tiaras once and had laughed herself half-sick.

Autumn knew exactly who she was.

She just needed a little *more*, that was all. Just a little more, because she knew a man like Bowie Fortune came along only once. He was harder to hold on to than a northern summer and there was no guarantee of good weather.

Still, she wasn't ready for fall. Not just yet.

He hung up the phone, then turned to look at her as if he'd known she was there the whole time. And Autumn didn't think she was imagining the way his gaze lightened. The way that heat returned.

And echoed in her, too. Brighter, maybe.

Just a little bit more, she told herself. *That's all. Then I'll be content to be let down however he likes.*

Bowie eyed her as if he could read all that on her face, but she was pretty sure he couldn't. Because if he could, no way would he have smiled the way he did then. As if he was happy to see her. As if this was real.

As if everything she felt, he felt, too.

You need to stop that kind of thinking, she lectured herself. *It will lead nowhere good.*

"Ready to go camping?" he asked, and the way he said it, it sounded dirty. In all the best ways.

Many of which she knew now.

She didn't think it was unreasonable that she wanted to know more.

Autumn smiled back at him with perfect, serene confidence, as if she spent nights like that all the time. And more, woke up in the morning with assorted men *right there*, then carried on as if everything was normal.

And then she smiled like she was the one who might be doing the letting down easy, come the day. Maybe she would.

"Oh, I'm ready," she said, and raised her brows at him. A direct challenge. "Are you?"

Twelve

When Bowie got the plane in the air—leaving his house, the beguiling lake, and remnants of Midsummer at the Mine, the scene of his crime, behind—he began to feel more like himself again. He could breathe better.

He always found his equilibrium in the air. That had certainly been true when he'd been a teenager, filled with too much testosterone and the deep desire to not be his overly responsible brother, forever the enemy of fun.

Flying had taught him the difference between the kind of fun he'd been attempting to have around Lost Lake and Hopeless—and real fun. The so-called fun he'd been into had been the usual teenage stuff, reckless and stupid and always with the potential to go horribly wrong. It was a miracle anyone lived long enough to grow up, as far as Bowie could see.

Flying had introduced him to the man he could be, someday, if he settled down in all the right ways. If he got serious about something. If he stopped worrying about being the anti-Quinn and started thinking about being himself instead.

Up in the sky, he didn't have to worry about such things.

Up here, he was always himself.

The skies had saved him after what had happened with Karina. Every spare moment of leave he could muster up, he'd spent flying. It had been a no-brainer to see if he could make a living at it once his time in the service was done.

Usually, the minute he took off, he was good.

This time, he couldn't say he was fully himself no matter how much he wished he was, because Autumn was right beside him.

Looking cool as a cucumber instead of rattled, the way she'd been the first time he'd flown her, which only made him feel . . . grumpier.

But grumpy was not his style. So he had no choice but to force himself to act like everything was normal. Because that was how she was acting. *At* him, to his mind.

He should have been acting that way, too.

Because Bowie didn't get torn up about women. He didn't let things get complicated. He didn't *do* this.

"You look entirely too dour," she observed from beside him, her voice bright and clear through the headsets they both wore. Headsets that he had never regretted were noise-canceling until now, when it felt like she was *in* his head. "Yet the sky is clear and blue. Is there something you're not telling me? A lurking snowstorm? Winter just over that ridge?"

Bowie ordered himself to get a grip. Maybe this time, the ten thousandth time since he hadn't ended this upon waking, it would take.

"This is Alaska, Autumn. Winter is always over the next ridge. If you don't prepare for it, you can be sure it will get its teeth in you but good."

She sighed. Pointedly. "Because, of course, I have lived my entire life on a tropical island and know nothing of this *winter* you mention. I've certainly never lived through one. In a state known for its long, brutal winters. You do know that Alaska isn't the only state in the union with weather, right?"

"You're the one who wants to go to a tropical island," he reminded her. "Personally, I like a little snow."

Autumn shifted in her seat at that, prompting him to cut a look her way. But she looked the way she always did. Pretty enough to make him feel downright foolish. And, today, obnoxiously *serene*. "Yes. Well. I'm told the mai tais are worth the trip."

He cleared his throat, but still sounded rough when he replied. "I would miss the mountains."

Another sigh he couldn't pretend he didn't hear, because it was right in his headset. "You do know that a great many tropical islands have mountains, right? On account of how they're volcanic and all?"

Bowie shot her a grin, and he wasn't even forcing it, which really should have concerned him more than it did. Especially given how he'd spent the last night. And the law he had yet to lay down about the upcoming night and all nights thereafter. Now was a perfect time to get in there and get it done.

Instead he asked, "But are they *these* mountains?"

He figured the Alaska Range scenery made the point for him but she didn't respond. When he glanced over again he saw her gazing out at the foothills as they flew, with the higher peaks towering imposingly before them. He'd been more than half in love with these mountains all his life, even though he was sticking to lower elevations today.

And that was all the love he allowed himself these days.

That was what he needed to remember.

An hour or so into the flight, he began the descent toward his favorite little slice of isolated heaven, winding his way down into a tricky section of hill and rock. Careful to watch his instruments as well as the view in front of him, because mountains were tricky. And these were trickier than most. Even down low compared to the stars of the range, like Denali up at its lofty twenty thousand or so feet.

And Bowie had been grumpy all morning, feeling a little bit swollen with self-recrimination and regret. Or not really regret, because he sure didn't regret a single moment of last night, but he couldn't say he thought too highly of himself for it, either. He'd known better before he'd kissed her. He'd sure as hell known better after kissing her, but he'd gone ahead and stood out there in the moonlight with her anyway, hadn't he? He'd been nursing his guilt all day like a sore muscle, but as he made his way down into his hideaway, he forgot all about it. Because he heard Autumn's indrawn breath. Crystal clear, right there in his ear.

Like she was still wrapped around him in his bed.

An image he did not need to dwell on while attempting to land a plane in a mountain lake, thank you.

He could have taken her camping back home. There were any number of sweet camping spots he knew there, especially in summer. But instead he'd decided to fly them out to his favorite spot. Not because it was his favorite, he'd assured himself. She'd wanted inaccessible and remote, and he'd delivered on that. It was the least he could do.

Also, it was the prettiest place he knew.

Deep inside, Bowie knew he was headed toward a reckoning. He kept thinking right but acting completely differently. There was no way that was going to end well.

He knew that. Better than most.

And yet, right now, he couldn't bring himself to care.

Because before them, a picture-perfect alpine lake glistened in the summer sun. Up above the tree line, white peaks surrounded it, still and always covered in snow.

And he set them down right in the middle of all that pristine goodness.

"Wow," Autumn breathed, her eyes wide and no sign of that irritating *serenity* any longer. This was the Autumn he liked best—all wide-eyed wonder and contagious joy, and he really needed to stop thinking about her that way. "This is . . . *wow*."

"I understand," Bowie managed to say, feeling a little too pleased. As if he, personally, was responsible for this little slice of Alaskan perfection. "That's pretty much the only appropriate response."

He brought the plane in toward shore, then secured the floats in the usual makeshift fashion he used while out adventuring. Autumn climbed out and started taking the gear onto the beach. When he was reasonably sure wind and any resultant waves couldn't damage anything, he jumped onto the rocky shore and headed toward Autumn.

A little too aware that for all intents and purposes, they might as well be all alone on the earth.

It was a different kind of quiet here. No generators. No motors out on the lake or power tools in the shop. No radio, no music. A primeval stillness here, he liked to think, because the wilderness was never actually *quiet*. It had wind and water. Wildlife. The crunch of his feet against the shore. The sound of his own breath.

The sound of Autumn, existing there at the water's edge, taking up too much space. Crowding out the riot of his own blood in his veins.

He walked toward her, each step too loud. And as certain as he was that this was all leading him straight to his own doom, he didn't stop. He didn't even slow down.

"Do you come here a lot?" she asked when he came to a stop beside her. She was looking all around, her whole face lit up, so that Bowie didn't have to ask if she felt that same sense of exhilaration that he did here. He could see she did. It made something in him tighten, then hum a little.

Worse, it made him imagine things he shouldn't. What-ifs that belonged to other men, maybe, but not him. Never him.

"I come here whenever I can," he told her, and his voice seemed too loud and insubstantial at once out here. "I found it a long time ago when I was scouting around, getting my flight hours in. I've never seen any sign that other folks come here, too. You're the only person I've ever brought here."

That was true. But he wasn't sure why he felt the need to say it. Especially not when she turned those pretty eyes of hers on him. And looked at him, for far too long. As if she knew all the things about him she shouldn't. His secrets. His longings.

What he wanted, badly, that he wasn't going to let himself have.

You seriously have to get it together, he growled at himself.

"You asked for remote," he said, and maybe he sounded a little more surly than necessary. But it was that or really, truly deal with how thrown he felt around her, and that was unacceptable. "Never let it be said that Bowie Fortune doesn't deliver."

"Good news. I would never have said that."

"See that you don't, killer," he said, grinning despite everything, and somehow that managed to put them back on reasonable footing.

Because you're suddenly deeply concerned with being reasonable? he asked himself as they started to set up their camp. He would have laughed at himself, if he wasn't too busy putting up his tent. Then pulling out the one he'd brought for her. And then . . . stopping.

There was no reason he should have been stopping.

"Are we setting up the tent for you?" He didn't look at Autumn as he asked it. He didn't need to look at her. He knew exactly where she was. Up on the beach and back from the water with him, where they were protected from the wind, but not fully swallowed up by the trees.

Exactly five feet away from him, squatting down over one of the bags he'd packed full of supplies. Looking at the mosquito head nets he'd packed like she couldn't decide whether or not to put it on yet.

She laughed, that rich, earthy sound that he'd heard too much over the past twenty-four hours, a lot like she was tattooing it inside him. Permanently.

Bowie took exception to that. He'd made it through his

entire military career without a tattoo, mostly because he was ornery. He liked his scars as they were. He didn't need to pretty them up, thank you very much.

He wished he understood what it was about Autumn McCall that made him want to change that. That made him think she would be the one tattoo worth having.

"I don't know that I need to put up a tent," she said then. He looked over at her and there was a little too much uncomfortable wisdom in that gaze of hers. "Do I?"

He was already looking at her. And then that was all he felt like doing for a while, even though everything inside him felt catastrophic.

Except not necessarily a *bad* catastrophe, and that was what he couldn't seem to take on board.

"Here's the thing, Autumn," he began, because he was going to do this. Right now.

But to his surprise, she groaned. "Bowie. I swear to God, if you take this opportunity for one of your let-her-down-easy speeches, I may not be responsible for my actions."

He pushed on. "I just want to make sure—"

"I do not recall sending out wedding invitations," she said, and the craziest part was that she sounded . . . perfectly calm. Amused, if anything. "I'm not going to pretend that I have a whole lot of experience in these matters, but I think you're freaking out."

Only if she'd tossed him into the frigid lake could she have shocked him more.

"Freaking out? Marines don't freak out. Pilots never freak out. You must be thinking of someone else."

She stood slowly, fixing him with that look she got sometimes, like she was seeing straight into his soul. "That could be. There's quite a crowd around here. It's easy to get faces confused."

"I'm glad you see that, Autumn. It's important to accept our own limitations."

"I owe you an apology." Her whole face lit up again in that way he liked most, bright and sharp. Letting him know exactly how ridiculous he was, which, for some reason, made him feel a lot less like he was playing some role. "I've obviously let myself become overwrought."

"That happens a lot," he said kindly. "It's one of the effects of my charm."

She let out a laugh, then contained it when he raised an eyebrow her way. "It is something," she agreed after a moment, clearly still working on that containment. "That charm."

"Lethal, you might even say."

Her nose wrinkled. "I wouldn't say that, actually."

"Many do," he told her loftily.

"That's me," Autumn said drily. "Always super concerned with blending in with a crowd."

Bowie would be handling all of this a lot better if he didn't *like her* so much. Hot bodies were great and all, but they weren't *confusing*. This woman confounded him.

So he ended the debate he didn't want to have in the first place by picking up the extra tent and carrying it back to stow away on the plane.

He stayed out there, standing on the pontoon and taking in where he was. Crystal blue water, untouched by any humans but them. So clear, he knew, that if he swam out into the middle of the lake and looked down, it would seem as if the bottom were right there, right within reach, when it was actually deep. Even now, at the water's edge, he could see every last stone that made up the lake bed.

All the times he'd come here before, that had been enough. More than enough. He'd let it all wash over him and make him feel new again. Him again. Like flying on solid earth.

But today, back on the shore like a dream come true, Autumn was moving around the campsite, gathering kindling and bringing it down to the ring she'd made closer to the water. He loved the lake and the towering mountains, but looking at her felt the same. The same rush. The same recognition. The same peace. Maybe it was just that she looked as if she would be perfectly happy here on her own. As if she didn't need him at all.

Maybe that was why it felt sweeter when she looked up to see him. And waved.

Then she quickly turned back to what she was doing, and he liked the way she focused on things. The tasks she set herself. Or him, last night. There was a ferocity to her and it called to that same ferocity in him, so much so that he felt something in him give way. Like a wall crumbling down.

As if it were never there at all.

He wanted to fight, but he blew out a breath, centering himself. He pushed aside his memories. All those safeguards he'd put in place, none of which had done a damn thing about Autumn. He set them aside, and then he considered the situation.

With his actual brain instead of one knee-jerk reaction after the next.

He was going to share a tent with Autumn. And he was only a man. Not a very good one, by any measure. There was absolutely no way he was going to turn himself into a saint tonight. Or any other night.

If he'd wanted that, he would have set up a tent for her and called it a day. He hadn't done that.

He wasn't going to do that.

And there with the mountains as witness, the clear lake below him like clarity, he told himself it was okay.

Bowie had made a promise to himself when he was little more than a kid, that he wouldn't get close to any other woman, and he'd kept that promise. He'd honored it. But he had also interpreted that promise in the strictest possible sense, because that had suited his grief at the time.

Maybe it still suited him sometimes.

He had decided that meant one night only, no extensions and no repeats. And it had served him well, because, truth was, he'd always lived a nomadic lifestyle. He still did, most years. He loved every moment of it. Just like he loved coming back home when he was done.

There was no place for permanence in his life. He'd made sure of that.

And everything about Autumn was temporary.

Even her name. Because the autumn here was a gleam of gold. The deepest blues. Crisp and lovely and brief. A little breath, then gone.

The season, and soon the woman, too.

All around him there was his favorite kind of quiet. The rustle of the wind. The call of a faraway bird. What some liked to call the pristine Alaskan wilderness, though there was nothing pristine about it. This was rugged land. The more beautiful, the more treacherous.

And like everything else, temporary. Today's beautiful weather could be tomorrow's dangerous storm. The pretty snow capping the mountains could be an avalanche at a moment's notice.

Nothing was permanent.

Neither was this.

"You look very serious," Autumn said, and he blinked, not realizing she'd drifted down from where she'd gotten the fire going. She wiped the back of her palm across her forehead and smiled at him in that disarming way of hers. Or maybe he wanted to be disarmed, for a change. "I can only hope that's because you're deep in the planning of our dinner menu."

"I have some MREs. They haven't killed anyone yet, so far as I know."

She didn't quite make a face. "Freeze-dried food. Everyone's favorite."

He laughed despite himself at her dry tone. "It's everyone's favorite when the alternative is not eating."

Now she really did make a face. "That's the survivalist mentality we love to see. I guess I should be happy it's not grosser. Like bugs."

Bowie let himself smile a real smile and worse, feel the warmth of it move through him, like this really was okay. "That generally comes after the gourmet MREs are used up."

"Note to self: don't camp that long."

But she didn't look concerned. She looked the way she always looked. Perfectly happy in her skin when he was crawling out of his.

And he told himself it would be fine. It *was* fine. This wasn't a relationship, this was a camping trip. A little moment carved out of a summer that would be over before he knew it. What was the harm? What would it really hurt to let himself engage, when he knew there was no hope for anything more?

So he jumped down from the pontoon and met her there on the beach.

Then he wrapped his arms around her, grinned down at her like he was a different man altogether, and indulged himself.

Starting with a kiss.

And then, because Bowie wasn't the kind of man who did anything by half, he did a whole lot more, out there beneath the endless blue sky and the watching mountains.

Until he forgot he'd ever questioned that he should do exactly that.

As often as possible.

Because soon enough, she'd be gone.

Thirteen

Did you like being a marine?" Autumn asked. They were lying in the tent, some ten days into their camping trip. She had her head cozied up on Bowie's arm like it was a pillow, a small joy in the swirl of much larger ones. They both lay on their backs, gazing out of the tent's panel toward the sky, still light this late at night. Though she liked to think she could see the stars peek through in the middle of the night these days. Just the slightest bit, as the midnight sun slowly released its grip. "I don't actually know what it's like to be a soldier."

"Clearly not." But she could hear the laughter in his voice. "You should know better than to ask a question like that."

"Is that an offensive question?"

Bowie gave out one of his long-suffering sighs that she knew by now were mostly for show. Maybe entirely for show. The man did like a show. But then, it turned out, so did she. A realization she was glad she couldn't share with her sisters, because she could already hear their responses in her head.

She knew that she'd spent the better part of her life witnessing grand dramas indeed, usually in the living room of her father's house, while never starring in any herself. No matter what her sisters might claim. She'd spent the last ten days starring in a different sort of show altogether here. And no one was as shocked as Autumn that she quite liked it.

More than she should—but she wasn't thinking about that. Not yet. Like the world that was turning ever closer to the winter darkness, it was coming. There was no escaping it. So really, why worry about it in advance?

"Darlin', you're killing me," Bowie was saying, sounding very much alive. "A marine is obviously the superior form of all soldiers so, yes, obviously I liked it. I would have thought that went without saying."

"Maybe to other marines."

"Oorah," he said, and laughed, like that was all the response needed.

And before, he would have stopped there. He would have turned the conversation into something else, made a joke, changed the mood.

But everything was different here, on their private lake a million miles away from anyone. He turned toward her, and she shifted her head off his arm so she could lie next to him and gaze at him in the summer light though it had to be getting near midnight.

They went to bed early here. Though not to sleep.

"I was proud to be a marine," he told her, reaching over to tuck a bit of her hair behind her ear. Because he did things like that now. She slept in their tent in a T-shirt and little else, though she kept more clothes within reach, should she have to exit suddenly. Which was always a possibility in bear country. He did not seem concerned about the potential intrusion of bears, so he was always as gloriously naked as he was now. But at the moment, what made her melt was the hand he hooked over her hip, proprietarily.

Though she knew better than to infuse these things with meaning.

Or maybe she didn't know better. Maybe she only thought she should, while swooning a little bit inside, every time.

"I wanted to make a difference," Bowie said. And this was the Bowie she adored. No wisecracks, no practiced smiles. The man she got on these long nights, the man she knew in the midnight sun—this was the Bowie who made her heart feel too big inside her. Like it might tip her over when she stood. "I might not want the responsibility that my brother has to all our friends and neighbors, but I wanted to do something with my life. Serving my country was something I believed in, totally."

"Then why did you quit?"

His smile started in his eyes then, and those were the ones she loved best. She could feel them inside her, like heat. "Don't really love getting shot at, it turns out. And the kinds of things I did for the marines, there were too many bullets."

Autumn knew every inch of his body now. She didn't have to look as her hand moved, of its own accord, to trace the scar on his arm. And another one on his side, jagged and wide. "I don't like to think of you getting shot."

"Turns out," he drawled, "neither do I." He liked to trace patterns over her skin. Maybe it was words he was writing there, but if they were, she could never make them out. "I think the better question is, Why didn't you join the marines? It's a time-honored way for folks to leave home and do a little good."

She laughed at the idea. But when she was done laughing, she considered it. "It never occurred to me to leave home. I never thought that was strange, but maybe it is. My sisters couldn't get out of Montana fast enough. I guess I always felt like I couldn't abandon my father."

"You're supposed to abandon him. You're the kid." He was intent on those patterns of his, as if he alone could see the masterpieces he made, using his fingers as brushes. "Besides, your father didn't exactly strike me as the kind of guy who needs taking care of."

"Thank you," Autumn said, and she wasn't kidding. "That's my work. He was a mess."

"After you lost your mother. You told me."

She'd told him so many things by now that it shouldn't have surprised her when he already knew something about her, but it did. Every time. "I don't think he meant to fall apart as completely as he did, but that was what happened. And I was the one who picked up the pieces. If I hadn't, I don't know who would have. And all my sisters are younger than me, so if I'd left, who would have taken care of them?"

"How much older are you?"

"Jade is two years younger than me. Willa is about two years younger than her. And Sunny is the baby. She's a year younger than Willa."

"So basically you're all around the same age," Bowie said. Autumn wanted to argue with him, because she had always felt *significantly* older than her sisters. But mathematically, he wasn't wrong. She found herself frowning. "For some reason, you were capable of acting like an adult at age fourteen, but they're still infants who need your help."

She turned her frown at him, even though she knew by now that it would only make him grin. This time he did that and also dropped a kiss right there where her brow furrowed. Autumn liked that a little too much.

But she reminded herself that she was making a point here. "Hey. Marine. Maybe you should be careful when talking about other people's families."

"You can talk about mine if you like." He ran his palm along that dip at her waist, another thing she thought was silly but that fascinated him endlessly, and who was she to argue with the man's fascinations? "I'll probably chime in."

"Anyway," she said, sighing a little because his hand was distracting, up beneath her T-shirt. "You successfully changed the subject from your Marine Corps career."

"It's all the same subject." He lifted his gaze to hers. And it turned out a person really could get lost in all that endless, fathomless blue. Even when she didn't want to get lost, she did, like he was the only night around. Perfect for wandering off into and never quite returning. "Seems to me that you and I basically did the same thing. Took on burdens not our own and made the best of them. The only difference is, after I did a few tours, I decided I was done playing by other people's rules. You probably would have stayed with your father forever if he hadn't met Donna."

Her sisters said things like that all the time and it always irritated her. But this was Bowie. He had no stake in this. Nothing to prove. Maybe that was why she couldn't seem to help but take that comment on board in a way she never did when it was Jade's.

Bowie rolled away while she was digesting it, sitting up and digging around until he found his jeans. He tugged them around his hips as he rolled up. He stamped his feet into his boots, then ducked outside.

She knew he was going to find something to eat, because they'd burned off their dinner twice already by now. And she was hungry, too, come to think of it. But she lay there another moment anyway, staring up at the sky and wishing she really could see the stars. Surely they would provide a little guidance.

Because . . . why hadn't she had a whole plan for her life? She understood why she'd done the things she'd done, but maybe it really was strange that she'd never balked. Even when her sisters were being awful, she'd never thought to herself, *I wonder what would have happened if Mom had lived and I'd had a normal life?* She wished all the time that her mother were still here. But she never thought too much about the fact that if Roberta were still around, there would have been no reason for Autumn to stay home. Or the life she would have had to go find after high school like everyone else.

Shouldn't everyone have a road not taken?

Why didn't she?

Because this summer, this contest, didn't count. This was something she'd seized upon as an opportunity after it was clear she had to figure something out. A way to kill two birds with one stone, and that wasn't the same thing. Though it dawned on her then that maybe that was the piece she'd been missing. That maybe a whole lot of lives were arranged around what happened when a person *had* to leave the nest and not so much what that person had dreamed about doing all along.

That felt a little heavy for a summer night on a lonely lakeside beach within sight of a gorgeous man.

"You need to keep your head in this game," she advised herself, her voice a little scratchy in the confines of the tent.

She pulled on her own pants and shoes, then zipped herself into one of her midlayers, too. Because Bowie was impervious to mountain temperatures, but she wasn't. And it still thrilled her to know such small, matter-of-fact things about him, like how little the weather bothered him on a cool July night. It felt like an intimacy. Autumn could see him off down the beach by the fire they kept far away from their tent so as not to tempt the bears, stoking the flames with the stick they'd been using as a fire poker since they'd arrived. She zipped up the tent behind her and then stood there a moment, just breathing it all in.

Because she wanted to remember this, always. The stillness. The expansiveness.

Him.

She didn't think she'd ever felt more alive. Part of that was Bowie. But a whole lot of it was this place, too.

This perfect, sacred place.

Autumn shoved her hands deep into her pockets to warm them, because the night was cool at this elevation, despite Bowie's flagrant half nakedness. She crunched her way down across the beach, the scent of the hot dogs that he was roasting for this middle-of-the-night snack dancing in the air. The smell of the dogs made her belly rumble, but it made her heart hurt, too. Because they were running out of the supplies they kept packed away in bear-resistant storage. They'd already gone beyond the original week they'd planned up here. She knew it was unlikely they could make it much past two weeks. Even though, Bowie had told her with his usual intense amusement, he always packed more food than necessary. *Because you never know*, he liked to intone.

It all made her ache because she knew that this was special, out here. Just the two of them. Because despite all the other things they'd packed, neither one of them had come with any defenses.

She didn't need another painful conversation about boundaries to know that wasn't going to hold when they left here.

And Autumn had always considered herself the very height of practicality in all things, but she knew there was nothing the least bit practical about the way she chose not to think about that.

Because there was no point worrying over something she knew she would never change.

Though it was maybe worse now, because if she didn't know better, she would have sworn that Bowie found her beautiful. *Her.* That he wasn't comparing her to her objectively stunning sisters every time he looked at her. She would have sworn that sometimes, he gazed at her as if she alone blew him away—

But wishes never were horses, Autumn knew. No matter how many times you tried to tell yourself you heard hooves.

He glanced over at her as she sat down on the shared rock they'd decided was their couch. And for a man who spent so much time behaving as if he was oblivious to the niceties of human interaction—at least, that was what he did back at Lost Lake—she knew by now that Bowie was far too perceptive. Especially where she was concerned.

Tonight, she didn't want him delving any deeper.

"I'm trying to decide why it is I never had a big life plan like everyone else," she told him as she settled on the rock beside him.

Bowie was turning hot dogs on his spit. "I think most people have a plan. Me, I knew I needed a little break from

Lost Lake. I wanted to see the world some before I settled myself down in one particular part of it."

"I know everyone else is filled to the brim with all that wanderlust," she said. "But I guess I liked the world I found myself in."

"You like it, sure, but you also want a tropical vacation away from it so much that you signed up for a random mail-order bride contest all the way up in the Alaskan interior."

Autumn blinked. *Crap.* She kept forgetting she was supposed to be an ambitious reality show contestant. She wasn't one. Not in the way she'd claimed she was. Not for the first time during this camping trip, Autumn really wished she hadn't had the bright idea to tell such an obvious lie. Given the fact that she was clearly the worst reality show contestant of all time. Something Bowie never commented on directly, but she thought it was only a matter of time.

No matter how often she remembered to talk self-importantly about *content.* Or mutter a few incomprehensible things about *branding*, a concept she'd given exactly zero thought to in her notably unbranded lifetime, she suspected she really wasn't convincing him.

Also she kept forgetting.

Because there was far too much to do here. She'd set all her traps and had found a bit of success. It was summer, as Bowie liked to remind her, and the wildlife was far more obliging because they hadn't hunkered down for winter yet. They'd brought ample supplies with them, but Bowie was teaching her how to use his bow, and she'd found the fish appeared to like her gill net just as much as fish did down in Lost Lake. And, sure, she'd certainly gotten all kinds of prime content for the contest, but she knew that wasn't what she was going to take away from this.

She kept telling herself that this was like any summer romance she'd ever read about or watched on television. It felt like this because it would end. If it was real, if it had staying power, it wouldn't make her feel too hollowed out with joy to bear it, some days. There was no way that was sustainable.

And that wasn't even getting into the sex stuff.

Because one day, when she'd processed everything that had happened here enough to be cool and sophisticated about it all, she was going to have to have a talk with her sisters. Not *the* talk, which she'd had with them many times over the years—not that she'd been a good resource on that subject, but she'd read a lot of books and lectured them extensively anyway. That was all behind them now, thank goodness. What Autumn needed to talk to them about was the way *they* talked about sex.

As far as she could tell, not one of them had ever had good sex in their lives. Not one, according to the stories they liked to tell her about their exploits. Because for all the carrying on about boys back in the day and men now, all the would-be lovers who chased them around, and all the nights they liked to sit around telling stories while sounding nonchalant and worldly, the tales they told didn't have one iota of the electricity Autumn felt with Bowie.

Not one single spark.

She was beginning to think that was because they'd never felt it and as their older sister and self-appointed protector, she couldn't let that stand. They had to *know.*

But she'd lapsed off into thinking about sex again, and he was handing her a hot dog on a stick like it was the greatest of delicacies.

She took hers, holding the stick in front of her like a Popsicle. "Here's the truth," she told him. "I know what I'm good at and it's not the kind of thing most people find exciting. I was telling your sister that what I'm really good at is being a housekeeper. But every time I look around for that kind of job, what people really want is a house cleaner. And I'm good at cleaning. I like it."

"I noticed."

"Your house is much neater than I thought it would be," she conceded. "I came prepared for squalor."

"I'm pretty sure that was supposed to be a compliment," Bowie said, his eyes dancing. "I'll take it."

"I find cleaning a house meditative." Autumn mused on that as she took a bite of her hot dog. "I guess I could go do that. It's honest work, and I like that. But I also know myself. I have a feeling that cleaning and recleaning the same houses would get old. I'm not afraid of hard work. But, you know. There's hard work and then there's fruitless enterprises for very little gain. I'm not a fan of those."

"I don't know anyone who is." They ate in their usual companionable silence, which Autumn could read entirely too much into if she let herself, and then Bowie shifted beside her on the rock. "Maybe your problem is that you don't think big enough."

"You mean like opening my own cleaning company?" She chewed thoughtfully. "I've considered that at different points. Especially now that so many gated communities are popping up in the Bitterroot. You know those people don't clean their own houses."

"You said you liked housekeeping, not cleaning."

"It's true." She leaned closer to him, wrinkling up her nose. "I think that in another life I was meant to be a grand lady in some stately home in England. You know. Ordering servants around and planning meals for twenty every night."

"I can't help you with stately homes," Bowie said. "That's not how we do it around here. But it seems to me that focusing on houses is the problem. What you need is an inn."

"An inn?"

"You'd be a fantastic innkeeper," he told her, as if he'd had the opportunity to judge a great many in his day. "You're organized. You have a portable whiteboard. You like cooking, cleaning, and managing people. Seems like a good fit to me."

Autumn opened her mouth to argue, but realized she didn't really have an argument handy. Because everything he said was true. She did like all of those things. "You are . . . not wrong."

"Here's a fun fact," Bowie confided in her, nudging her a little with the gloriously naked expanse of his arm that she found she enjoyed even through her layers. "I'm not often wrong. People don't like to admit that. It ruins my mystique."

"Do you have a mystique or a reputation?" she countered, though her head was still turning over that innkeeper thing. "I guess an innkeeper who has the bad luck to be without an inn is just . . . What? Destined for a sad motel somewhere?"

He gave her a reproachful look and another nudge at the shoulder to go with it. "That sounds like defeatist talk. You need to believe in yourself a little bit, Autumn. You only just this hot second discovered the purpose of your life. Maybe give it a minute to settle in before you throw in the towel."

"I should build an inn right here." She grinned at him. "All tents and mosquito nets. And hot dogs on sticks. I'll have to turn them away in droves, assuming they ever find their way here."

"If that's your way of saying, *Yes, Bowie, you sorted out my entire life and I owe you everything, how can I ever thank you enough?* I accept."

She shifted closer to him, tipping her face up so she could get closer to his. And again, the joy in her moved like a kind of madness, burrowing into her, hollowing her out. Like the only thing she could hold was this. Him.

But that was how she knew it wasn't real. Because real life wasn't tunnel vision. She knew that all too well. Real life was compromise, and settling, and all the things she'd watched her friends do over time no matter how happily they'd started out. It was fighting on holidays, cold silences, and sometimes, taking it out on the people around you. She'd seen all of that in her time, most of it in her own family, and she understood. That was real. And real was hard.

Still, here and now, this felt better than real. And she

figured she ought to hold on to it—to him—as long as she could.

"Thank you, Bowie," she said, with great solemnity to match the occasion. "For solving my life as only you could. Maybe when we get back to Lost Lake, an inn will magically appear." She kissed him, then pulled back so she could get a little more of that dark blue. "Maybe it will be a traveling inn that can come with me wherever I go."

"I think you're going to have to let go of the tent idea," he said, right there against her mouth, like these were love words. "Folks are picky. I'm pretty sure they like an inn that has walls to keep the critters out or really, it's just camping."

Then she stopped thinking about it, because he was pulling her into his lap and kissing her with that hunger that seemed to grow more intense every day.

Making their own light to match the endless summer.

And she didn't feel *realistic* when she was kissing Bowie. She felt reckless and glorious. Autumn never wanted it to end.

But on the morning of their fourteenth day out by their own, private alpine lake, she woke up to find herself alone in the tent. That wasn't necessarily unusual, though Bowie had showed a marked preference for waking up together, inventively. She pulled on her clothes and crawled out of the tent, shivering a little as she looked around because the morning was cool. She did her usual alfresco bathroom run, then walked out to the water to wash her hands. When she straightened, she saw Bowie standing down the beach near where he'd moored his plane.

She walked to him, thinking about another day in this paradise of theirs. She needed to check her traps. She still intended to do some tanning later in the summer and hoped that she might add to her collection of skins.

But when she got to Bowie, he was . . . different. Distant even though he stood right there.

Autumn knew in that moment. She knew.

He confirmed it in the next breath. "It's time to head back."

"I figured," she said, though it cost her something to sound so casual when really, she wanted to cry. "We ran out of hot dogs two days ago."

"We shouldn't have stayed the extra week," he said gruffly. "I do still have a business to run."

And it felt like an accusation even though she knew, rationally, he hadn't accused her of anything.

"Oh no," she said, trying to sound like she was actually sorry instead of . . . epically not sorry at all. "Did we keep you from something?"

He turned then and she knew that look on his face. And she was even less interested in seeing it now. Now that she knew all the other things about him. All the things he could do to her. All the ways he was when they were alone.

God, she sounded like an overwrought teenager in her own head.

"Please don't insult me by saying whatever it is you're about to say," she managed to say before he could start. "I'm not an idiot. You've made it abundantly clear that anything that happens between us is temporary. At this point it's like beating a dead horse."

"It's not you," he said.

He really said it.

"I know who it is," she retorted. And all the things she didn't let herself think about, all the feelings she kept at bay, all that terrible joy and the ache in her heart, seemed to roll up together inside of her. She wanted to cry, but she wasn't a crier. She was the one who wiped tears away for others. Autumn drew herself up. "Because maybe you haven't noticed, Bowie, but I'm *fantastic*."

But that didn't really give her the girl-power hit she was

going for there, because Bowie only shook his head. "No one's denying that. But that's not the point."

"Then what is?" She shook her head at him. "Because you act like someone who doesn't want this to be temporary. Day in and day out. And yet every now and again, it's like you suddenly remember—"

His gaze was a dark storm and she hated it.

"I like to think I keep my promises," he said, as if the words hurt him as they passed his lips. "That's why I don't make many of them. When I do, they're forever. And I knew I shouldn't have let this happen, because it's too tempting to break my promises with you."

A terrible notion bloomed inside of her. "Are you married?" Something in her belly turned when his mouth flattened. "Are you?"

"Look," he said, shoving his hands into his hair. "I accept responsibility for this. I don't know why I thought I could cross lines with you then act like it didn't happen. But don't worry. It's not going to affect this contest for you. It's all over the contracts we signed. There's no expectation of a relationship. All they really want is pretty pictures."

"Bowie." She didn't scream his name and she would never know how she refrained. "You can't actually think that you can spend two weeks with me, intimate in every possible way, and then *not tell me* whether you're *married* or not when you start talking about keeping promises. You know that's unacceptable, right?"

"I'm not married," he bit out.

Her heart was still pounding. Her head hurt. "That's a relief. Because I didn't have *adulterer* on my bucket list."

But it wasn't really a relief. In the sense that she felt no easing of anything, really.

Because all he did was nod. Then again, like he was taking blows. It was maddening. "I told you I take responsibility. I mean that. All you need to do is tell me what you need and it's yours."

"I mean, off the top of my head, I'd say sharing with me what promise you made that you must now dramatically keep would be a good start."

He looked less like he was bravely fending off blows then, and more like he didn't like her tone. "Everyone has secrets, Autumn. I don't see how telling you mine is going to make this any better for you. Because it isn't going to change anything. It doesn't matter what I tell you. We're going to go back to Lost Lake. You'll either stay out the summer or you won't." He moved a hand in the space between them. "This? You and me? That's done."

Later, she thought, she might be grateful for the simple brutality of that. Because he was right. It didn't matter what he said. She wouldn't accept it. She didn't *want* to accept it. So what was the point of arguing about it?

And suddenly, it became absolutely crucial that she not show him how hurt she was by this. It was okay if he thought it was her pride. But Autumn would walk off into the woods and feed herself to the bear population before letting him think for even one second that her heart was involved.

"Thank you for the clarity," she said instead of all the things she wanted to say. "I'll go pack."

She was proud of the way she walked away from him, with her back straight and her head high. Not storming away, but not lingering, either. Like there wasn't a single thing broken. Certainly not her.

Though she could admit, when she got back into the tent, that one of the reasons she'd been able to stroll away like that was because she'd been hoping he might call her back.

He didn't.

Instead, they packed up their camp completely and stowed everything away on the plane. And much too soon, they were in the air again. Autumn had no choice but to stare down at that sweetly perfect lake, the high mountains in the distance, and face the fact that she would likely never see it again.

Stupid heart. It just kept breaking.

But she settled in for the flight and tried to get her bearings the way she always did. She stared out the window at the gloomy cloud cover while she tried to come up with a plan for how she intended to handle the rest of the summer. It was July now, but still early in the month. It was a long, long way to Labor Day.

"Bowie," she said, even though she'd partly been planning to never speak to him again, "did you realize we missed the Fourth of July?"

And at first, she thought the blue streak he swore at that was some kind of veteran's response to missing such a patriotic holiday.

But it quickly became clear it wasn't. He was saying something into his radio, but then swore again, as if maybe the radio wasn't working—

"Hold on," he shouted at her, right before every instrument in the cockpit seemed to go wild and something loud happened entirely too close to the plane.

And then they plummeted from the sky.

Fourteen

The storm came from nowhere. That was the trouble with mountains, and with these mountains in particular. They were sneaky, and sometimes they hid, especially when storms rolled in fast. This one with too much lightning for Bowie's taste.

Thunder crashed too loud and too close, a ruckus that only called attention to the lightning that hit them once. Then again.

Normally that would be fine, if not ideal. Planes were built to withstand lightning—but this time, the lightning got lucky and knocked out his instruments.

That shouldn't have been a problem. Bowie was well trained. He knew how to fly by sight and feel, but visibility dropped dramatically. He had to roll the plane midair to try, belatedly, to get around the storm that suddenly seemed to have it in for him.

He spent more time than he should have trying to fight his way through the worst of it, but the worst of it kept coming.

Then a major microburst hit, and he was out of choices.

He had to take the plane down because it was going

down whether he liked it or not, hard and fast. A mountain he hadn't expected reared up in front of him as he worked on steadying his descent, and getting his bearings suddenly became urgent.

He had been in bad spots before. But not with Autumn beside him.

But he couldn't think too much about that, or it would be all he could think about, and that meant certain death for both of them.

He expected her to scream, but she didn't. He couldn't risk a glance over to see if that was because she'd passed out, so he hoped not.

Or maybe, if things didn't go his way, it was for the best.

But he couldn't think about that, either.

Bowie kept his hands steady as he took them lower, doing calculations in his head as they dropped.

He flew in and around these mountains all the time. He knew the way to his secret lake like a map in his head, and even though he pretended to keep it a *complete* secret, Noah knew where it was. He was reasonably sure that he knew how far off course he'd gone while fighting to get around that bastard of a storm, how it had blown them around, and how he'd rolled out . . .

Meaning he *thought* he knew where they were. He'd radioed out, or started to, but that had been before the worst of the microburst.

But that was going to have to do, because the weather was getting worse.

Bowie took the plane down, cruising alongside a monster of a mountain and looking for the canyon he hoped like hell was where he thought it was, because there was about to be a significantly worse visibility situation than the bad one they already had going on—

And at the last moment, the ground rushing up before him, Bowie banked hard to the left, and saw a glimmer of water. Right where he wanted it to be, so there was that.

He always had been luckier than he deserved.

There was no time for finesse. He landed hard. The pontoons hit the water, and then everything was a jumble, hard and sickening.

Then everything was quiet.

Ominously quiet.

Bowie didn't think he'd passed out, but that didn't matter. What mattered, when he had his wits about him again, was taking stock of the situation. He did that quickly, first a quick survey to make sure all of his parts were in serviceable order. Then he turned to the side to find Autumn, looking woozy but with her lips pressed tight together, like she was toughing it out.

There was no time for the pang that barreled through him at the sight of her. "Are you hurt?"

"I don't think so."

Bowie did a quick scan of her and saw no blood, no visible injuries. Her pupils were normal, her breath and color good. She was in no immediate danger. That was good.

He released himself from his seat and tried to take a look around, moving carefully in case he had the kind of injuries that waited a minute to present themselves. But aside from what he'd consider normal dings and scratches after a landing like that, he was good. He did a quick recon of the plane, which was neither in pieces nor on fire.

That was also good.

"Pretty sure we did a full flip," he said, too much noise in his head, still, to really pay any attention to how rough he sounded. But he felt it in his throat and tried to smooth it out a little, in case she was more scared than she was letting on. "Which is good. It's better than ending up upside down."

"I'm pretty sure we hit something," she said, her voice a little funny. His head whipped back to her to assess any damage, but she was only performing her own examination of herself, running her hands over each leg. "Not the thunder. But there at the end."

He remembered, then. It was almost lost somewhere in the jumble of it all after the pontoons hit the water. And how desperately he'd tried to keep his hands on the controls as the plane had bounced, then flipped. His fingers ached. Looking down at them, he was only dimly surprised to find that he had a decent slash across the back of his hand. He dismissed it—it was a literal flesh wound. What mattered was that he was standing. He'd been in enough tough spots to know that this one was, at the very least, survivable.

At least for the moment.

But that was all that mattered. This moment, then the next.

It took some doing to climb out of the cockpit, but he did, not surprised to find that Autumn was right behind him as he went. He took another hard look at her, seeing for himself that she was okay. Again. She winced a little as she moved. There was a shadow on her cheek that he knew would become a bruise.

But she was alive. She was in one piece.

None of that had been a given up there in that storm. He wasn't a man much inclined to give thanks, but he aimed a few upward then. Because he really hadn't known if they were going to make it.

Outside, it was raining. Visibility was crap. But they were in another lake, this one much smaller and he saw that what they'd hit wasn't a giant rock or mountain, which was why they were still alive. Because this lake barely qualified for the name. It was shallow and they'd run aground, hard.

Meaning his Cessna was damaged.

It took him a handful of hours to determine to what extent. While he did that, Autumn picked her way to shore and surveyed the area by foot. Every time he looked up, she was in a different part of the land, exploring this place where they found themselves.

When she waded back out to him, he was feeling all those aches and pains that adrenaline had hidden from him before. He could see that bruise blooming on her face, and the way she was favoring one leg, he bet she had a doozy there, too.

"You want the good news or the bad news?" he asked her as he hauled her up out of the water. Not that she needed his help.

Accept the fact that you want to touch her, he ordered himself. *You just survived a plane crash. These are extraordinary circumstances.*

"I've never understood the question," she was saying, that frown already in place. It was ridiculous how comforting he found it. "Everybody always wants all the news. That's the nature of news."

"We're not going anywhere," he told her, not trying to pretty it up. Because she could take it. After all, she'd handled him ripping off another Band-Aid back at the other camp well enough—and he didn't want to ask himself why he felt bad about that now. "And I have to do some repairs."

"Can you do repairs? Without a hangar and all your . . . plane stuff?"

Bowie realized he was still holding on to her arm. Maybe that was why he didn't tease her about using the very technical term *plane stuff*.

But he did force himself to let go.

"You got the bad news in one, killer," he told her. He nodded toward land. "So I hope you found us a good spot to camp. We might be here awhile."

A week later, Bowie wouldn't have said that he was resigned to their situation, exactly. He was too pissed about the fact he'd crashed. And now had to not only repair what he could of his hardy little plane, but figure out how to do it without his usual array of tools and the internet to guide him through anything he was fuzzy on.

Because no one was coming for them. No one knew where they were.

Not exactly—and this was Alaska. *Not exactly* could be all that stood between life and death.

When he found himself awake in the middle of the night, that was what he thought about. Being stuck here when the weather turned. The storm that had brought them down was only a precursor to what was coming.

He needed to get them out of here.

Not that it was torturous here. He couldn't pretend otherwise. If he forgot that they couldn't leave, it was a nice enough place to stay. At the moment. Because it was July, and fall was a ways off yet. There were a lot worse times he could have crashed down here. Bowie tried to remember that.

He and Autumn were okay. That was what mattered. That first night, they'd set up their tent in the rain and then crawled inside, huddling up against each other for warmth. And to shake a little, together, as all the adrenaline and fear worked its way out of them.

And then, sometime in the night, they'd woken up and turned to each other, fierce and desperate while the rain drummed against the tent. As if it didn't matter what state they were in as long as they could find a way to come together. Again and again.

A fierce little celebration of the fact they'd lived.

That they were *living*.

In the morning, they'd surveyed their new home for the foreseeable future. The shallow lake was mountain fed. There were some woods. The first thing they did was lay out logs and stones on the beach, spelling out HELP so it could be seen from above. They got a signal pyre burning and gathered some oil-soaked rags and green boughs to use to make huge columns of smoke that could be seen from miles away, should a plane fly overhead. But mostly, all around, there were inhospitable mountains and a reality that Bowie kept hoping would change without him having to do anything too extreme, like figure out a way to hike out of here with Autumn, and survive.

But it didn't change. Every day, it was the same. They'd been blown off course. His radio was shot. Until he figured out how to get this plane in the air, or could figure out how to make what looked like a near-impossible hike up the river that fed into this canyon less deadly, they weren't going anywhere.

"Surely people will come looking for us," Autumn said on the first day they woke up here. They were both sore. Visibly. He could see the way she favored her right side, and that bruise on her face was livid. He was favoring a few choice spots himself. But neither one of them talked about that.

"I radioed right before we went down, and that should trigger a search," he had to tell her. "They could be searching right now. But we got blown around up there. I figure we're at least twenty miles away from that call. Probably more like fifty."

He didn't have to point out that in a place like the Alaskan bush, twenty or fifty miles of rough terrain meant that any search party was pretty much doomed before it started. And he hated when he saw the realization dawn in her face.

It should have scared him, maybe, how much he wanted to protect her from that.

"So." She cleared her throat. "We're stuck here."

He wasn't afraid of her scowl. He wished she was scowling at him now, because he liked it a lot better than the current look on her face, not so much sad as resigned. "Exactly."

Other women would have fallen apart at that. Bowie thought he might like to fall apart himself. But Autumn only nodded. Once or twice, like she needed to let it settle in some.

"Okay then. Well." She smiled at him, like she was convincing the both of them that this was all fine. The way he figured she had when she was a kid. "I guess we're going to have to do this pioneer thing for real."

Bowie spent a lot of time the first couple of days checking and rechecking the tools and supplies he always carried with him on the off chance that he could wish his shop and hangar into existence here.

But that wasn't productive.

Together, he and Autumn walked around the little valley they found themselves in. Bowie had flown over it before, but he'd never come down to investigate, because it had always looked questionably narrow. It was. They were surrounded by steep walls of rock on all sides, and though Bowie had done his share of rock climbing in his day like any thrill seeker worth the title, he didn't see the two of them climbing their way out of this unless there was no other choice. Meaning, unless winter was coming in and it was a choice between falling to their deaths or dying here.

"It's okay," Autumn said after they'd walked up and down the whole of the canyon and were back at their new campsite. "I understand the situation."

"Glad you do. I'm not sure I do."

"We can't walk out."

He studied the fire. He thought about the state of his plane. "If I can't fix the plane by mid-August, we're going to have to try. The water is coming in from somewhere. An inlet means an outlet, in some form or another."

Bowie didn't point out what she'd probably already realized on her own. That the last-ditch effort to hike out was just that, and likely to end as badly as attempting to winter here would.

She was sitting cross-legged in front of the fire. Her gaze when it met his was steady. "That means you either have to fix the plane, or we have to prepare to live here indefinitely. Or at least until mid-August."

"That's not a good thing, Autumn."

Her gaze didn't get any less steady. "It's not good or bad, Bowie. It's just how it is."

Bowie learned a lot of things about himself in that first week. He thought of himself as a hardy individual, rugged and capable. He liked to live off-grid. The marines had taught him that a great many of the skills he'd learned as a child could serve him all over the globe.

But it was one thing to choose to live the way he did. It was another thing to be forced to.

Autumn, by contrast, seemed to bloom.

She didn't throw a fit. She didn't lie down for a few days, the way anyone else would have. She didn't even complain about the bugs. Instead, all of those things she'd been doing for the contest—the bushcraft, the survival methods—she put into real action. She went out and set traps all over the canyon. Not only the ones she'd brought with her from home. She also fashioned other ones, too, using sticks and rocks she found here. She moved her gill net around, vowing to keep it up until she caught something. Some days she went hunting. Sometimes using traditional methods and sometimes using the rifle he always carried in the bush for bear protection.

Today, a week in, she'd come back from checking her traps with a reasonable bounty, waving it at him from the beach so he knew there was dinner in the offing. He'd come in to clean the meat, set some aside to preserve for their potential big hike, and prepare the skins the way she liked them so she could work on tanning them. And the last he'd seen her, she'd been doing something in the woods.

Bowie had spent the whole of the morning wrestling with the plane and he needed a break. So after he handled the meat and stored it safely away, he walked out into the woods to find her.

He came across her some ten minutes later, standing with her hands on her hips and that frown on her face, staring at the side of the mountain.

"If you're expecting the mountain to move for you," Bowie drawled, "it's going to be a long wait."

She jumped at the sound of his voice, but then smiled. And he didn't want to admit he'd come to depend on that smile. It was one of the great many things he wasn't thinking about lately, because what was the point when they might not make it out of here?

Autumn shoved her braid out of her way and pointed straight ahead of her. "I found a cave."

"A cave?" Bowie asked, though he followed where she was pointing. "Or the den of something with fangs that's not going to want to share?"

"Here's hoping it's just a cave, though you never really know until the temperature drops." She wrinkled up her nose, still frowning at what he now realized was the mouth of the cave. "It doesn't go very deep. But I've been looking all over, and I think this is the one. The most protected. The woods are more scraggly than I'd like, this being Alaska, and not much of a windbreak, I'm betting. But this will do. The stone is cold, but we have the tent and our provisions and I think we can make a decent shelter if we start cutting trees and saplings to make a protective front."

"What's wrong with the tent on the beach?" he asked.

Autumn was quiet, so he turned back to look at her and found she was studying him with a sharpness he wasn't sure he liked.

"There's nothing wrong with the tent on the beach. Now. But it's going to get cold. Fast. I expect the snow will start in September." She indicated the cave she'd found. "This could be the difference between surviving or not."

Something a little too intense to be a shiver worked its way through Bowie then. "I don't intend to be here when winter hits. One way or another."

"I hope we're not," she said quietly. Too quietly. "But if we are, we can't stay out there. It's too exposed."

But he could tell she knew he was aware of that.

It somehow made it worse.

Another week passed. Bowie made incidental progress. It required creativity. Thinking outside the box and banging his head against the wall until all that banging gave him a new idea to try.

Over and over again.

Sometimes Autumn helped. Other times, when she was between projects, she'd come and sit with him while he swore and kicked things and then started again. He liked those times the best. He would tell her about life at Lost Lake. All the festivals in the Mine. Huddling down in his parents' house while the wind blew so hard it was a miracle the house stood. In return, she would tell him stories about growing up on her family's little ranch in Montana.

"My take on ranches is that they're an endless amount of work," Bowie observed after a set of such stories. "And none of these tales you keep telling me are convincing me otherwise."

The weather couldn't decide what it was doing today. It had rained this morning. Now it was sunny. And it was almost warm in the sun, which was nice. It felt like a proper summer. Especially with Autumn lying on the undamaged pontoon, her face tipped up to the sun, pretty enough to stop a man's heart.

If he didn't know they were stuck here, Bowie might have said it was a delight. Their bruises had faded. The lake here was shallow, and terribly cold, but it allowed them to wash their bodies and their clothes and better yet, drink as much as they liked. They had food to eat and prepare for later, small game and some plants and the odd fish.

When he stopped worrying about how he was going to get them home, Bowie could admit that there was a kind of liberty in having only the one thing to think about. The one worry.

It made everything else simple.

During the day they worked. At night they huddled together by the fire and then in the tent. There was sex and there was sleep, and in the mornings they woke up, heated up the frigid water by the fire for washing, and then did it all over again.

It wasn't a bad life, really. But that would change come fall.

And he could feel more of fall every morning now. There were teeth in the wind, a harbinger of things to come.

They were running out of time.

"I never had much to compare it to," Autumn was saying now. "But I'm with you. A ranch is a thankless task. But for my dad, it's the only work he knows how to do. Folks around us are selling. There are always refugees from California who want to build themselves fancy ranch houses on the land, but do none of the work, so we could always sell. But my dad really likes working the land. Sometimes I think the struggle of it was the only thing that kept him going after we lost my mom."

Bowie almost worked a little sorcery with a wrench, but couldn't quite make it happen at the last moment. He set it down and wiped at his brow, which was better than throwing the wrench into the water. He'd only have to go get it. "Funny, I thought what kept your whole family going was you."

Autumn shaded her eyes as she looked over at him. "I've had a lot of time to think about my family while we've been out here. It occurs to me that maybe pushing everybody to carry on was less my enormous saintliness and more me not dealing with my grief. On an epic scale."

That hit Bowie a little harder than he liked.

But that was Autumn. Always with the unexpected bombs when he least expected it. Never about the shallow water when there was some deep nearby.

"I've never understood the way people say that," he said. He was aware, on some level, that he wouldn't have had this conversation a couple weeks ago. Not even on their camping trip, where they'd talked about all kinds of nothing, all day long. Everything was different here. In this canyon he was so determined would not become their tomb. "How is a person supposed to deal with grief? It seems to me that mostly people want to move on and act like nothing happened. See if time dulls it. But it doesn't, does it? And all you accomplish is making sure that it will rip you open each and every time it comes for you."

He didn't like how exposed he felt, standing there with her gaze on him, so he followed her lead and tilted his head back to let the sun dance over him instead.

"Grief is going to do what it's going to do," Autumn said after a moment. "All you can do is try to distinguish between healthy ways to grieve and the more unhealthy ways."

"Maybe they're all just grieving," he retorted gruffly.

Too gruffly, he acknowledged, because she looked at him a moment more, then changed the subject. She told him about her sisters and how funny they were, especially as they tried to protect her from afar. "It feels like they're trying to reverse our whole childhood these days. It's a lot of texts and I pretend to be annoyed, but I like it."

"My brother and sister don't text a lot," Bowie told her, feeling surly. Because maybe he didn't want to change the subject. Or maybe he wanted to be the one who did the changing. *Or maybe you're just surly.* "But they're perfectly happy to drop by without an invitation whenever they feel the need, especially in winter when they can make a ruckus with the snow machines."

Autumn's smile widened. "So basically the same thing, just Alaska."

Bowie should have gotten back to work when she got up and headed into shore. But first he was mesmerized, the way he always was, by those impossible curves of hers and the way she walked. So briskly, as if she had no idea what the sight of her did to a man. He knew all of those curves intimately now, for which he was profoundly grateful daily, but that didn't lessen the impact of them. If anything, it made it worse.

He kept watching her as she went to put more fuel on the signal fire, out on the little spit of land surrounded by water that they planned to keep burning as long as they could. In the hope that smoke might make it out of the canyon and inspire someone to come looking. And he was still watching as she made her way back to camp, gathering the makeshift basket she'd made that he knew she liked to use when she was headed out foraging. Something she did often, even though there was less to show for it here than there had been back home.

She wandered along the water's edge awhile, then disappeared into the woods.

And she didn't look back even once.

Later that night, they sat out by the fire long after they'd eaten a bit of dinner, then cleaned everything up so as not to attract any wildlife. There were no bears in the canyon as far as Bowie could tell, but that didn't mean other creatures couldn't make themselves known.

Tonight they had a rousing discussion about western water rights that had led into a debate on wildfires and forest management, all of which counted as a sport here in the Last Frontier. But now, they were quiet. The midnight sun was doing its thing, but the nights were getting longer by the day. Soon enough, they would be headed toward the dark months.

He needed to get them home well before then.

"So," Autumn said from beside him. "Are you ever going to tell me what promise you made? The one that isn't that you're married?"

Bowie's knee-jerk reaction was to cut off all possible mention of Karina, immediately. But everything was different now. They had no choice but to live here, and it was entirely too possible they would die here, too. Or die trying to get out of here. And she talked about grief like she knew it.

He knew she did.

And anyway, there didn't seem to be any particular point in holding on to secrets in a situation like this. After surviving a plane crash together, it seemed almost churlish.

But he was just making excuses, he could tell.

For the first time in his life, he wanted to talk about this. Not just to talk about it. He wanted to talk about this with Autumn, specifically.

Only Autumn, he thought.

There was something in that he was going to need to examine. Something in him that felt a lot like a tuning fork, singing out a low, sweet note he didn't recognize. But that could come later. If there was a later.

He stared into the flames, then took a breath.

"Her name was Karina," he said.

Fifteen

Autumn hadn't actually expected him to answer. She wasn't sure what she'd expected. Maybe for him to grimly tell her, once again, that nothing would change between them even though it had.

She had no idea why she'd even asked. She certainly hadn't expected a *name*.

But then, wasn't that the lesson here? To overthink less and do more? If there was a lesson in crash-landing in the remote Alaskan mountains, that was, where their imminent death was all but certain.

Death was always certain, of course. She knew that, the way everyone knew it. And Autumn understood it more than many, because she'd spent her formative years watching her mother die. Mortality had been a companion for her in ways it wasn't for a lot of other people ever since.

None of that had really prepared her for this, it turned out.

Autumn tried to be practical about it. Logical. They would survive for a bit. Maybe even awhile. Maybe they would climb these steep walls and walk out of here. Maybe someone would happen along and rescue them. But it seemed more likely that they no longer had the life expectancy she'd assumed they did before the plane went down. Having a sell-by date changed things. The sun seemed brighter, the water colder, every breath in her body a gift she tried to savor.

This man's hands all over her body, the scrape of his beard against her skin, all became songs of praise.

Aside from all of that intensity, she'd discovered that her impending demise also . . . made her chatty.

Bowie, who was always chatty in the usual course of a normal day, had gotten quieter. Yet when he did speak, it seemed more real. More truth, less banter. Like the name he'd thrown out just now, when she'd been expecting a deflection.

Ask and you shall receive, she told herself. *You have only yourself to blame.*

"We were both eighteen," Bowie said. His voice was grave. He was gazing into the fire, fiddling with the stick he used as a fire poker in those strong, capable hands of his. "I met her on a beach in California, like something out of a Beach Boys song. She was a surfer girl who thought seventy degrees was cold. As far as I could tell, she and the California sun were one and the same." He shook his head, his mouth curving at his own memories. "We were each other's first. She was like dessert and every second I could get away, I spent with her."

He found Autumn's gaze, and she'd already forgotten that she'd winced a little at the sound of another woman's name. Because all she could see was that darkness in Bowie's blue gaze and she didn't know why she was holding her breath.

"Her parents did not like me. At all. I like to think it was a marine thing, not a personal thing, and I get it now. Who wants a half-feral jarhead just out of boot camp around their innocent daughter? But who knows? What I do know is that the more we had to sneak around, the more convinced we were that we were supposed to be together forever."

Autumn felt a kind of pressure in her chest, and she

didn't know what it was. She wished she hadn't asked him this. She was afraid he was about to tell her things she truly did not want to know—

This is not a mystery, a voice inside her suggested. *You already know how this ends. He told you before you got on the plane. You don't want to hear about the woman he still loves so much that he will never, ever love you.*

And they were out here, a million miles from anywhere and highly unlikely to be rescued, so there was no lying to herself. Autumn was exactly that small. There was no point pretending otherwise.

She was also in love, but no good could come from mentioning that. Especially now.

He was answering the question she'd asked him. So this was on her. If she really loved him, maybe she could try listening to him talk about his obviously painful past without thinking only of herself.

She flushed a little and was glad he was still staring into the fire.

"My first tour, she waited for me. Being apart was like torture. We talked whenever we could, but it didn't make us miss each other any less. I figure her parents hoped she'd forget about me, but she didn't. So the next time I was on leave, we eloped."

Autumn definitely wished she hadn't asked him about this, but there was no going back now.

"We didn't tell anyone," Bowie said, as if the words were hard to get out. "She was going to get her parents used to the idea while I was away again. Ease them into it. But she never got the chance." He shook his head, his beautiful face suddenly looking like a stranger's. "She got in a car accident. The day before I left. A drunk driver came out of nowhere and T-boned her car. Her friends lived. She didn't." That dark gaze of his found hers and held. "She'd been my wife for a day. In secret."

"Oh, Bowie," Autumn breathed. She was no longer thinking about herself. She was thinking about him, still a teenager himself and grappling with something so cruel and incomprehensible. "That's so horribly unfair."

"I never told anyone," he said then, the words rushing out of him like he'd never dared speak them out loud before. Autumn reached over and laid her hand on his leg. Just to remind him he wasn't alone. "It didn't seem right. I could have told her parents, but what would be the point? They didn't like me that much to begin with. Why add to their suffering? We hadn't told anyone when we could have, so running around afterward telling people that it had happened once she was gone felt wrong. And the longer I kept it to myself, the more impossible it became to tell anyone."

"What about your family?"

"They didn't even know Karina existed," he said, his voice a mix of old bitterness and loss. "How was I supposed to tell them that I dated a girl, married her, and lost her all before I had a chance to bring her home?"

And maybe she'd been feeling small and petty and insecure a little while ago, but in this moment, all Autumn wanted to do was soothe him. With every part of her heart. She rubbed her hand against his hard thigh, wordlessly giving him her support.

He looked down at her hand, and something seemed to move through him. She almost pulled her hand back. But instead, he moved to cover hers with his.

And for a while they sat there while the fire danced before them, mourning the senseless loss of someone he loved.

Something Autumn was only too familiar with.

"My mom was ill for a long time," she told him quietly, after a long while. "And the only thing that's good about that is that she knew what was happening to her. She made sure that she said everything she needed to say before she went." She looked down at the place where their hands were joined and slid her free hand on top, like the hug she doubted he would accept. "One of the things she told me was that people might not be eternal, but love is. Love is every time you think of her. Love is everything that reminds you of her. Love goes on and on, as long as your heart beats, and beyond that, too, in all the stories you told about her to those who follow after you. Love never ends."

She had believed that for most of her life, but never more than now.

Bowie nodded jerkily. "After I finished my tour, I went back to California and I spent a lot of time at her grave. It's pretty there. Quiet, with a view of the ocean. She would have liked it."

Autumn imagined a cemetery by the sea. A young Bowie, ravaged by grief. She held his hand a little bit tighter.

"I sat there and I made her a promise. Everyone else might not know who we were to each other, but I did. I promised her that I wouldn't forget her. And that there would never be another woman who could take her place."

"And there won't be," Autumn said at once. And fiercely.

Because she could only imagine teenage Bowie in his uniform and a California girl who loved to surf. They belonged to each other. She felt ashamed that she'd ever had a moment of worrying over a ghost. When she knew firsthand that one of the greatest gifts of love was how huge it was. How all-encompassing. There was room for all. That was the point.

He moved his hand so he could play with her fingers, tracing the length of one and then the next. "I've made sure there was never an opportunity. When I told you it was me, Autumn, that wasn't a line. It is me. It's the promise I made Karina a long, long time ago."

"I understand," she whispered.

She wasn't just saying that. She really did understand. But that didn't mean that it didn't hurt. Autumn's heart ached. It *ached*, and she could no longer tell if it was because she ached for Bowie and what he'd gone through, or if that was her own heart breaking.

But it didn't matter. Love was love, whether it was returned or not. Love was love, and it mattered, no matter what became of it.

Autumn had to believe those things, or she never would have come here in the first place. And, okay, maybe she could think of a lot of places she'd rather be than plane-wrecked in Alaska with no real hope of getting out, but she couldn't think of anyplace better than being with Bowie.

Even plane-wrecked and unlikely to live out the year.

Because she either believed what her mother had told her or she didn't. Love either mattered or it didn't.

But she did believe her mother. She always had. And she knew, then, that the love she felt mattered. Even if this man who would never have looked at her if he hadn't been trapped with her in a makeshift reality show didn't feel it, it still mattered.

And if it mattered, if it was as much a part of her as her own heart, then there was only one thing that she could do.

That was love him because she loved him. As best she could. For as long as she could.

Because she'd been over every inch of this canyon and had even tried a little climbing on her own, without Bowie glowering there behind her and telling her how unsafe it was, just to see. And so she knew beyond the shadow of any doubt that in the end, love was going to be the only thing they had here.

She couldn't fix a broken plane. She couldn't make his radio work or summon rescuers with the force of her will. She'd tried. Every day she tried.

But she could do this. She could understand that he had given her a gift tonight. He'd showed her *him*. And she could treasure him.

She turned on their little stone so she could face him, and she took his beautiful face between her hands. He had a beard now, but it in no way detracted from that edgy beauty of his that she was fairly certain was lodged forever inside her. Or maybe it was just that she was inside out when he was near.

Autumn searched his face, though she could not have said what she hoped to see. Because she liked looking at him, maybe. Or because, for all her high-mindedness, she still wanted to see that particular gleam there that she knew was all hers.

When she did, she kissed him.

They had enjoyed each other so many ways by now. They'd feasted on each other as if that alone could ward off the coming winter. He'd done things to her she couldn't even name, she'd returned them in kind, and she'd loved them all.

But this was different. This was sacred.

She kissed him again. Then again. She kissed him until his hands moved beneath her layers to find her skin, and without meaning to move, she found herself sitting astride his lap.

Autumn stood then, pulling him up and onto his feet and then tugged him behind her and into the tent.

Inside, it was still hushed, still sacred, still a ceremony. She stripped off her clothes and then she went and knelt over him, pushing his hands out of the way when he would have pulled her up the length of his body. Instead, she pulled him free of his trousers, wrapped her fists around him, and took him in her mouth.

Bowie groaned. It was a rough, sweet music, and it made her tremble in reaction.

He muttered something about not wanting to finish like that, but she ignored him. Instead, she used all the skills he'd taught her to bring him to the edge, keep him there, and then toss him over.

Bowie lay there for a moment, panting, and then he jackknifed up and tugged her to him. First he kissed her wildly, as if he could barely contain himself. And then he spread her out before him on top of their zipped-together sleeping bags and returned the favor she'd just given to him.

Except he took longer. And he went slower. And kept her on the edge, then tumbling over it, then on the edge again until she hardly knew her own name.

And only then, when they were both half-crazed with

wanting each other and naked at last, did Bowie roll her beneath him and find his way inside her.

With something like reverence.

And with every thrust, she thought, *love.*

Love was what mattered. Love was what would last. Long after they were gone, love would sustain them in the memories of those they left behind.

But here, now, there was this. Love made electric. Love so deep and so good they became part of each other.

Love, whatever came next.

Love so that they would face it, together, without fear.

Because fear and love could not occupy the same space, she understood that now. Not only that, but love was so vast, so huge, it couldn't matter how much of it any one person had. What mattered was the fact of it.

Love, she thought as they hurtled toward that edge again, together this time. Love, she thought, and then, together, they caught fire.

And she was still thinking about love like that a couple of weeks later when Bowie let out a huge whoop out by the plane. When she raced out to see what had happened, he caught her up and danced her around on the slippery pontoon until they both toppled over into the water.

"I got it," he told her when they surfaced, shivering. His grin took over his whole face, and she felt his joy inside her even before he told her why. "It's going to be a rough ride, but I think I can get us home."

And what she would remember, she thought in that single, stark moment, was that she was torn.

There was the part of her that was overjoyed. That they would live—or at least leave here—when she'd been trying so hard to come to terms with what had happened to them. When she'd been trying to think about how to live through the winter, not give up at the first snowfall.

But there was that other part, too.

The part that wanted to stay here forever, because here, he was hers. No matter what.

She had to tuck that part away as best she could as they packed up their camp, both of them too excited—or too ashamed, in her case, and maybe a little worried, in his—to say much. They both climbed into the plane and Autumn belted herself in tightly, not letting herself think about that last plane ride and their tumultuous, terrible drop out of the sky.

Bowie muttered about flying by sight instead of instruments and a whole lot of other technical things she didn't think she wanted to understand, but she kept her gaze trained on the beach where they'd camped. The path she'd made to the cave in the woods. The sheer, dizzying height of the mountains all around them.

The shallow water that was a bit shorter than anyone would want a runway to be.

"You're going to have to go straight up, basically," she said.

Bowie looked at her, his face serious. His eyes intense.

"Good thing I've spent my whole life practicing reckless maneuvers exactly like this," he said. "It should be a breeze."

She didn't know if she believed him, but it didn't matter. He was starting up his engines. He was shifting into that space that she'd seen him access only out here. It was a certain stillness that reminded her that he'd once had a different profession. And that, in all likelihood, he'd been pretty good at it.

Autumn wanted to screw her eyes shut and block it all out, but she couldn't. She *couldn't.* She intended to take part in this, even if it was the end of them.

Because even if they made it over the mountains, even if they flew all the way home, it was still the end of them. She didn't want to believe it, but she did. She couldn't help it. The intensity of this place would fade out there in the real world and he would remember that promise he'd made. Autumn could practically see it play out before her.

"Hold on," Bowie told her, but she didn't need telling. She was gripping the arms of her seat like she wanted to rip them out.

Part of her did.

He took off then, racing the plane down its unreasonable runway, then launching them into the air, straight at the tallest, most forbidding mountain—

Only to execute a tight turn that should have been impossible, at the last possible second—

Autumn didn't think either one of them breathed until they cleared the walls of the canyon.

Even then, it was impossible to relax in a plane that might shatter to pieces in midair no matter how careful he'd tried to be with what he'd had on hand. Autumn hadn't needed him to outline the risks. She understood them.

You understand we might . . . ? he'd tried as they waded away from their beach for the last time.

I understand.

But she'd been resigned to dying with him in that canyon. If the plane exploded midflight, well. That would be quicker. And still with him.

The flight went on forever, tense and quiet. Autumn was no aviation expert, but she could tell that they were flying at a much lower elevation than she remembered from before. She didn't ask about it. If she was interpreting his muttering correctly, it had something to do with visibility and all the controls she could see weren't working.

Maybe she did close her eyes a time or two—when there was a bump, or a spot of turbulence—but otherwise she stayed as she was. Eyes wide open, bearing witness to her own life.

And when, at last, they came through some cloud cover and she saw the jagged shape of Lost Lake below her, she found herself more emotional than she would have believed possible.

"We made it," she whispered.

"I should mention that I have some concerns about landing," Bowie said then. Abruptly.

"What?"

"Just a few minor, piddling concerns, that's all," he said, and she could tell that he was trying to regain that easy, friendly sort of patter he'd been all about before. But he couldn't quite get there. They weren't the same people they'd been then. "It might be a little rough going in, that's all I'm saying."

"Rougher than that time we crash-landed in the mountains and had to live by our wits for a month?" she shot back.

"You say that like it wasn't fun."

Their eyes met then and it was like a bolt of light. She actually laughed, though none of this was funny, or it shouldn't have been. At any moment, the plane could come apart at the seams. Or maybe they were going to crash-land again, and who could possibly walk away with only a few bruises from a *second* crash in one summer? They would have gone to the trouble of escaping their fate only to meet it here, back home.

Everything was terrible. Objectively.

Still, it was the two of them, and it was ridiculous, and what else was there to do but laugh with him as they went down this time?

Bowie began his descent, but they were both laughing now. And that bolt of light still connected them. And maybe it was maniacal. Maybe it was sheer panic.

But if this was the end, at least it felt like a roller coaster ride.

At the end of the day, wasn't that just life?

No one got all the time they wanted. What mattered was enjoying the time you had.

Even if it was one short descent into a pretty lake.

So she laughed, and he laughed, too. And the lake seemed to spin around beneath them, but she told herself it was a roller coaster, that was all. And when they landed on the water, they bounced too high, then skipped like a stone.

But this time, they didn't flip over. They didn't run aground.

They seemed to skid across the water, Bowie was fighting for control, and when they finally slowed down, Autumn could see a big red cluster of houses before her, cascading down the side of the hill until they joined up with the Mine.

She had never been so happy to see a big old abandoned mining town in her life.

There were already people running down the hill and some of them jumped into motorboats anchored on the beach, then headed out toward them.

"Well, damn," Bowie said, and though his voice was casual, when she glanced over, Autumn could see all that emotion she felt inside her on his face. "Looks like they missed us after all."

"It's nice to be missed."

That seemed like such an inadequate thing to say when she'd just been given a second chance at a life she thought she'd lost.

"Looks like you were *really* missed." Bowie pointed at one of the motorboats coming toward them. "That looks a lot like your sisters."

Autumn was overwhelmed. Turned inside out again. There was water on her cheeks and that was how she realized she was crying, or maybe that was what the laughter had turned into on the way down.

She looked out the window and sure enough, she could see three blonde heads and her father and Donna, too. Another boat was full of Fortunes. All of them grim-faced and white-knuckled as they raced for the plane.

Because they didn't know that she and Bowie were okay yet. They didn't know what they were coming to find.

But Autumn knew time was running out, no matter how happy she was to be here. She turned to Bowie, reaching across the cockpit so she could touch him, maybe one last time.

"I love you," she said, not in a rush. Not emotionally. But like it was the most serious thing she had ever said out loud. Because it was. His eyes widened slightly. But she couldn't stop. "I'm in love with you. I was prepared to die out there with you, and as unfair as I found that prospect, there was a peace in it, too. I'm going to remember that."

"Autumn . . ." he began.

"I don't need you to say anything. I just need you to know. I know you can't love me back. I knew that from the start, when I saw that look." She smiled when he frowned. "I know that look. That's what happens when you're the ugly duckling in a family of swans."

"What?"

She squeezed his arm with both of her hands. "I know that everything is going to change now that we're back. But before it does, I just wanted you to know. That's all."

"Autumn," he said again, and he was frowning at her. Bowie Fortune, who always defaulted to a smile, was *frowning* at her. She decided to consider it the love letter he would never write her. "You have to be the most—"

But he never finished that sentence, because they'd made it back to the world.

And the world came crashing in to greet them at top volume just then, like it or not.

Sixteen

It was chaos.

But a sweet kind of chaos, Autumn thought, when she'd woken up this morning absolutely sure that she'd never see any of these people again.

She and Bowie were loaded into separate boats to be taken back to the Mine. And there were so many shouted questions and fierce hugs that Autumn felt as if she were being shaken around in some kind of jar even before the boat started heading toward shore.

Nothing felt real. Or maybe it felt too real.

And yet all she was really aware of was that she wanted to bury her face into Bowie's chest and feel his arms around her, but couldn't, because he was in a different jar.

"What are you all doing here?" she thought to ask her sisters at some point as they clustered around her, as if physically unable to stop touching her. She could see Bowie in the neighboring boat, receiving much the same treatment. Piper had her arms around him. Quinn had an arm over his shoulders. His usually stone-faced friend Noah was almost actually grinning.

"What are we *doing* here?" Jade demanded. "Are you kidding? We've been here for ten days already."

Autumn tried to take that on board. "Ten whole days?"

"Autumn," Willa said from beside her. "It's August?"

"You've been gone since the end of June," Sunny said fiercely, her eyes bright with tears.

And Autumn knew this, of course. She'd tracked the days in the canyon. But it was different to imagine, now, how those days had been for these people she loved, and who loved her. Maybe she hadn't wanted to imagine that, out there. Maybe she'd been protecting herself.

Once on land, Donna cried and her father cleared his throat and pinched his nose a lot, but both of them hugged her again and again. And hard.

"I can't lose you," her father said gruffly when it was his turn. He ruffled her hair, then held her tight. "I can't lose you, little one."

The *little one* almost killed her. Her father hadn't called her that in a long time. Since long before her fourteenth year, when they'd all changed, and maybe Autumn and him most of all.

Autumn was swept into the Mine, and found herself seated on the couch in front of the fireplace with Bowie beside her. Beside her, but soon pushed down to the other end of the couch, as there was so much family in between.

And there were a lot of things she was trying to process at once. That she'd told that man she loved him. That she didn't regret it or feel the slightest hint of shame.

That it was August. She and Bowie had left on their camping trip before the end of June, and all of July was gone. That her whole family was here, clearly all of them half out of their skins with worry. Or in some cases, fully out.

What she really wanted was to sit in a quiet room with Bowie and breathe a little. And maybe attempt to make sense of the fact that they'd actually made it home. With him, the only other person who could possibly understand.

But no one looked likely to let either one of them out of their sight.

Piper came over at some point and hugged Autumn, too. "Never do that again," she ordered, in a thick voice.

Then the rest of the Fortunes came over, each of them taking a moment to make sure she really understood how concerned they'd been.

"I thought he'd done you in," Lois said in her direct way, and actually hugged her. Autumn had been under the impression that Lois did not hug unless pressed. Levi grabbed her hands and held them a moment. Quinn put an arm around her while Violet hugged her. Even Noah smiled, like he meant it, and for a brief moment, pressed his shoulder to hers.

Like they were her people, too—but she needed to not torture herself like that.

"All of you back off," came an authoritative voice. "I've never seen two people who needed a good meal more and how can they eat in the middle of this dogpile?"

Mia Saskin came barreling through the crowd, bearing a platter. Two of her grandchildren, Amie and Garnet, trailed behind her, bearing trays. And in short order, Mia cleared the couch and set up a meal on the low table in front of Bowie and Autumn.

"Eat," Mia ordered them. "You have the rest of your life to tell the story."

Autumn stared at the food in front of her as if she hardly recognized what it was, even as her stomach rumbled. She realized three things at once. One, that she was starving for food she didn't have to hunt, trap, prepare, or eat on a stick and with her fingers. Two, that she *had* the rest of her life again. And three, that Mia Saskin was some kind of psychic, because she needed this. She needed focus on the simple task of eating instead of all these *feelings*, hers and everyone else's.

Being thrust back into the midst of so many people, all

of them unwilling to stop talking about how much they loved her, was wonderful. Truly wonderful. Especially after she'd been isolated with Bowie for so long.

But her head was spinning.

"I've always loved Grand Mia's chili," Bowie rumbled from beside her in a low voice that she associated with misty mountain mornings and quiet, cold beaches. Right now it felt almost as good as her face pressed tight into that hollow in his chest. "Maybe never so much as right now."

His eyes met hers, and she let out a small sigh, because she could see he was as taken back as she was.

"It was a hard landing," he said in that same undertone that was for her ears only. "In more ways than one."

All Autumn could do was nod, overwhelmed. She found it was a relief to turn her attention to the food before her. And much better than asking herself what he might mean by that. *In more ways than one.*

Did he mean her declaration of love?

But there was a sturdy crock of thick chili before her, rich and just the right kind of spicy. It was so good on her tongue that she thought maybe she might have started crying again. There was a round little loaf of bread beside it, straight from the oven. She cracked it open and the warm, yeasty smell almost knocked her over. She would have said she hadn't been around the Mine long enough for anyone to know her preferences about anything, but there was a stout mug of black coffee, strong the way she liked it, and a can of real Coke, and for all the love that Autumn had received since she'd crawled out of that plane, she could *taste* this love.

It made her warm, sitting there in her little bubble with Bowie while their families and friends talked all around them.

It was that breath she'd wanted. A small moment to reset.

She ate up every bite.

And when it was done, she felt like a different person.

Bowie looked as if great weights had dropped from his shoulders. They looked at each other for a moment, as if to say, *Can you believe all this?*

Then they sat back and told everyone what had happened.

"We were very relaxed about the whole thing," Bowie said after he finished the story. He lifted a brow in Autumn's direction when she frowned at him. "We knew you fine people would come find us, sooner or later."

"There's not a whole lot of later to go around," Levi replied, his gaze intense as he stood by the fire. "The snow comes early up there."

"Early and often," Lois agreed. Gruffly.

"Next time you take my daughter camping," Hunter suggested, sounding crotchety and mean when Autumn could see he was still emotional, "maybe let someone know exactly where you're going."

"Noah knows the general location," Bowie protested. Mildly. "I threatened to drop him there once."

"True story," Noah allowed. "But you might remember that you waved your arm at what was basically everything west of Mount Foraker."

"Anyway, that would only have taken you to our original campsite," Bowie said. "The storm knocked us around some."

Quinn shook his head. "We've had a few of your friends running daily flights over the area after we pinpointed your last radio signal, but we couldn't find anything."

"Good thing I managed to MacGyver my plane back together, then," Bowie said, and grinned as if it had all been a lark. "All's well that ends well, I guess."

And he sounded so cheery and dismissive in the face of so many frowns aimed his way that it finally dawned on Autumn *how* dangerous it had all been. And what a good pilot Bowie really was to keep the two of them from dying when they'd crashed the first time. Not to mention, flying them all the way back home in a vessel that likely shouldn't have been in the air.

But Autumn didn't really want to dwell on all the ways they could have died. She found she was enjoying not being dead.

"I really did think you'd both be dirtier," Jade said at one point. She doubled down when everyone stopped and looked at her. "What? You think a plane crash in the mountains and then foraging about in the wilderness to survive, you don't think *clean*, do you?"

"My first thought was the Alaska State Troopers or the FAA," Bowie replied in that lazy way of his. "Not hygiene."

"That new doctor from down in Hopeless is coming up tonight or tomorrow to give you two a checkup," Mia Saskin told them, but she was looking mostly at Bowie. "Don't argue."

"Also it's still summer." Autumn looked down at the clothes she'd worn and reworn the whole month they'd been gone. "We washed every day *and* washed out our clothes. It would have been different if it was winter."

Everyone went a little quiet at that, because a whole lot of things would have been different if it was winter. Including this happy little reunion.

"I hope this means you're ready to go home now," Willa said then, sounding as bossy as she usually did only during Christmas, when she became a decorating monster. "I think it's time. Obviously the Alaska reality show thing isn't really working out."

"Less of a reality show," Quinn interjected. He folded his arms as he stood behind the chair Violet was sitting in. "More a promotional vehicle. Officially speaking."

Bowie let out a long-suffering sort of sigh that made his brother grin.

"I think we can count this as an epic disaster," Jade said, clearly agreeing with Willa. "Everything will be better when you're back home where you belong, Autumn."

"You've lived in Montana your entire life and never came this close to death," said Sunny, with a great deal of authority for someone who was five years younger than Autumn. "We can help you pack."

And then everyone in the whole of the Mine seemed to look at Autumn expectantly. Except for Bowie, who was suddenly making a study of his jeans.

"I don't want to go home," Autumn said, calmly enough.

Her sisters looked baffled. Donna and her father exchanged a look she couldn't read. Most of the actual citizens of Lost Lake made a lot of noises that sounded like *damn right*, especially Piper.

Bowie kept up his contemplation of his jeans. But he smiled.

And it seemed to warm her up like a hit of sunlight.

"What are you talking about?" Sunny was demanding. "You love being home. You're always home."

Willa was nodding vigorously. "No one understands why you ran away to Alaska in the first place."

"Maybe it was an experiment." Jade sounded almost philosophical. As if she was sitting there on the arm of the sofa *musing*, unbidden, about Autumn's life. When Autumn was still adjusting to having gotten it back. "A learning experience, sure. But there's no need to drag this out."

All Autumn could think about was the month she'd just lived through. And the month before that, really. All the bushcraft things she'd trotted out because she'd wanted to win a contest, and was glad she had, because she'd had to use most of them after the crash.

Sitting here on this couch, feeling sleepy after gorging herself on Mia Saskin's chili, it occurred to her that she hadn't thought once about content for social media the entire time she and Bowie had been at the crash site. She was finding it difficult to imagine ever thinking about it again, in truth.

Out there in the canyon, she'd just been happy that she knew how to do practical things that made it more likely they might survive. Now that was over and they were safe, she could admit that she'd been terrified. If only to herself. That it had been less logic and determination and skill every day, and a lot more panic.

Luckily, panic didn't freeze her in place. It never had. Panic made her capable. Focused.

Panic was why she'd tried to fill her mother's shoes when she was still a baby herself. It was why she'd scouted out that cave and had already been implementing her plans on how to winterize. It was all the jerky she'd made so they could eat it when the weather turned cold, or carry it with them when they tried to hike out of that canyon.

Because panic was how she did the things that she hoped might forestall disaster. Or, at the very least, give her a fighting chance.

And she knew her sisters loved her. But she also knew they panicked, too. They didn't even see the ways they treated Autumn like a parent, not a sister. That was probably her fault for acting like a parent all this time, but now they didn't see her as an independent person. Not really. She was theirs and she belonged where they'd left her.

Autumn understood. She felt that way about her father.

But she wasn't the same person she'd been when she'd left Montana.

"No one understands why you did this anyway," Sunny said reproachfully.

As if Autumn had "done this" *at* Sunny.

Autumn's belly was full of moose chili and perfect bread. Her heart was overflowing. There was an ache there, too, and she figured that when all the adrenaline of having made it back here wore off, she had a good long cry waiting for her. But at the moment, she wasn't sure she'd ever been better.

Or maybe it was just that nearly dying made a person understand how to live. At last.

"You," she said.

Sunny looked startled. "Me?"

"You," Autumn said again. She looked at her other sisters. "And you two, as well. All three of you. That's why I'm here."

"I thought it was for a tropical island," Bowie said from beside her.

Autumn ignored him. She kept her gaze on her sisters. "I love you all," she told them, and she meant it. "You know I do. But sometimes, you're impossible."

"Hey!" Jade made the loudest sound of protest, though her other sisters joined in.

And it did occur to Autumn that *maybe* she should have waited until it was only their family unit for this, but she hadn't. And she didn't feel as guilty about that as she should have. Her trouble was, she was too comfortable here. It really did feel like a homecoming, to come back to this place, these people, that she'd last seen at Solstice. She didn't even question why Bowie had come to this end of the lake instead of down near where he lived, because she was pretty sure she knew.

Setting them down near people gave them a better chance of surviving if things had gone wrong. But they'd lived, so this was a celebration. And it meant so much to her that all of these people were here. Because all of them had worried. All of them cared.

It made her feel almost as warm inside as Grand Mia's food.

Maybe that was why she was able to face her sisters so calmly.

"I spent a lot of time caring for Mom before she died," she said quietly. "And she told me a lot of things. About how she'd lived and how she hoped we would. And what she would have done with her life if she'd had more time. But mostly, she talked about happiness. She hoped we'd all be happy, her girls, because she loved us. But she wasn't worried about us. She was worried about Dad."

She could see her father didn't like being the center of attention, because his jaw went granite in that way it did when he was uncomfortable, and he shifted his weight where he stood. But Donna was beside him and she held his hand, the way, Autumn knew, she always would. She had been loyal to Hunter and the McCall family for a long time now, though she got precious little credit for it.

"Mom wanted Dad to move on," Autumn told her sisters, and her voice was still quiet, but she'd gotten serious now. "She would not have been a fan of those years before Donna."

All of her sisters looked thunderstruck. But Hunter nodded. "That's a fact. Your mother always said I had no business getting into the whiskey. Can't hold it. Makes me mean. She would've been dearly disappointed that I couldn't hold it together after she passed." He looked at Donna. Then Autumn. "I'm not proud of it."

"Then Donna came into our lives and let Dad be Dad again," Autumn said, smiling at him because it was okay. She understood. "He was happy. Donna makes him happy. She's doing it right now."

Donna flushed now that it was her turn in the spotlight. "Your dad is a good man, girls. Really he is."

Autumn stood up then, so she could face each of her sisters in turn. And because she needed them to really, truly hear her. "Mom would have loved Donna," she told them fiercely. "She's kind. Patient. Unbelievably generous. And most of all, she loves Dad *and* all of us."

Hunter looked down at his wife, and it was so obvious to Autumn that he was proud of her. He adored her. And that didn't take away from how he'd felt about their mother. And probably still felt about her. If anything, she thought he was capable of loving Donna so well *because* of their mother.

"Mom would have loved all of this so much that she would have sold her jewelry by hand, herself, if she thought it would help," Autumn continued.

She saw the way her father reacted to that. And how her sisters began to frown.

So she kept going. "I know you think about that jewelry

from time to time. Jade, you wanted to get it out last Christmas. And I think we can say that Mom did sell that jewelry. Because she would have wanted Dad's wedding to someone as perfect for him as Donna to be perfect. That's who she was."

"Wait," Willa said. "Are you saying—"

Autumn cut her off. "I decided that I needed to buy that jewelry back, before any of you found out it was missing, because I knew—" She had to raise her voice over her sister's protests. "I *knew* that if you found out about it, you'd blame Donna. Who you already call your wicked stepmother, *to her face*, when as far as I can tell, she's a freaking saint."

"Okay, now," Donna said, bright red but still sounding as calm as ever. "That's a bit too far. It doesn't take a saint to love all of you. That's just common sense."

"You're making my argument for me," Autumn said. She pointed a finger at each of her sisters in turn. "So that's why I'm here. To win the prize money, so I can buy the jewelry back. And before you argue with me, ask yourselves, Would Autumn really do something so extreme if she didn't mean it? You know I wouldn't. I'm never extreme."

"You're making up for it," Jade muttered.

"I couldn't ask any of you for help, could I? It never even crossed my mind to try, and I know that's my fault." Autumn blew out a breath. "I took on too much, too young, and I never put it back down."

All three of her sisters were looking at her then with the same wide eyes, and Autumn knew she was doing the right thing here. But she would have preferred it if she didn't feel like she was kicking them while she did it.

"I don't think that's your fault," Hunter said then, sounding grave. "Pretty clear that it's mine. Just like the jewelry."

"I'm going to get it back," Autumn promised him.

"There's no need for that," Donna said gently. She looked up at Hunter, then smiled a little sheepishly. "I bought it back after you left in June and snuck it right back where it belonged in the ranch house, hoping none of you would ever know it had been missing."

Now it was Autumn's turn to stare.

"This is never something you should have worried about, Autumn," Donna said in her bighearted way. "I hate to think that you put yourself through this ordeal because of me. It seems to me that there's been enough of that in your life."

And it was only because Autumn already felt too much that she wasn't knocked over by this revelation. All she could do was whisper her stepmother's name.

"I was handling this," Hunter told his wife. "I hate to think of you spending your money on my foolishness. I'll pay you back."

But Donna only squeezed his hand. "It's our money. It doesn't need paying back."

For a moment, they were all quiet—or winded.

Autumn thought, *this*.

This was what she wanted.

"I'm done acting like your mother," she told her sisters softly. "Because I'm not her. Nobody could be her."

"Autumn," Sunny began.

Autumn held up a hand. "I'd like to be a big sister, for once. Just a big sister. We have a marvelous stepmother. And Dad is right here. Maybe, finally, we can just be *us*, you guys. The family we've made."

Hers were not the only damp eyes, she noticed. But she held her breath, because she was sure her sisters would explode . . .

And they did, but not the way she'd imagined. Instead, there was a sudden torrent of apologies and recriminations, but all of them swallowed up in a big, McCall family group hug that went on and on until all of them were laughing and sniffling at the same time.

When it broke up, and everyone was surreptitiously wiping at their eyes, she found Bowie watching her from where he lounged on the couch with a considering light in those Montana night eyes of his.

Looking at him made her feel like she was home.

And for the moment, she chose not to focus on how dangerous that was.

"And here I had you down as a reality star for the ages," he drawled.

"I would be a terrible reality show contestant," she told him. "Think about it. There would be machinations and allies and all that jockeying for position and there I'd be, outraged that my lists and plans were ignored. I'd be sent home before the first episode was done."

And for some reason, those words seemed to spin out between them, like some kind of confession.

But she was caught up by her sisters again, and the next time she looked back toward the couch, Bowie was gone.

She told herself that wasn't an omen.

But it was August already. And she didn't need to win this contest any longer. She'd survived long enough to come home and see all the people she loved in one place. What more could one person ask for?

Everything, a voice inside her whispered. *You should ask for everything.*

But she already had. She'd told Bowie that she loved him.

Autumn had to face the fact that this was his answer.

Just the way he'd told her it would be, from the start.

Seventeen

Bowie didn't get drunk. That wasn't his style.

But that didn't mean he wasn't prepared to nurse his whiskey right and proper, like a man should when he cheated death.

He'd done it a lot, so he should know.

Then again, this wasn't anything like the other times. Everything about today felt different. Because everything was threaded through with Autumn, and if this separation he was enduring right now—when he knew she was right here in the same building—was any indication of how it was going to be, well.

Maybe he really should get drunk.

"Time was, you used to enjoy your death-defying stunts more," Noah observed from beside him.

"What makes you think I'm not enjoying myself?" Bowie asked. "I'm alive and well. I have a whiskey in my hand at my favorite bar, surrounded by all the friends and family a man could want. I'm basically the physical embodiment of enjoyment."

Noah took a pull from his beer. And laughed. "That's you. The embodiment of something."

Bowie should probably go home. It turned out a person couldn't crash a plane in the state of Alaska without a hassle, so he had that waiting for him. If he was smart, he'd get a good night's sleep in a proper bed before attempting to deal with the numerous authorities who were interested in all the details—and not, probably, because they wanted to compliment him on flying that plane out of what would surely have been his and Autumn's certain death.

Yet he couldn't bring himself to leave.

Maybe it was because his family was still gathered here, a lot like they were attending his wake. The whole community had turned out, which was gratifying on some level. A person did wonder, every now and again, who might show up at the funeral.

He could hear Grand Mia banging around in the kitchen, because the woman was magic and was always prepared to feed every last soul in Lost Lake on a moment's notice. Not necessarily with a smile. He saw assorted Saskin cousins shooting some pool over in the corner. Amie and Silver were bickering near the fire.

Quinn was having what looked like a very serious conversation—so it would be about something the community would eventually vote on—with a selection of the gray Fox sisters and old Harry Barrow, who looked unusually sober. His sister and Violet were holed up at a table with Abel and Rosemary from down in Hopeless. And his parents were holding court with a selection of folks from their generation, telling stories, by the look of it, no doubt of exploits past. Either Bowie's, or, far more interesting, their own brushes with particularly Alaskan deaths over time. The way they were laughing, like it hurt, made him guess it was the latter.

His place. His people.

And yet there was that yawning thing inside him, voracious and wide, that only wanted Autumn.

In all the ways he couldn't have her.

"I'm the last person to lecture anybody on ghosts," Noah said from beside him.

"I can already tell I don't want to have this conversation. I'm not sure a lecture on ghosts is going to sit any better."

His best friend ignored him. "You and I have some of the same ghosts, Bowie. We handle them differently, you and me."

Bowie knew the only way to ward off Noah in lecture mode was to make it funny. To steer it in a different direction. He was usually good at that. The best.

Instead, he found himself looking down at his whiskey like it might help him when he knew better. Whiskey didn't help anyone. Usually it made things worse.

That was its charm. His charm had, apparently, been left behind at an alpine lake.

But that was fine with him. Because with every moment that passed here in the Mine, it was clear to him that he'd left behind a whole lot more than that.

I love you, she'd said. And then, in case he'd missed her meaning, *I'm in love with you*.

He felt his heart kick it up a gear or three inside his chest, just remembering it.

Beside him, Noah gave him one of those looks that seemed to tunnel deep inside him. It was annoying. After all, Bowie hadn't decided to live his life in such an isolated place because he wanted to be known so easily. Pretty much the opposite.

Noah was still seeing way too much, despite Bowie's attempt at a poker face. "One of the reasons we're friends is because we've both never met an ideal we couldn't take to its extreme."

"And here I thought it was my irresistible personality and keen eye for gifts."

"A lot of folks join up in peacetime," Noah continued. "But us? Only the few, the proud would do. And then we stayed in."

"Just for a spell," Bowie offered. "Not like those maniacs down in Grizzly Harbor, still running missions like they're twenty."

"You could argue that the act of living here, when there are an infinite number of easier places to live, makes us our own special kind of maniac, friend."

"You could argue that. But why would you? The very fact that the perfection of Lost Lake escapes most people is one of the reasons we live here."

"You're making my point for me," Noah said quietly. "It's who you are, Bowie. The patron saint of lost causes. And yes, I know, I could teach a hermit about alone time. But this isn't about me."

"Are you sure about that?" Bowie tried to keep his voice light, not an easy task when he wanted to break things. "Because it's long been my observation that anyone who doles out advice is only ever *really* talking about themselves."

Noah smiled. Slightly. "Okay, let's talk about me. But let's pretend that instead of being me, I'm you, a lonely-ass man who's closer to his collection of Cessnas than he is to another human being. Until now."

"Is this the same kind of pretending we're going to do to keep not talking about the person you'd like to be close to?" Bowie asked, an edge to the mild tone he was aiming for. When Noah cut his dark gaze to his, Bowie only shrugged. "I'm not Quinn, buddy. His head would explode. You know all I'd do is delight in giving you a hard time."

"It doesn't matter," Noah said, very distinctly. "Because it's never going to happen."

Neither one of them looked over toward Piper.

"I saw the way you were looking at Autumn today," Noah said in a low voice, so low and controlled that Bowie almost felt bad about throwing his little sister in his friend's face. Almost, but not quite. "I also saw the way she was looking back. I figure you probably put the brakes on that the way you do with everything."

"I made a promise," Bowie gritted out, slamming his shot of whiskey back down on the bar, untouched. "That means something."

"To who?" His best friend demanded, looking him dead in the eye. "Karina is dead. She's been dead a long time. She doesn't care what promises you made. You've been mourning her longer than she was alive. And a whole lot longer than you knew her."

Bowie made a series of anatomically impossible suggestions.

Noah ignored them all. "Here's one thing both you and I know about the dead, Bowie. They don't come back. No matter how much you wish they could. Nothing you do will ever change that. So the question has to be, What the hell are you doing with your life?"

And this time, he didn't wait for Bowie to throw his words back in his face. He tossed back the rest of his beer and stalked away, without even glancing at Piper's table as he passed it by.

Leaving Bowie with nothing to do but stand there.

While his heart kept kicking at him like it was trying to break free.

And since breaking free wasn't a great idea, Bowie decided it was high time he exited his own wake, and headed outside.

He could remember Solstice too clearly, that was the problem. He stood out front for a moment, deeply resenting the ways that Autumn was in everything. He had lived here all his life and had a thousand memories of this place. It was his home. Yet all he could see was Autumn. Talk about ghosts.

Autumn dancing, her head tipped back, her red dress clinging to her while she moved heedlessly, recklessly.

Joyfully.

Autumn on market days, fascinated by everything. Just as likely to get into an in-depth discussion about weaponry as jewelry, and even better if a single item was both. Autumn down on the lake, arguing with him about fishing methods but happy to let him take her in the motorboat to set her net. Canoeing, sliding easily through the water in a hushed, bright evening, while he sat behind her in the stern, contemplating that perfect hourglass shape before him.

Autumn everywhere, and she was something far worse than a ghost.

Because Noah was right, damn him. Bowie had been carting Karina around with him wherever he went for years. But she was a memory of a specific time and place. She'd never touched any part of his life but that year in California. She'd been his secret ever since, hidden away inside.

Meanwhile, Autumn was everywhere. He didn't have to hold her apart from his life. She'd been suffused in it. She was part of it.

And if he was being completely honest with himself—something he liked to say he was all the time when, really, the truth was more complicated—he knew Autumn a whole lot better than he'd ever known Karina.

Partly because he knew himself better. Because he wasn't eighteen and neither was Autumn, and how much could any eighteen-year-old truly know themself? Much less another teenager, no matter how much they wanted to?

There had been hormones, sure. A connection. He didn't want to deny that.

Yet for the first time since California, Bowie stood there and asked himself a question he'd been avoiding for a very long time.

If Karina had lived, would they have made it?

He knew the statistics. He knew how many of his friends' marriages had busted up, whether because they couldn't quite get their heads around coming home even when they were home, or because the family they'd left behind found too many distractions while they were gone. Either way, the military was hard and it wrecked marriages.

Bowie had to wonder if they'd ever had a chance, he and

the girl he'd married so fast. She'd never even seen where he lived. They hadn't had time to work out the details. Would Bowie have given up Alaska to live in crowded, mystifying California with her? Or would he have taken her away from everything she knew, even and especially her parents, who might have hated him—but Karina had been their only child and they'd loved her?

It had been easier, all this time, not to ask himself such things. It had been easier to hold on to the image of that smiling, happy surfer girl on the beach. To imagine that the life they'd been robbed of would never be anything but more of the same.

When life wasn't that way. He knew that. Life could take a simple little camping trip and turn it into a plane crash with the high possibility of a slow, inevitable death over the course of an unforgiving winter. Or an attempt at a highly dangerous climb out of a canyon that would, at the least, make the same relentless death come quicker.

One of the primary gifts the marines had given Bowie was that he no longer feared death. His or anyone else's. He'd seen too much of it. He'd mourned too many people. It was one of the reasons why he always took care to live what was left of his life to the fullest.

But it hadn't been his life he was risking out there this last month. It hadn't been his life that he'd been worried about losing.

He would have liked to tell himself that it was Autumn alone that concerned him, and it was true that keeping her safe had been a driving force. But he also knew, little as he wanted to face it, that it hadn't been *only* that. He'd been worried about *them*.

As if, despite all his efforts to the contrary, they'd gone ahead and become an us.

While he wasn't looking.

Bowie felt something else in him crack open at that.

"You all right?" His brother's voice came from behind him, snapping Bowie out of whatever state he was in. He felt himself smile automatically and felt a little too aware of his own crap just then. A little too aware of what he did and how he did it, and worse still, why.

But he didn't drop his smile when he faced Quinn. "You mean that philosophically? Spiritually?"

"I was thinking physically. You look like you've been knocked over the head. Hard." But Quinn grinned. "If so, I'd like to shake the hand of the fine individual who did it."

"You know me," Bowie said, still flashing his smile. The finest combat gear he'd ever known. "Too hardheaded to die. Turns out I can crash a plane without even a hint of a concussion."

Quinn shook his head, which wasn't the laugh Bowie was going for. He reached out, disarming Bowie completely, and threw his arm over Bowie's shoulders.

"You're a pain in the ass," Quinn said gruffly. "But it turns out, I wouldn't know what to do without you."

"Good," he replied, his voice a lot rougher than he would've liked. "Because I'm not going anywhere." And they stood there a moment, side by side, in this place where their family had been forever. Where they would be forever, brothers to the end. "And I'm glad you're feeling the love." Bowie had to clear his throat. "Because I need a ride home."

Though it took him longer than he cared to acknowledge, back there in a house he'd built entirely to suit himself that now seem stained with Autumn's abscncc, to realize he was waiting for her to show up.

Even though he knew she wasn't going to.

His mother and sister dropped by the day after he got back, his mother bearing a tray of her comfort lasagna before her and Piper trailing after her with sharp eyes and all the gossip.

"You're too skinny," Lois barked at him, sticking her lasagna in his oven right then and there, with a look on her face that told him she intended to stand over him while he ate it. "And that scraggly beard doesn't do you any favors."

"Thanks, Mom," Bowie said cheerfully, leaning back against his counter while his mother and sister made themselves comfortable in his kitchen. "I love you, too."

And then he got a lump in his throat when his mother, usually hard as nails in all things, came over and grabbed him in another fierce hug. His sister came in from the side, her grip almost as tight.

"We thought you were gone," Piper said, her voice muffled because her face was pressed against his shoulder.

"Don't do that again," Lois warned him, and then laughed as she stepped back, even as she wiped at her eyes.

And then she fed him gooey lasagna and watched him eat it, like every bite would protect him against all future potential plane crashes.

That part was sweet. But Piper was there, too.

"Autumn's dad and stepmom left today," she said innocently, and smiled blandly when Bowie threw her a dark look. "They went down into Hopeless and caught a ride to McGrath. Had to get back to the ranch, you know."

"That's the thing about ranch life," Bowie said, though he felt something stab at him, too sharply, because he remembered having this very same conversation with Autumn. "You can't take a break from it. Ever."

"The sisters are staying," Piper continued, pretending that she was just addressing her lasagna. "They rented one of the summer cabins. Jenny Benco was thrilled. She didn't think she'd get more rental money this summer."

"Lost Lake is a great vacation spot," Bowie said without inflection. He wanted to confiscate his sister's comfort lasagna, if she was going to be actively uncomforting. "Good for them for taking advantage of it."

"It's less vacation and more guard duty, I think." Piper smiled sweetly when he looked at her. "But Autumn refuses to leave before Labor Day because she signed a contract. And for some reason, I can't think why, they're all under the impression that she isn't entirely safe here."

"She's perfectly safe," Bowie said, dispensing with any

pretense that he was in a smiley, happy mood. "I would die to keep her safe, Piper. I almost did."

And he didn't want to talk about that. Just like he didn't particularly want to sit there and witness the expression on his sister's face. Much less his mother's. So he pushed back from the table and stalked away.

Still, he waited around the whole of the next day, and not because of the numerous phone calls he had to make. Not because he cared about a contract or the contest he supposed they were still in, technically. But because he guessed he really did expect Autumn to turn up.

She didn't.

And he couldn't say he really enjoyed the feeling that he was haunting his own house. Even going so far as to stand in the doorway of the room she'd slept in, trying to see if the air smelled like her.

That was when he knew he had to deal with this situation, once and for all.

So on the third day, even though he was only about halfway through his headache with the state of Alaska and worse by far, the FAA, he helped himself to one of the fine planes in his hangar and took off.

Because he had some ghosts he needed to see.

Before he became one himself.

Eighteen

Bowie's plane flew in overhead a week later and did not land near the Mine this time.

In case Autumn might have missed this, even though she was sitting outside making a miserable failure of her basket-weaving project with a full view of the lake and the sky above it, every single one of her sisters came out to tell her they'd seen him. Or his Cessna, anyway, because they'd all learned in their time here that it was only Bowie who flew in that low, affording the entire community the opportunity to note his arrival.

"Thank you," Autumn snapped, glaring at Jade. "I actually have eyes. I saw him fly over myself."

"Terrific," her sister replied, completely ignoring the fact that Autumn had just taken her head off. That was only more irritating, as far as Autumn was concerned. They had been tiptoeing around her all week and it was doing her head in. "Maybe now we can go collect the rest of your things."

Because that was what Autumn had told them when they'd rented this little cabin near the Mine. That she didn't feel right heading down the lake and collecting her stuff from Bowie's house while he wasn't there—and everyone knew he wasn't there. That he'd flown off a couple of days after they'd come barreling back home had been the main topic of conversation around the lake for the better part of the week. No one knew where he'd gone. No one knew when he'd be back.

Autumn had cautioned herself not to take his departure personally.

While taking his departure completely personally.

Still, *it would feel too much like I'm burgling the place*, she'd told her sisters every time they suggested she actually settle into the cabin with them if she insisted on staying here for the rest of the summer. Which she could only really do if she went and packed up that guest room at Bowie's house.

Autumn suspected her sisters knew perfectly well that the real reason she didn't want to get her things was because . . . She didn't want to get her things. She didn't want it to be over.

She was in love with him and she didn't want to let go.

No one had to tell her that was sad.

The past week had been an exercise in love. She knew that, even if her heart was feeling a little battered and besieged these days. Her sisters had thought they'd lost her and they needed to stick close by for a while. Autumn welcomed that, she did. She even felt the same way.

Besides, they were horrified by all the things she'd said in the Mine when she first got back. All three of them had told her privately that they wanted to change things, because they didn't want to be the wicked stepdaughters who had inspired Hunter, Autumn, and Donna to go to such lengths to save their feelings.

We sound like monsters, Willa had said, but like she expected someone to contradict her. No one had.

I don't want to be a monster, Jade had protested.

Sunny had been more blunt. *We're definitely the monsters here, so.*

There had been a lot of tears, especially with Donna.

Her sisters had all decreed that they were going to stay here awhile and help Autumn.

Am I an invalid? Autumn had asked, but they'd ignored her.

Jade had rented the cabin. Willa had sorted out groceries. Sunny had conferred with Mia Saskin and had been in charge of linens and other necessities. It was all very sweet. And within twenty-four hours of their "help," Autumn had happily released them back to their own pursuits. Because her sisters had about as much interest in tanning hides or weaving baskets or checking a gill net as they did in picking up and moving back to Montana. They found the summer weather frigid and spent most of their time wrapped up in down coats with hats scrunched down on their heads, trying their best not to complain too bitterly about the cold while they were within Autumn's hearing.

If she hadn't almost died out there, they definitely would have spent the week whining.

And it had been like falling back in time to share a cabin with her sisters like they were kids again, Autumn thought now. There'd been a lot of laughter, endless stories and memories, and it had been fun, too, to spend time on this side of the lake. The cabin was an easy fifteen-minute walk to the Mine, all of it along the shore of the lake. They could wander over to have a drink. Eat breakfast in the diner. See what Grand Mia had going on for dinner. Depending on who was around, they could even get a fancy coffee and sit outside, because the Mine was also a café with one of the best views around.

At night, Autumn lay in her bunk bed, restrained herself from kicking Jade's form above her, and mostly thought about Bowie.

She'd had no idea that it was possible to physically ache for another person. To miss his presence. His body that she'd grown so used to touching casually, as if it were an extension of her own. The way he smelled. The way he moved. How his eyes found her and then crinkled in the corners.

Maybe what she was doing was processing everything that had happened. From Midsummer at the Mine to bouncing their way across the surface of the lake to safety, it had been quite a ride.

Autumn still felt as if she was on it.

She was sure that was the problem. Maybe she needed to get off the ride, really and truly, and to accept what her family kept telling her. That it was all over and she should probably just go home. The first step was going to Bowie's house and gathering up her remaining things.

And she refused to do it.

"You're not sleeping," Jade said now, settling herself on a chair on the porch of their little cabin. Willa was working on her nails on the step. Sunny had her face in a book, wrapped up in a blanket in the farthest chair. "We hear you tossing and turning every night."

"I don't think that's surprising," Autumn replied, as calmly as she could. She was sitting cross-legged in the dirt out front, scowling ferociously at the tangle of grasses and rushes that looked nothing at all like a basket, despite the fact this was her second day of working on it. "I slept on the ground for a month. A bed takes some getting used to."

"Also it's a trauma response," Willa said, matter-of-factly, without looking up from her nails. When everyone else was quiet, she glanced up from her filing. "You went through something intense. Just because you're safe now, that doesn't mean you've dealt with it."

"I had no idea you were a psychologist," Jade said, and while she wasn't actually smirking, they could all hear it in her voice.

Willa sighed. "I read, Jade. You should try it sometime."

"I'm dealing with it fine," Autumn interjected before they launched themselves at each other. They'd been on such good behavior all week. They had to be *itching* for a fight.

"Right. Super fine." Willa shook her head.

"That's why you're still trying to win a contest when

your reason for entering it no longer exists," Jade said. "Mom's jewelry is safe. Dad and Donna are good. We've seen the error of our ways. The only person who isn't taken care of is you."

For some reason she remembered that beer she'd signed for at the bar in the Mine. *Care of Bowie Fortune.* She had to repress a shiver.

Autumn gave up on her pile of grass and aimed a smile at her sisters. "I don't need an intervention, Jade. Though I love that all of you are here for me. I really do."

"This isn't about the contest," Jade continued in a know-it-all sort of voice that Autumn recognized, and did not like. It was hers. "This is about Bowie."

Autumn laughed at that, but her other two sisters were nodding soberly.

"We've been talking ever since you gave us the sex lecture," Sunny offered.

"I stand by everything I said," Autumn told them now. She climbed to her feet, brushing the dirt off her pants. "There's a lot better sex out there than you've been having, and I love you too much to stand silently by when I know the difference. You'll thank me."

"You're in love," Sunny pronounced, like it was an accusation in a court of law.

This was not news to Autumn. She'd said as much to Bowie. She'd curled herself around her own lovesick heart every night in her bunk bed. She'd stopped actually saying it to herself, because there was no need. It was tangled up inside her. It was layered over everything. At this point, it was who she was.

But it was still a kind of gut punch to hear someone else say it.

"You're completely, head over heels in love with him," Jade agreed.

"It's obvious," Willa said.

"I'm still thinking we might need to carve out his heart and feed it to the wild animals around here," Sunny said in the way she said all psychotic things. Sweetly and calmly. "Because everybody needs a ritual to move on."

"Is that a ritual?" Autumn shook her head at her baby sister. "Or a cry for help? One that I think you'll find will be answered with the presence of law enforcement."

Sunny waved a hand. "But obviously that's not appropriate. If you don't actually want to move on."

And then they all sat there. Staring at Autumn expectantly. Sunny set aside her book. Willa actually put down her nail file.

"Are you telling me or asking me?" Autumn hedged, trying to get her bearings for this unexpected development. Three pairs of matching, unamused blue eyes stared back at her. She sighed. "Yes. I'm in love with him."

"So this is what we don't understand," Jade said, cocking her head. Very much as if she was issuing a challenge. "What, exactly, are you doing?"

"I beg your pardon?"

"This is not the Autumn McCall we know and love," Willa said, almost sorrowfully. "Where are the sixty-eight plans of attack? Or any plan at all to get out there and win him over?"

"I would have expected a spreadsheet, at the very least," Sunny agreed with a sniff. "*Several* spreadsheets and a whiteboard for overflow. Because there's always, always overflow."

"Instead, you're wafting around in the woods, skinning things—which I think we can all agree is worrying—*basket weaving*, and gazing off into the distance a lot." Jade shook her head. "If I didn't know any better, I might think that the unstoppable, indomitable Autumn McCall was wallowing."

"You never wallow," Willa said, her expression filled with reproach. "We're the ones who wallow. All the time."

"I could give lessons in wallowing," Sunny agreed.

"It's like you came back from that camping trip a different person," Jade continued, as she was clearly the self-appointed leader of this intervention. Autumn almost admired the initiative. "And I don't mean that in a good, *you found yourself in the jaws of death and came out stronger* way. I'm a little bit afraid that all that time scrabbling for food in the wilderness made you forget who you are."

That took Autumn's breath for a moment. She wished she was sitting down, but she thought that if she shifted to sitting now, too much would be read into it.

Then she realized that she was, in fact, sitting down. When had that happened?

"But don't worry," Sunny said, sitting up in her chair. "We're here."

Willa was nodding vigorously. "And we're going to remind you that you've never taken a single thing in life lying down."

"When we were kids I didn't know you actually slept like the rest of us," Sunny told her. "Since I never saw you do it."

"It doesn't make sense that you're reacting to a man like this," Jade said then. "You, of all people. You're the one who taught me that there was absolutely no point having relationships if I wasn't prepared to fight for what I wanted and stand up for myself. Which usually includes asking for what I want. Directly."

Autumn tried to take all of this in, looking back and forth between her sisters, who, as usual, were arrayed there on the porch before her like a beautiful blonde wall.

She blew out a breath, annoyed that it was shaky. "I had a job to do with you three, and I'm glad I did it. Mom was very clear. *Take care of your sisters*, she told me. *They're too pretty for their own good*. It was my job to make sure I got you ready for life. The way she would have wanted." She lifted her hands, then dropped them. "It was different for me. I think you all know that."

For a long moment, all three of her sisters stared back at her. And then, for another long moment, they stared at one another.

When they looked back at Autumn, they were all wearing identical frowns.

"Hey, Cinderella." Jade shook her head slightly. "You know she said that to me, too, don't you?"

Autumn hadn't known that, but she nodded. "Good. I'm glad the both of us were looking out for Willa and Sunny like big sisters should."

"No," Jade said. Intently. "I mean she said the exact same thing to me. The exact same words. *Take care of your sisters, they're too pretty for their own good.* All of my sisters, Autumn."

"She said the same thing to me, too," Willa chimed in.

"And me," Sunny agreed. "She didn't single you out. It wasn't, *Take care of the pretty ones and also Autumn, the family troll.*"

"I never thought she was singling me out," Autumn gritted out, though something inside her seemed to quake, like she might fly apart at any moment. "I'm just the oldest. It was my job to take care of you."

"You're focusing on the wrong part." Jade pointed at Autumn. Then she looped her finger around in the air to encompass the rest of them. "You're determined to believe that there's some separation between us and you. There's not. Mom thought you were too pretty for your own good, too, Autumn. She wasn't wrong. I don't think that she expected that you'd be so busy worrying about how pretty we might be that you forgot to accept the fact that you are, too."

Autumn ran her hands over her face and refused to accept that they were trembling. "That's very sweet. But I don't need you to make me feel better about myself like this. I know how I look. I also know how you look. Reality doesn't upset me."

"No." Sunny rolled her eyes. "It just escapes you."

"We all look like Dad." Willa waved her currently sparkling pink nails in the air. "We're tall like him. Blonde like he would be if he ever took that cowboy hat off and let the sun get in his hair. And we're all built the same way he is, too."

"Rectangles," Sunny pointed out dourly. "We're all shaped like rectangles."

"Yes," Autumn said drily. "I can see that it must be a huge hardship to be skinny and lean."

"And flat as a board." Jade narrowed her eyes. "Literally shaped like Dad, Autumn."

"Not exactly the picture of femininity," Willa agreed with a tight smile. "As I was reminded repeatedly in the seventh grade, when all the other girls were developing and I was not."

Autumn shook her head, bewildered. "I guess seventh grade was hard for everybody?"

"Autumn," Jade said, and now her tone was gentle. Autumn didn't know quite what to do with it, only that she quaked even more inside. "You look like Mom."

And suddenly, Autumn found that her knees had gone precarious again. She couldn't quite breathe. She wanted to cry.

"Body like a goddess," Willa said matter-of-factly. "And the face of an angel. That's what Dad says every time he sees a picture of Mom. So does Donna, for that matter. And that's you. It's always been you."

But all Autumn could do was shake her head.

"You're going to have to face facts sooner or later," Sunny told her, the blanket around her shoulders like a cape. "You're gorgeous. So whatever weird, Autumn-y thing you've been telling yourself about how you're the ugly duckling and all men feel let down when they look at you and whatever other nonsense you fill your head with, you need to let that go."

"There are no ugly duckling McCalls," Willa assured her. She waved a sparkly hand. "Swans one, swans all."

"Or put another way," Jade added, with a little more edge, "you might want to consider getting your head out of your —"

"I saw it!" Autumn cried, the words tumbling out of her. As if that quaking had torn them loose from somewhere deep inside her. "When I walked out the door and saw Bowie for the first time, I saw the expression on his face. You can talk all you want about swans and Mom, but that's not what happened. And that's not what usually happens, while we're on the topic. So as sweet as this all is, and it really is sweet, it's not what's going on here."

"Unfortunately for you," Sunny said in her usual blunt way, but with a smile this time, "we were all there, too."

"The man took one look at you and just about keeled over." Willa smiled. "And not because you're ugly."

"Why do you think we didn't want you going off with him?" Jade asked. "He's not the first man to look at you that way, big sister. But he is the first man I've ever seen *you* look at in the same way."

"None of this is what actually happened," Autumn protested.

"He was smitten," Sunny pronounced like that was the final word on the subject. "At first sight."

Autumn opened her mouth and then had to close it again, because nothing came forth. She didn't know when she'd stood up, but she wished she hadn't because her knees were barely working. She wasn't feeling any more confident about her ability to draw breath. That ache in her heart had grown to three times its size, and she would've said it was already too big to stay inside her chest. Now it felt as if it were prying her ribs apart.

She wanted to reject what her sisters were saying to her, but she couldn't. Not the nonsense about swans, but about Bowie. Because, for all that she might have lectured her sisters on the importance of life-altering sex, she was the one who'd actually had it.

She just didn't have it in her to believe that only her life had been altered by it when she'd been sharing all those moments with Bowie.

And if she believed that he had been as affected as

she was, was it really so hard to imagine that he might have been as blown away at their first meeting as she had been?

Even though it flew in the face of everything Autumn had ever known to be true about men and herself and life in general?

Then again, wasn't that the Bowie Fortune experience in a nutshell?

"Guys," she managed to say. "I love that you think so highly of me, but I don't really think—"

"You don't have to think," came the voice that Autumn had been waiting to hear for a week now. Gruff and amused and glorious in every way. "You can just ask."

All of her sisters whipped their heads around. But Autumn was facing the cabin, so all she had to do was stare as Bowie sauntered around the corner, hands in his jeans pockets, looking the way he always did.

Absolutely splendid, from head to toe.

Her eyes moved over him, drinking him in. He had shaved the beard, but not today. So his jaw was back the way she liked it best, the kind of stubbly that made her want to go and run her hands along that perfect, roughened line. His dark eyes gleamed like every night they'd spent together. He had thoughtfully packaged himself in a Led Zeppelin T-shirt and a pair of jeans that were old enough to fray in places, but not so old that they didn't cling to all the strength in his thighs and that butt of his that she had developed a particular fondness for.

Because she was alive and had eyes.

"Bowie," she said. Weakly.

That was all she could say. She hadn't seen him since they'd landed in the middle of Lost Lake, were force-fed chili, and were suddenly not dying before spring. She hadn't seen him for an endless week when she'd spent every minute, more or less, of the most intense month of her life constantly in his presence.

She recognized that ache now. She knew what it was.

It was what happened when a person realized that they

had another half, but it was missing. That half of her heart was his, forever, and there was no getting it back. There was only loving him. Basking in him.

And hoping that someday, if she was lucky, he might give her half of his heart, too, so that each of them could have a whole.

Otherwise, she understood, she could look forward to a lifetime of aching, just like this.

"While we're on the subject," Bowie said, offering her sisters a courteous nod, then returning his attention to Autumn. The full force of his attention. She could feel it like another quake straight through her. "Your sisters are right."

"You shouldn't say that in front of them," Autumn managed to say, though her voice was barely above a whisper. "It gives them ideas."

"I took one look at you and knew you were going to wreck my entire life," Bowie told her, his voice low and his gaze intent on hers. "Skinny blonde girls are a dime a dozen." He seemed to remember himself and threw a glance toward the porch. "No offense."

"None taken," Willa said grandly.

Jade shrugged. "Is it a very shiny dime?"

"Not untrue." Sunny was nodding, almost thoughtfully. "See every murder movie and television show ever made."

Bowie only smiled a little, turning his attention back to Autumn.

"But it got worse," he told her in that same way, as if he was testifying. Before the grand jury of the McCall sisters, though it was all for Autumn. "Not only are you every dream I've ever had come true, you're funny. You're fascinating. You're . . . *you*. A woman of projects. Plans. You like cleaning, for God's sake."

She thought she would die if he didn't stop. She knew she might die if he did.

He didn't stop. "Autumn, inside and out and in every particular way, you're the most beautiful woman I have ever known. Does that clear it up for you?"

She couldn't take it in. She pointed in the vague direction of her sisters. Then at him. "But they . . . but you . . ."

"Let me put this another way," Bowie suggested, sounding almost lazy.

Though not one thing about him was actually lazy. She knew that all too well.

He closed the distance between them in a single step. Then he took her hands in his and she thought, *yes*. Finally, *finally*, she was touching him again.

She had no idea how she'd survived this long without touching him.

"Bowie," she began, and the worst part wasn't that she was shaking, everywhere, but that she couldn't seem to hide it.

"I love you," he said, cutting her off with his Montana night eyes ablaze. "I love you, Autumn. How's that?"

Nineteen

One look at Autumn McCall and he was a goner.

He had that same thought back at her father's ranch, that very first day. And here, now, on the shores of his favorite lake in the world, it was even more true than it had been then.

She looked 100 percent Autumn. Out here surrounded by rushes and long grass, for some reason. Her hair was pulled back in a smooth ponytail, looking particularly strawberry and gold today, and her hazel eyes seemed to catch every last bit of sun. He could see the hides she'd clearly tanned hanging near the porch. She was wearing a T-shirt and pants he'd taken off her a thousand times, and had a heavy apron wrapped around her waist. A working sort of apron, not a cooking sort. Though she could do both.

This was what he liked, he understood now. What he needed. She was so pretty. And she was innately practical. A woman who could tan hides for the fun of it, then put on a red dress and dance like the heartbreaker she was. A woman who had found herself plane-wrecked and had straightened her shoulders, looked around, and got to work.

A woman who'd sat beside him as he told her his biggest secret, even though she couldn't have liked hearing it, and had offered him nothing but her support.

It didn't hurt that she was also so hot in bed that he could break a sweat just thinking about it.

And right now she was looking at him as if he'd personally climbed up into the Alaskan sky and restored the stars to the summer sky instead of waiting for fall like everyone else.

"You love me?" she asked now, her voice soft.

Bowie wanted to tell her where he'd been. That he'd gone down to California and spent some time at Karina's grave, updating her on things. Letting her go. And he would have stood by his inclination to never let her parents know the full truth of what had happened between them, but he'd looked up at one point from where he'd been squatting down, having a heart-to-heart with his one-day bride, and found himself face-to-face with Karina's father.

He'd frozen there, not sure what to do.

I'm so glad to come across you here, the older man had said with a kind of urgency. *Patricia and I have thought about you often over the years. I know we treated you harshly, and we regret it.*

Bowie had found himself telling Karina's father everything, and then going back the following day to the house Karina used to sneak out from to see him, to tell the same story to both her parents.

I'm so glad she knew that kind of love, her mother had said when he was done. She dabbed at her eyes with a tissue. *It's one of the things that has eaten away at me, that she died too young to know. I'm glad I was wrong. And I hope you've found it again, Bowie. I think without love, neither one of us could possibly have survived losing her.*

I am in love, Bowie had said without meaning to. And somehow, it hadn't been strange at all to make a pronouncement like that to these people who once, long ago, had thought so little of him. *But before I committed myself, I had to clear it with Karina. I made her a promise.*

And he couldn't wait to tell Autumn all of this. Because it was all because of her. He would never have gone down to that cemetery again. He would never have found a way to connect with the other people Karina had loved so much.

He would never have understood what Autumn had been trying to tell him back there in that canyon. Love was the only thing that mattered.

Love was all there was.

"It's okay if you're reconsidering it," Autumn said then, though she looked stricken.

"Um, no, it is not," said one of her sisters, he couldn't tell which one. He didn't care.

It hadn't been his intention to do this with an audience, but then, if he thought about it, it made sense that they had one. This was how they'd started, after all.

He wasn't intimidated by a gauntlet of Furies.

"I have reconsidered," he told Autumn. "But not the way you mean. I had to go to California first. I had to make a new promise."

Her eyes widened, then grew damp as he watched. "There by the sea? Where you made the first one?"

"I wanted her to know," Bowie told her, and this was the important part. This was what had become so clear to him during the long flight down the West Coast. "That I kept my promise. I didn't go out and replace her. I would have been happy to wait forever, but then you came along. And you loved the man I am now. You showed me who that was. Not the man I was only just becoming back then. He was hers. But it's changed everything that you love the me as the man who lost her, Autumn. Everything."

There were some murmurs from the peanut gallery, but he only had eyes for Autumn.

Her gaze was overly bright, and she moved closer to him, tugging her hands from his so she could slide them up his chest. Then around his neck and on to his jaw, tipping his head down so she could look at him—but it was as if they were all alone.

The way, he figured, it always would be when she was around. Because she was the only thing he could see.

"I love you," she whispered, like it was a vow.

A promise.

This one theirs, not his.

"I love you, too," he said. "I think it hit me the first moment I saw you. But it took me a while, Autumn, because I was so wrapped up in the past. I'm going to regret for a long time how long it took me to realize what I had in front of me here. I was afraid that opening up to another person meant letting Karina go. And then you came along, so fearless about everything, and now I don't know how I lived so long like that. Or how I almost lost you because I was afraid to let go of a ghost."

"Fear and love can't occupy the same space," she whispered. "Ghosts can't occupy anything but our memories. And Bowie, you know this already. Deep down you do. Love is the only thing that can be in two places at the same time."

She slid one of her hands to cover his heart. Then, holding his gaze, she moved it to her own.

His own heart was beating so hard, so deep, that he was sure it echoed all up and down the lake. And he welcomed it.

Because if Bowie Fortune was going to do a thing, he liked to do it big.

"I love you, Autumn," he told her, because he couldn't say it enough. "So when I was finished in California, I took myself up to Montana. Because these are modern times we live in, despite your pioneer ways, but I had a feeling that you're the kind of woman who would like a man to consult her father before he takes it upon himself to ask you a very important question. Not because he owns you or I want to. Because he loves you, and so do I."

"Bowie . . ."

She couldn't seem to form any other words.

He stepped back and smiled a little at the sighs from the porch. He pulled out the ring he'd been carrying in his pocket since he left Montana, held it before him so it could catch the light, and then knelt down before Autumn.

Right there in front of her summer cabin, where anyone out on the lake could see. Knowing his friends and family, they'd had their binoculars trained this way since he'd headed over here in the motorboat after he'd seen to a few things back home.

The more, the merrier, he thought.

"Autumn McCall," he said now, his eyes locked to hers. "We've already been through a lifetime together. In a little over two months you've been my mail-order bride, my roommate, my friend. You've been so much more than that. Kissing you on Solstice is the best decision I ever made. And I know we haven't talked about it, but as little as I wanted to die in that canyon, knowing that we'd be there, doing it together, made it better."

"Not okay," she whispered, nodding as tears ran down her face. "But better. The best part of a bad deal."

"But then we made it out," he continued. "And it became clear to me, pretty much immediately, that having already done life and near-death with you, I wanted more. I wanted everything."

"Bowie . . ." she whispered again, her voice choked.

"I've lived a week without you now," he said. "That seems like punishment enough. I want to repeat that as little as possible."

"I agree," she managed to say. "I agree in every respect."

"Autumn McCall," Bowie said, and it was funny to feel a little punch of nerves now. He hadn't felt nerves when the storm took them down. Or when he'd had to use every trick he'd ever learned to get that plane out of the canyon. He'd been in mission mode then. Right now, he wasn't a seasoned pilot, a decorated former marine. Right now, he was just a man in love, handing his heart to a woman who could smash it with a single syllable. So he got to it. "Will you marry me? Will you spend the rest of your life, which is hopefully a lot longer than it seemed about a week ago, with me?"

And she didn't even hesitate. She didn't even pause. "Yes," she said. "*Yes.*"

Everything inside him went still.

Still and good and almost too bright to bear, and then he began to ache. Because it was joy. Pure joy. And it was so intense, it hurt.

He took the ring and slid it on her finger.

"Your father gave me this ring," he told her. "After he laughed at me and reminded me that he told me so, way back when. And he did. I didn't think anyone could wreck my life, but Autumn, I'm so glad you did."

"It's my mother's ring," Autumn whispered, her eyes round with some kind of wonder, even as tears tracked down her cheeks.

Bowie had thought the ring was pretty when Hunter had given it to him. But on her hand, it was like the diamonds took on a different dimension. The bigger one in the middle and the two flanking it, like the past, the present, and their future. Like the three lakes they'd fallen in love beside, this summer alone.

"Your father told me your mother would have wanted you to wear this," Bowie said, standing up and taking her hand in his, so he could look at her. This woman who would be his wife. Who would, if he had anything to say about it, grow old with him. "And that he wanted it, too."

"I'm honored to wear it," Autumn said solemnly. And then, gripping his hand, she turned toward the porch. "But only if it's okay with all of you, too. She wasn't only my mother."

Bowie had forgotten her sisters were there. They were huddled together in a big clump of a hug, hands over their mouths and tears streaming down their faces.

"I'm going to love looking at your hand and seeing it there." Jade's voice was choked. "Like Mom has been here with us all along and always will be."

"It's *perfect*," agreed Willa, thick and fierce.

"I will hurt you if you try to take it off," said Sunny.

Then, speaking in some sister language he couldn't penetrate, Autumn clearly called them all to her, because they rushed her. And before he knew it, he was caught up in a McCall sister group hug that involved a lot of tears and a lot of punches on the shoulder from Sunny, too. Not all of them love taps.

But he lifted his head and there was Autumn. His Autumn. Glowing right at him.

"Are you sure you want to marry me?" she asked over three blonde, mostly weepy heads, all bent down to really let the emotion swell between them. "I come with sisters."

Bowie only smiled. "I wouldn't want you any other way."

And that wasn't strictly true. What he really wanted was to get Autumn alone, but first there was celebrating with those sisters. Then the whole McCall brood came down the length of the lake with him to tell his parents. Lois and Levi were so pleased they called in the rest of the family, and they all spent the evening there by the lake outside his parents' house. Noah actually hugged him. Violet got misty-eyed. Quinn looked proud enough to burst. And Piper was beside herself. She even hugged Bowie without pretending to hate him, making them both a little sappy.

"I always thought I was so lucky to have the two best brothers," Piper said at one point, with an arm around both Bowie's waist and Quinn's.

"Well," Bowie drawled. "One, anyway."

"Idiot." Piper shook her head, but she squeezed both of them. "But then the two of you gave me the present of two sisters, too. And not just any sisters, but the very best sisters anyone could have."

The three of them looked down the hill, where Violet

and Autumn were standing in a group with Autumn's sisters, all of them laughing.

All of them lovely, Bowie thought, but only one of them his. In every possible way.

"You planning to lock that down, big brother?" he asked Quinn, because everything was a little too sweetness and light and that wasn't the Fortune family.

"Seriously," Piper said. "What if she changes her mind and runs, screaming, away from you, Quinn? Nobody wants pre-Violet Quinn back."

"Nobody," Bowie agreed.

"Don't you worry about me and my professor," Quinn said, grinning. His eyes on his woman. "She already made it through a winter here. We're good."

It was getting on toward ten o'clock when Bowie finally took his woman home, after a stop by the Mine to get a drink and drop off Autumn's sisters near their cabin. One drink had turned into an impromptu party with the various folks who'd still been around.

Only after they'd celebrated awhile did Bowie get Autumn to himself.

"It feels like seven lifetimes since I've been here," Autumn said as they walked up the yard toward the house. "I didn't want to come back while you were gone. It felt wrong."

"I know this is a weird house." He stared up at it. Then looked at her. "But I want this to be your home. I'll tear it all down and build you what you want, just say the word."

"I love this house," she said, her eyes shining again. "I love you, Bowie. I love the life we're going to build here."

And he kissed her then, at last, deep and long.

The way he'd been dreaming about for a week.

But then, instead of picking her up in his arms and carrying her off to that bed upstairs that would be theirs now, he pulled back. He slid his hands to her shoulders and looked her in the eye. "There's something I want to show you."

Her smile widened. "That's sweet, Bowie. You do know I've already seen it, right?"

He laughed at that, but then he took her hand and tugged her with him into the woods.

"I did not expect a hike," she said from behind him. "Is this what marrying you is going to be like? Nonstop surprises?"

"If you're lucky," he said. "And baby, I think you know you are."

It wasn't a long walk. Only a few minutes and then he pulled her out of the woods into a clearing. There was a meadow that rolled down to the water's edge. Better still, there was a big old barn sitting there at the top of the hill, a remnant from a time some or other Fortune had made plans to do more with this land.

"That's a pretty barn," she said. Because she was Autumn and no matter what, she adapted. A crashed plane, a barn in the summer twilight, it was all the same to her.

God, he loved this woman more and more by the second.

"It would make a prettier inn," he said gruffly.

And he watched, with pleasure, as her mouth dropped open. "Bowie. No. Really?"

"Really." Her hands flew up to cover her mouth. "We'll have to clear it with the community first, but don't worry. Every one of them has at least one relative they'd rather they didn't have to put up at their house when they come visit. I don't think they'll be a problem."

"*Bowie*," she breathed. She dropped her hands as she looked at him. "You found me my inn. And it's not a tent."

Now he pulled her into his arms. Now he lifted her up, tilting his head back as she wrapped her legs around him and held on tight.

"You found me when I didn't even know I was hiding," he said, holding her up like she was the moon. "I figure that must be your secret weapon. The perfect compass that finds the things everyone else has lost, and then gives them back."

"That's not my secret weapon," she said, smiling so wide it made him happy just to look at her.

"It's a knife, isn't it?"

She gazed down at him and then bent to kiss him, with all that heat, all of that joy. Everything that was theirs and always would be.

"It's not a knife," she said. She kissed him again, then shifted so she could tip her forehead against his. "It's my heart. My dad always said no one could withstand it. All of this relentlessly practical goodness, with Mom's heart, too. My secret weapon."

"And now it's mine," Bowie said.

Then watched her melt in his arms.

"Forever," she promised him.

They were halfway through August and already, there was darkness creeping in at a quarter to eleven. But tonight, the deep summer blue night seemed to wrap them up in softness.

So he took her down with him into the grass of the meadow, there within sight of the inn they would build and the life they would live here, and recommitted himself to every curve, every sweet inch of her.

And let the summer night marry them as surely as he would, just as soon as she'd have him.

Because Bowie Fortune never backed down from a dare.

Especially not this one.

Because if it involved loving Autumn for the rest of their days, he already knew he would win.

Twenty

They didn't win the contest, which Autumn felt unduly aggrieved by. It went to the couple in the lean-to in Takotna.

"Show-offs," Autumn muttered.

"Technically, you failed to meet the minimum standards," Quinn told her over a family dinner after Labor Day. "You didn't post a daily picture the entire month of July. Or a video."

"I'm sorry we didn't have social media access while *plane-wrecked*," Autumn retorted.

Quinn only shrugged, a corner of his mouth kicking up. "I don't make the rules."

"That's factually incorrect," Violet piped in from beside him.

Bowie took her to a Caribbean island anyway. Where, it turned out, he found all kinds of ways to entertain himself. Lying around in the sun, staring at palm trees, enjoying a private pool with a view, and indulging his appetite for Autumn.

Who was equally voracious in return.

They went to Montana and visited with her father and

Donna, then properly moved Autumn into Bowie's house later in September. And as the weather turned, the world growing darker and the cold coming in, she was grateful for their cozy bedroom that let in the stars, and on some nights, the aurora, too.

And when the winter solstice came around, she was there in the Mine to dance it in, too.

Just like she was there the next month when, a year to the day Violet had showed up at the Mine, Quinn married her there. With the community around them and a few shell-shocked friends of Violet's all the way from San Francisco.

"I guess that now you're engaged to Bowie, you won't be telling us all his secrets," Rosemary said that night. "*Such* a bummer."

"Whatever you're imagining?" Autumn waited until Rosemary leaned in, and then grinned. "It's much, much better."

Autumn spent the winter studying up on innkeeping and hospitality. Come spring, the Lost Lake community trust voted to allow the lake's first inn. That meant that after the spring breakup, Bowie and Autumn worked feverishly—with the help of pretty much everyone they knew—to get the barn renovated and up to inn standards for summer.

They had their first three guests—her sisters, who had insisted, and refused to take the friends-and-family rate—on the fourth of August, one year to the day since she and Bowie had come hurtling out of the sky back to Lost Lake.

Back to life, and what a life it was.

Autumn vowed, daily, that she would never take it for granted.

It took them another year to actually plan a wedding They had the ceremony down in Montana, though they threw another big party at the Mine. Which was also where, at Midsummer at the Mine later that month, Autumn told her brand-new, beautiful husband the happy news that she was pregnant.

And their life was already so good. She had her little inn at last. She had Bowie, and her family, and his family, too. For someone who never knew what she wanted to do with her life, she now found she got to do pretty much everything she wanted, all the time.

They even went back to camp at Bowie's favorite spot that summer. They didn't go back to the canyon. Because their life was about love, not fear. There were no ghosts allowed.

And in the spring, when their daughter was born, they named her Roberta Karina—Robby for short—for the two women who'd made them, and whose love they depended on, every day.

And when she was old enough, Bowie took his daughter up in his favorite plane and taught her how to fly.

"Because," he told Autumn when she asked, "I want to make sure she knows how love feels, right from the start. So maybe it won't take her so long to find it."

And this was how forever worked, Autumn discovered. One kiss at a time. One day, one night, and then the next, on into eternity.

Two hearts made of halves, stitched together with hope, with laughter. With tears and *I love you*s, forgiveness and joy. Stories that were only theirs, told and retold. Time and wonder, bright smiles and secret kisses.

Two hearts made into one life, forever theirs.

Autumn intended to love every single minute of it.

And she had always been indomitable, so that was exactly what she did.

ACKNOWLEDGMENTS

All my gratitude to everyone who worked on this book. You made it shine! I would be lost without you!

To Lisa Hendrix, my Alaska guru. If there's a mistake, you can be sure Lisa told me to fix it and I went ahead and left it in anyway.

And as ever, to Jeff, for inspiration, plot-hole excavation, and too many meals I would have forgotten otherwise to count.

Keep reading for an excerpt from

BOLD FORTUNE

by USA Today *bestselling author*
M. M. Crane, now available!

Violet Parrish, PhD, should have known that her long-distance, never-consummated romance with Stuart Abernathy-Thomason—also a PhD, though the sort who viewed any inadvertent failure to acknowledge his doctorate as a deliberate assault—was doomed.

Looking back, there had been signs of his inevitable betrayal from the start. The long distance itself, because surely it wasn't *that* difficult to fly from London to San Francisco, and yet the much-discussed flight had never occurred. *It's been such a busy year, hasn't it*, Stuart had always said mournfully. The failure to engage in even the faintest hint of any intimate acts over their computers, when Violet had read too many articles to count that had insisted that said acts were *how* couples maintained their relationships across distances. *I want you, not a screen*, Stuart had told her, and could never be budged.

The glaring fact that when she'd excitedly told him that she was coming to London to visit, after making certain he had a gap in his schedule, he'd initially been excited—then had come back the next day and told her that he'd been called away on those exact dates. *What bad luck!* he'd said in his plummy voice.

These were all signs Violet would very likely have continued to ignore had there not been the naked-webcam incident.

"I don't understand," her boss and mentor said to her now, peering across the length of his crowded desk at the Institute of San Francisco, a small nonprofit with an academic pedigree and lofty ideals. Irving Cornhauser, too many degrees to choose just one, was often confused for a man in his eighties. He was fifty. "What does a *web camera* have to do with our work here?"

"I don't think we should focus on that," Violet said. She remembered all too well the office-wide effort to teach Irving how to use social media. They'd concluded he didn't *want* to understand. She slid her glasses up her nose and braced herself. "The issue is the relationship with Dr. Abernathy-Thomason. *My* relationship with him. My *former* relationship, that is."

She should have felt heartbroken. Wasn't that the typical, expected response to catching one's significant other in an intimate embrace with another woman? Then again, maybe this *was* heartbreak. Having never been in a relationship before—by choice, as Violet liked to remind her mother, because she was an intellectual with other things on her mind—she had nothing to compare it to.

She had not expected it to feel like heartburn, acidic and anger-inducing. With a deep and growing sense of outrage that she was now forced into this position. Standing in Irving's office on the first working day of the new year, confessing things that could only embarrass them both.

"Your personal life is your business, Violet," Irving said in faintly censorious tones, as if Violet had pranced in here for a cozy giggle about boys. Having never done anything of the sort before, in all the years they'd worked together. "The less said about it, the better. Our role here at the Institute is to lend our considerable focus to small environmental matters that make big differences, and in so doing—"

Violet wanted to scream. But she refrained, because she was an academic, not an animal. "I know the mission. I helped write our mission statement, actually." But he knew that, of course. "I'm not making a confession because I want to go on a double date with you, Irving."

He blinked at her in astonishment. Her fault for making reference to the fact that he even had a partner. More personal details he did not care to share on the job. Irving liked to think of these walls as a place of philosophical and intellectual purity. The less reference to the fact that they were humans, complicated, and with lives of their own, the better.

A philosophy Violet had always heartily supported, and yet how the mighty had fallen—to a con man dressed up in a pretty accent. She was surpassingly ashamed of herself.

"The problem is that I discussed my research with Stuart," she said before Irving could reply, because she wanted to get this out. Stuart's betrayal and her stupidity had been burning her alive all throughout the Christmas break, when no one at work—especially Irving—answered calls or emails. She'd tried. "And worse, our paper based on that research for the spring conference. I thought it was a circle of trust and I was mistaken. Badly mistaken."

The acid inside her lit her up all over again as she relived the whole nightmare.

It had been Christmas Eve. She had been at her mother's place in Southern California, hiding away from too much Prosecco, a selection of white plastic Christmas trees, and the near-constant caterwauling of off-key carolers at the palm trees in her mother's beach-adjacent compound. She and Stuart had talked as planned, and she hadn't given much thought to the kinds of questions he always asked her. He was so supportive. He was so *interested.* Despite her mother's dire warnings about the lonely lives of sad girls who lived in their heads, he was *involved.*

Violet had found someone who not only supported her work, but understood it, as Stuart was part of a think tank dedicated to the same issues. She'd been congratulating herself on that score after the call had ended while enduring a series of frustrating questions from her mother's sixth husband, who appeared to think Violet taught elementary school students. No matter how many times she corrected him.

Then she'd escaped to the guest room and seen that her laptop was still open. Upon sitting down at the desk to close it, she'd seen that Stuart had not turned his camera off.

It had taken Violet longer than she cared to admit to understand that Stuart had not, in fact, been playing some kind of game with that woman. Right there in his lounge in his tiny flat in London that she knew so well, after a year of looking at it through this same screen.

Naked.

She'd cleaned her glasses with great care, but no. It was still happening when her lenses were clear.

Maybe it really was the heartbreak and the betrayal that made her stomach hurt so much, but on the flight back to San Francisco the day after Christmas—after a holiday packed full of recriminations (hers) and justifications (his), until he'd sneered at her and told her that he'd been using her all along—all she'd really been able to think about was how *insulting* this all was. And how embarrassing it was going to be to explain to her colleagues.

She'd met Stuart at a conference in Nice last summer. They'd had one marvelous dinner, followed by a perfect kiss, before Violet had raced to catch her flight home. And their romance ever since had involved a great many letters—okay, emails, but she'd felt like a modern-day Austen heroine all the same—and the odd video chat when their schedules allowed.

Far fewer said chats than there probably should have been, she saw that now. And none of them naked. But Violet had been so proud that *at last* she was having the relationship of her dreams. Not the *shattered glasses against the wall, screaming bloody murder* nonsense she associated with her parents' bitter union—finished before she was born but reenacted during custody skirmishes throughout her childhood—and most of their many marriages since.

Her relationship with Stuart had been cerebral, not physical. Violet had been sure that the next time they saw each other in person, the physical would catch up. How could it not? Everyone knew that sexual attraction started in the brain.

Better than the belly, she thought now, while hers continued its protest.

"I'm afraid that I was wrong about Stuart," she made herself confess to Irving now, because she might have made a horrible mistake but she, unlike Stuart, was capable of facing her own actions. She straightened her shoulders. "Terribly, horribly wrong."

"Right. Er. Well." Irving now looked as if she'd slapped him. "I suppose we can't all be lucky in love."

"Irving." Violet was beginning to feel desperate. It was the dread, she thought. It had sat heavy on her this past week and had gotten worse as she'd prepared to come to work today—and that was before she'd seen the press release. "You don't understand. Stuart has taken our paper that we intended to unveil at the conference—or all its major points, anyway—and has presented it as his. His center sent out an announcement this morning with excerpts. He's claimed all of our theories on new technology avenues for brighter environmental solutions as his own."

This time, Irving understood her. She knew because he had a tell. She watched, with a strange mix of apprehension and relief, as her boss's bald head slowly and surely turned an alarming shade of red.

Like a shiny tomato of fury.

Finally.

Irving wasn't a yeller. He was a seether. He stared at her for a long moment while he grew ever redder, then turned his attention to the computer before him, banging on his keyboard as if it, too, had betrayed him.

But no. Only she had.

Violet's heart kicked at her, because she loved this place. Because they were such a small nonprofit, they functioned more like a research team—reminding her of her doctoral days. Her colleagues were more like friends and each paper they presented was a communal effort. Their most recent project—half a year of research and debate followed by half a year of drafting the kind of paper that had the potential to shift high-level thinking—had been about specific technologies that might or might not aid in certain proposed environmental protections in remaining wilderness areas, like the Alaskan interior. She wanted to beg Irving not to fire her. She wanted to offer him a host of rationalizations.

But she stayed where she was and she stayed quiet, because she hoped she was woman enough to accept whatever consequences came her way. She'd assured herself she was since Stuart had showed his true colors on Christmas Eve.

Still naked. So naked, in fact, that she'd kept getting distracted by the blinding whiteness of his narrow chest while she should have been laser-focused on his perfidy.

When she heard Irving's hiss of a breath, she knew he'd found the headlines from the usual industry publications, all of them lauding Stuart for his innovative findings.

Her findings, damn him. Her colleagues' findings.

"This is a disaster," Irving whispered. His bald head was still getting redder, which wasn't a good sign. "Violet. This is a *disaster*."

She might have had a week to prepare, but she still wasn't ready.

"I wanted to be the one to tell you." She sounded stiffer and more wooden than she would have liked. But there was no helping it—it was that or crying, and she hadn't cried yet. She refused to cry *here*. It would be humiliating and also, it might kill Irving. She held out the sheet of paper she'd been holding since she'd walked in here. "I've prepared my letter of resignation."

"I don't want to accept it," Irving said, shaking his head.

"You know I don't. I recruited you out of graduate school myself."

Which wasn't the same thing as not accepting it, she noted.

"I understand." Violet swallowed. "I prepared a statement. Explaining the situation to everyone here, so there can be no doubt that I'm taking complete responsibility for my lapse in judgment."

That was the part that really burned. Violet had always considered her judgment unimpeachable. She didn't like this discovery that she'd been wrong—that she'd apparently been human and fallible all along.

"Your taking responsibility is all well and good," Irving said, rubbing his hands over his face. "But there's the upcoming conference to think about. What do you propose we present now? What will we tell our donors? You know a huge part of our fundraising is based on the reception our papers receive."

Violet felt a surge of temper, but she tamped it down. She'd always objected to the Institute's insistence on focusing on only one idea at a time. Surely, she would argue in meetings, their small size should allow for nimble navigation between many ideas. Not so much communal focus on one thing—though that was what had given the Institute its sterling reputation for intellectual approaches to modern environmental dilemmas. The application of those approaches—in places like universities and corporations or, better still, more broadly in the world insofar as that was measurable—was what excited their donors. Violet had always thought they therefore ought to present several papers each year, to better have more nuanced discussions in more directions. But she suspected that if she broached that theory again today, it would be seen as self-serving.

Worse, she honestly couldn't tell if it would be or not, since as of a week ago, she'd stopped trusting her judgment.

One more reason to detest Stuart.

"We're going to lose our funding," Irving moaned. But

at least this was familiar ground. As the CEO of a nonprofit, he spent the bulk of his time concerned about funding. And his head was noticeably less red.

Violet was grateful that she'd had this week to plot. To do what she was paid to do here and think outside the box. To frantically research all the projects that had gotten away, either because there hadn't been enough in-house enthusiasm to make them *the* idea of the year or because they'd tried to get them off the ground in their initial debate stage, but had failed for one reason or another.

And she'd circled around and around again to the same place. To the big one.

The one dream project that could bring her back into the fold, not just having paid a debt for her sins, but as a rock star.

The very small nonprofit version of rock star, that was, but she would take her polite applause and strained smiles where she could, thank you.

She shoved her glasses into place and cleared her throat. Irving frowned at her.

"As a matter fact," she told him, "I have an idea."

Three days later, Violet found herself on an extended layover in the Anchorage, Alaska, airport.

Some people might consider having to suffer through a thirteen-hour layover a kind of penance, but she was choosing to see it as a celebration. Because she'd convinced Irving—and the rest of her colleagues, because, yes, she'd had to face that firing squad of mortification—that she could do this thing no one else in their field had managed to do.

Yet, she told herself.

Not that anyone at work really believed she was capable of the task she'd set herself, of course. She knew better than to believe they had that kind of confidence in her. It was far more likely they were sending her off into the literal dark of the Alaskan frontier in winter because they thought she might very well get eaten by a bear. An effective way for the Institute to wash its hands of her. She could see the solemn statement of genteel regret to the press now.

But bears or no bears, she was doing it. Violet was a thinker, not a doer, and she avoided outside things like the plague—but she was *doing this.*

She had no choice but to do this.

When it was finally time to catch her plane, one of three weekly flights to a tiny village in the Alaskan bush, it felt a lot like vindication.

The flight was rough—or the plane was small. Maybe both. Her stomach, fragile since Christmas Eve, threatened a full-scale rebellion as they bounced around the clouds. Violet screwed her eyes shut and tried to think about anything else. Anything at all but the fact that she was *bouncing* in midair over the wild Alaskan tundra she had researched feverishly over the last few days while trekking back and forth between her apartment in the Marina District and REI in SoMa for the approximately nine thousand things she thought she would need to survive Alaska.

The trouble with the research she'd done was that she knew too well that she was currently flying over some of the most inhospitable terrain on the planet. Knowing that did not exactly help her stomach.

She thought instead about Irving and the way his tomato-headed fury had turned to disappointment, which was worse. She thought about the colleagues she had considered friends, many of whom had been unable to meet her gaze at their last meeting. Even her closest friend at the Institute, Kaye, had looked flushed with quiet condemnation when Violet had dropped off her enormous rabbit, Stanley, who Kaye had agreed to watch for the foreseeable future.

I'm going to fix this, she had declared to Kaye. A little bit fervently.

I wish you'd told me about Stuart, Kaye had replied

softly, clutching Stanley to her chest as if using him as a rabbit barricade, her eyes wide and reproachful. *He has a reputation.*

I'm going to fix this, Violet had said again.

The cargo plane bounced again, hard.

She gripped the armrest, hard enough for her fingers to start cramping, and hoped she'd live long enough to even try fixing it. Something that seemed touch and go for a while there.

Later, happily alive and on icy, snowy, but solid ground, Violet huddled beneath all the blankets on offer in the hotel room she'd booked. And had been lucky to book, as there had been only two options for lodging here in this town of some three hundred souls that was nonetheless considered the regional center of the Upper Kuskokwim region. The area appeared on the map of Alaska as part of the vast swath of wilderness off to the west behind mighty Denali in the Alaska Range. The hardy town of McGrath hunkered down in a curve in the Kuskokwim River called an oxbow, which meant it was surrounded on three sides by water, all of it frozen solid at this time of year. She'd seen it as her plane had come in.

It was only her first stop, however. Tomorrow she needed to figure out more local transport options deeper into the interior toward her final destination in a part of the world that measured distance in air miles. Not only because the distances were vast, but because there were no roads.

She clutched her trusty, much-read guidebook to her chest, having marked many of the pages with stickies—cross-referenced with the other guidebooks that hadn't made the cut, but which she'd read through two days ago in the bookstore—so she could more quickly reference the important parts when she set off on this adventure.

Like the bear population here in McGrath. Brown bears, grizzly bears, black bears, bears in colors yet to be discovered—she was worried about them all.

But there were no bears in her cozy little hotel room,

buffeted by the January winds outside. So instead, she found herself considering the no-less-overwhelming problem of Quinn Fortune. The grumpy, forbidding representative of a critical land trust and the reason she was trekking into the land of endless night and terrifying bears in the first place.

Quinn Fortune, whose response to the well-researched appeal she'd sent him the same day she'd made her confession to Irving was a very short email in return. Blunt, unfriendly, and to the point. He'd announced that he only did business over a beer at his favorite bar and if she wanted to discuss anything with him, he'd see her in the frozen wilderness he called home.

Only he'd used far fewer words.

Violet doubted very much that he expected her to take him up on that offer. But she, by God, was nothing if not prepared to defy expectations if it could get her out of this mess.

And that was how she found herself heading even deeper into the wilderness the next afternoon in an even smaller plane. Because, apparently, Alaskan bush pilots would fly anywhere in any weather, no matter how alarming the flight. The chatty pilot she'd met over breakfast at her hotel kept up a running commentary on the Kuskokwim River that wound around below them as well as the remote, mostly Native communities spread out along its banks, stretching some seven hundred miles from Mount Russell near Denali to the Bering Sea far to the west. Violet listened closely, making notations in the margins of her guidebook when appropriate. The pilot told her of past and present mines that brought settlers here from the Lower 48. He talked about the Upper Kuskokwim Athabascans, who tended to live Western these days while still hunting and fishing in the tradition of their ancestors. He offered many an opinion about the way city folks didn't really understand the reality of the people who lived out here.

Violet took her notes, nodded along because she suffered from that same lack of understanding, and kept her gaze out the window as much as possible.

Alaska was like a different planet.

Violet had gone to school on the East Coast and had thought she knew her way around a winter, but this was something else entirely. The scale of it was so different. Epic. The guidebook had told her so, and she'd prepared accordingly, but seeing it with her own eyes was astonishing.

There was more snow here than people, a humbling sort of thought.

It was dark again when her new friend landed in Hopeless, home to 103 residents, according to the internet. It seemed to be little more than a handful of hardy, utilitarian buildings clustered together against the howl of the wildness outside.

An actual howl, that was. A metaphor couldn't have rattled the plane as it bounced to a rough landing.

Or sliced straight through her outside the Hopeless General Store after her mercifully brief walk from the spot where her plane had taxied, her glasses fogged up the moment the air hit her.

Inside, the store was ramshackle and cozy at once. There were nonperishable groceries on a selection of shelves, with refrigerators and freezers lining the back wall. The air smelled of hamburgers and coffee, and her belly rumbled as if she hadn't eaten her weight in hash browns at breakfast back in McGrath.

"You look lost," came a deep voice.

She looked up and found a man watching her from behind the counter. At first she thought he had to be as ancient as he was large. But a closer look suggested he was merely magnificently bearded and much younger than she'd first imagined, with that slouchy hat and all the plaid.

"Am I in Hopeless?" Violet asked. He nodded. "Then no, I'm not lost. I'm trying to get to Lost Lake."

"Why?"

She reminded herself that she was out here in a place

where there were very few people. Maybe intrusive questions no one would ask in San Francisco were the norm here. Her fingers itched to make a note of that, but she restrained herself.

"I'm looking for Quinn Fortune," she told him.

The man studied her, not even remotely friendly. Which flew in the face of everything Violet had ever heard about small towns and their supposed charms, but maybe not everything could come with pie on demand and a cheery attitude. "He know you're coming? Because I figure even Quinn Fortune would come on down and meet an invited guest." And there was a not-so-subtle emphasis on the word *invited*.

Violet considered lying but thought better of it. "He does not know I'm coming, as a matter of fact. Though an argument could be made that maybe he should. He issued a challenge and I accepted it."

"Some challenge," the man drawled. "It's hard to get here. Especially from way on down in the Lower Forty-eight."

Violet didn't ask how he knew she wasn't from, say, Anchorage. As she thought about it, in fact, not a single person she'd encountered so far—the hotel owner, the bush pilot, this man—had asked her where she was from. For the first time, it occurred to her that their failure to ask wasn't because she fit beautifully into these harsh surroundings, despite having bought herself every single thing her guidebook had suggested. Quite the opposite.

She beamed at him as she adjusted her glasses. "I like a challenge."

And was taken back when, after a moment, the man's face broke into a broad smile.

"Rosemary!" he bellowed, which didn't make a lot of sense to Violet until a woman came out to join him at the counter. She looked like someone Violet might encounter on the streets of San Francisco, not way out here in the hinterland. Pierced and ethereal, her presence recast the man beside her.

Because she'd expected many things in the Alaskan wilderness, like bears. Lots and lots of bears, hence the bear spray in her pack. What she had not anticipated were hipsters.

"This lady came all this way to see Quinn Fortune," the man said. "On a dare."

Rosemary moved to the edge of the counter, jutting out a hip to lean against it, her gaze shrewd. "Do you know Quinn Fortune?"

"Only by reputation," Violet said. And a great many internet searches, but she kept that to herself.

"And you came anyway?" Rosemary asked. Which made the man beside her laugh.

Violet ignored the laughter. "I can see on the map that Lost Lake is some twenty miles away. I'm going to go out on a limb and guess there's not a taxi service around here. I'm hoping I can charter something to get me there? Or rent some snowshoes, maybe?"

The woman before her looked entirely too entertained. "I'm Rosemary Lincoln. This is my brother Abel. Don't you worry, we'll make sure you survive long enough to meet Quinn Fortune. Who doesn't know you're coming."

Violet looked back and forth between them. "That sounds ominous."

They laughed again. And as neither one of them looked inclined to share why, Violet didn't ask.

"I'm not usually a taxi," Rosemary confided. "But this I have to see for myself."

She disappeared back into the kitchen and when she re-emerged, was dressed for the cold. She murmured something to her brother, then led Violet outside into the dark night.

The dark night that had fallen at about 4:20 P.M.

Rosemary stowed Violet's pack on a sled connected to a snowmobile parked outside, then indicated that Violet should take the high passenger seat to the rear. She climbed on in front, and then took off.

The snowmobile's headlight gave only rushing, flickering impressions of the small frontier town that quickly gave way to nothing but snow and snow-drowned trees. The engine was loud, and the ride was not particularly smooth, and Violet found herself smiling wider and wider as they bumped along.

Because up above, the stars were their own wilderness in a night sky without the faintest trace of light pollution in any direction.

It was glorious.

Time lost all meaning. She would have sworn that there was no one else alive, anywhere. A stranger was taking her farther and farther away from anything that bore the slightest resemblance to civilization, but she couldn't work up any sense of alarm.

Violet couldn't stop smiling, even laughing a little to herself. Not when she'd lived her whole life so far without understanding that she could feel like this. Wild and free and filled with awe, hurtling forward through the endless dark without the faintest shred of fear.

This was what she'd always thought falling in love was supposed to feel like.

Though it certainly hadn't with Stuart.

When she saw the first light in the distance, she thought it was some kind of subarctic mirage. But as they roared closer, the lights only grew brighter. They were approaching the side of a hill, where it looked as if someone had stacked up a set of buildings like enormous children's blocks. She had the impression of a kind of big warehouse, red and wide, commanding the base of what seemed to be a haphazard pile of little red houses. There were other winter vehicles parked at all angles in front of it, enough to suggest they weren't at someone's home, but she couldn't imagine what kind of public establishment this was, twenty miles from what passed for a town.

Rosemary parked the snowmobile and when she turned off her engine, the silence seemed to rush in like a hard wind of its own. She swung off the snowmobile, then set about pulling Violet's bag from the sled in back.

Violet climbed off after her, took her pack, and looked around as she tried to slide the strap over the puffy shoulders of her brand-new parka. She gazed up at the hill, still not quite able to make sense of the jumble of red buildings.

"They call this Old Gold," Rosemary told her. "Once upon a time it was a gold mine. Trouble was, there wasn't much gold. Once the men who dug up the land moved on, the folks who stayed on here claimed it for themselves."

Violet patted her pocket where her guidebook waited, filled with careful maps. "The mine?"

"The mine, the land, and the mineral rights."

"Who lives here now?"

Rosemary headed toward a wide set of red and white doors that reminded Violet of barns. Or, more accurately, the pictures of barns she'd seen. "That depends on whether the youngest Fox grandchildren are here or in Fairbanks. But it's never more than twenty."

"Twenty," Violet repeated. She saw more people on the way out of her apartment building in San Francisco every morning. "Twenty people count as a town?"

"It takes twenty-five to be a proper municipality. This is a community." Rosemary nodded her head to the door before her. "And this building is called the Mine."

She pulled open one set of doors, crossed the small vestibule, then pushed through the next. Violet followed, dazzled by the sudden shock of heat and light. Her glasses fogged over, so she took them off and when she wiped them clear and popped them on again, she found herself standing in . . . an entire little town in one vast space, like a rustic, rural version of the Ferry Building back in San Francisco.

It was magical.

There weren't the farmers' markets and high-end food stalls of the Ferry Building here, but there appeared to be a variety of different shops and stalls packed into the big, open room. There were post office boxes to one side, a small grocery, a couple of shiny new ATVs parked near another set of doors closed against the weather. In one corner she saw a woodstove and leather chairs and, if she wasn't mistaken, a tiny library. In another corner there were couches arranged around a large fireplace. There was a bar at one end and some distance down from it, a space that looked like a diner, complete with a few booths and another set of doors shut tight. Longer tables and comfortable, well-loved chairs were scattered here and there, and Violet was so taken with the bright lights and the airiness of the rambling space that it took her a moment to realize that there were . . . people.

Staring directly at her.

"I knew Abel would call up here," Rosemary muttered from beside her, but Violet barely heard her.

Because a figure detached itself from the bar at the far end and something in her hummed a little, because it was a man.

Only not just any man.

Her heart kicked at her, and she had the sudden sensation that she was back out there on that snowmobile, hurtling through the heedless dark.

He had to be at least six feet and he wore his height with a kind of careless ease that made Violet's poor, abused stomach flip over and over. He wore utility boots and the kind of heavy-duty all-weather trousers she could see with a quick glance that almost everyone else was wearing, too. He had on a knitted hat that didn't quite contain all of his unruly dark hair. But this man was also wearing a T-shirt, of all things, that strained to contain a shockingly well-carved chest and biceps that made her feel deeply, inarguably silly. On a cellular level.

But she promptly forgot all of that, because his face had to be one of the great wonders of the world.

He had cheekbones to die for. There was a hint of dark hair from beneath his hat, and his dark eyes gleamed enough that she suspected at once they weren't black at all, but something more fascinating, like navy. *Midnight*, whispered that silly part of her. He had a mouth that should have looked out of place on a man who exuded such rugged masculinity with every step, but didn't. Maybe because his jaw was unshaven and his lips, sensual though they might be, were pressed together in what looked a whole lot like irritation.

Full-on grumpiness, in fact.

Violet couldn't breathe and told herself it was a knock-on effect of the cold. That was why everything was tingling. It had to be why.

More amazing, her stomach had finally stopped hurting.

"I'm Quinn Fortune," he rumbled, but she already knew that. She'd guessed the minute she'd seen him. She'd *known* on that same cellular level. His voice was as rough and wild as the landscape outside, and it made her feel silly and warm straight through. What was happening to her? "I could have saved you a long, grueling trip. Whoever you are, whatever you want, I'm not interested."